Sabina Saves the Future: Complete Trilogy

Martin Lundqvist

Published by Martin Lundqvist, 2019.

SABINA SAVES THE FUTURE: COMPLETE TRILOGY

First edition. September 15, 2019.

Written by Martin Lundqvist.

Also by Martin Lundqvist

Divine Space Gods
Divine Space Gods: Abraham's Follies
Divine Space Gods II: Revolution for Dummies
Divine Space Gods III: Rangda's Shenanigans

Sabina Saves the Future
Sabina's Pursuit of The Holy Grail
Sabina's Quest to Open the Portal in the Sun Pyramid
Sabina's Expedition to Stop the Apocalypse

The Divine Zetan Trilogy
The Divine Dissimulation
The Divine Sedition
The Divine Finalisation

Standalone
Matt's Amazing Week
James Locker The Duality of Fate
The Portal in the Pyramid
Money Laundering in the Laundromat
Pyramidportalen

Matts Fantastiska Vecka
Divine Space Gods Trilogy
Sabina Saves the Future: Complete Trilogy
Diez Historias Aleatorias y Muy Cortas
Ten Random and Very Short Stories
Dieci Storie Casuali e Molto Brevi
Dix Histoires Aléatoires et Très Courtes
Zehn Zufällige und Sehr Kurze Geschichten
Cinco Historias Aleatorias y Muy Cortas
Five Random and Very Short Stories
The Fall of Martin Orchard
Masa Depan Putri Sabina

Watch for more at martinlundqvist.com.

Chapter 1: About Me.

My name is Sabina Hines, but I secretly prefer Sabina Eisenstein. I was born in 2019, and I have just turned 18. I was born in South Africa, but I have been living in Sydney, Australia, for many years now; since my parents migrated there as the racial tensions in South Africa turned violent.

Some people say I am beautiful, and maybe they are right. I would describe myself as tall and slender, with symmetrical features and a clear complexion. My hair is blonde, and my eyes are blue, sometimes even glowing when *she* is talking to me. There is nothing unique about my beauty though, as beautiful girls are a dime a dozen, and physical beauty fades as we age.

No, what is unique about me, is that I have lived in a previous life. Before I was Sabina Hines, I was Sabina Eisenstein. I know that many of you will scoff at this, and my claim itself doesn't sound that unique. After all, countless people are claiming to have been everything from Napoleon, to Hitler, to Elvis in their past lives, and reincarnation is a major belief of significant religions such as Hinduism and Buddhism.

But my reincarnation story is unique. You see, my short life as Sabina Eisenstein was in the distant future: I lived between 2875 and 2887. Born to a Martian revolutionary by the name of Keila Eisenstein, the True Maker tasked me to stop the extra-terrestrial Xeno queen, Rangda, from corrupting the Zeto Crystals, and to stop Rangda from tyrannising and destroying the Milky Way Galaxy. While there is a grand total of seven primordial Zeto Crystals in the Milky Way, I was tasked with protecting the Terran one, as the other ones were inaccessible to me.

I failed at this task during the interplanetary wars and galactical Armageddon that occurred, and Rangda killed my physical body, forcing the True Maker to destroy Rangda. But, when doing so, the True Maker also inadvertently destroyed the entire Milky Way Galaxy, shattering it to micromolecular debris. Just before the massive explosion and the *End of Times*, I begged the True Maker to give me another chance to set things right, and *she* answered my pleas by resetting time so that I could be born again. The True Maker tasked me with defeating Rangda, before her demonic prowess grew too powerful. Looking at my options, I decided that 2019 was an excellent year to be reborn, and I got to pick my parents.

2019 was a good year, for several reasons. The technology was advanced enough to enable me to reach my goals, while there was still a lot to be discovered. I like that. More importantly, 2019 was the year that two individuals with suitable DNA to be my parents, could meet so that I could be conceived. It wouldn't be easy, though, as they were both already in relationships, and my father, Marvin Orchard, would develop incurable cancer a few months later and die before I was born. Using my telepathic powers, I influenced my biological parents to meet and have a short tryst in a restaurant, while their partners were waiting at their tables. I witnessed the whole thing, and while it wasn't glamorous, and I am not particularly proud over what I did, it just had to happen. I convinced my mother to not have an abortion and to not tell my *dad*, John, that I am not his biological daughter.

Well, I guess that's all you need to know about me for now, so let the story begin.

Chapter 2: Daydreaming in School.

I was daydreaming in school, thinking about how I could convince John, to pay for a trip to Jerusalem. The city wasn't safe for a girl to travel alone, and I didn't want my parents to come with me, as I had an objective that could get them in trouble. Maybe I could use religious zeal as my reason for going? John would certainly be happy if I visited the holy city of his ancestry, since he is a devout Jew.

While I was busy daydreaming, Joshua approached me. Joshua was every teenage girl's dream: Good looks, charming, a first-team player in rugby, soccer, and cricket. However, he wasn't my cuppa tea. I wasn't particularly interested in sex or boys, and my good looks were more of a curse, than a blessing, as boys kept approaching me.

"So, I am having this party Friday night ... Would you like to come?" Joshua asked.

"But Josh, I thought you were playing Rugby on Saturday morning?" I could tell that my reply made Joshua slightly uneasy, but he found himself quickly.

"Well, I guess I'm doing both." Josh replied.

"That's okay, you're still young and should be fine." I said.

"So umm, do you want to come?" Joshua asked nervously.

Did I? The answer was a definite no. Taking different substances to disbalance the chemical responses in my brain, what a dumb idea! But then I remembered something: My secret half-brother, Eric Orchard, who was the same age as me, had spoken about his feelings for this girl, Lindsey, from my class. If Lindsey was going to the party, I could help my brother out. Eric has suffered from depression, mainly from growing up without a father, and while partnering him up with Lindsey wasn't necessarily the best long-term solution, I wanted to see him happy.

"Are Lindsey McGowan and Eric Orchard coming to the party?" I asked.

Joshua looked at me with a puzzled expression, and replied, *"Yeah, Lindsey said she was thrilled to come. As for Eric, why do you ask? No-one likes him."*

I considered telling Joshua, that Eric had a purer soul than he had, and that there was more to life than good looks and success, but I realised that such a prissy approach wouldn't yield any favourable results. Instead, I took Joshua's hand, looked him in the eyes and spoke with a soft voice, *"Please invite him for my sake, he is lonely, and he won't cause any trouble."*

I could sense that Joshua was aroused when I held his hand. While this was a bit off-putting to me, it was also a relief. It pained me to reject someone who genuinely liked me, but in Joshua's case, he was merely sexually attracted to me, and he would be fine. I studied his face to get a hint of his thought-pattern, and, eventually, he spoke. *"Yes, you can bring your gay friend to the party if you want."* I thought of pointing out that Eric wasn't gay, but I didn't. It served everyone better, if Joshua perceived Eric to be gay, and not a competitor for my affection.

Chapter 3: At the Chess Club.

Later the same day, I was playing chess against Eric. Chess itself was just a reason to meet up in a safe and friendly environment. Eric didn't know that we were related, that we had the same father. I had withheld the information from him, because I had foreseen that telling him the truth would not be a clever idea. Either he would believe that I was a crazy liar, or he would believe me, and I would have destroyed his memory of his father, Marvin Orchard. Eric had a glorified image of his father, the father that died when he was only a couple of months old. Destroying that image, by claiming that his father had an affair just a few months before his death, was not the way to go.

I enjoyed spending time with my half-brother. Although, because he didn't know that we were related, he tried to kiss me once, and I freaked out.

This day, I decided to lose the chess game in 37 moves. My mental connection to the True Maker made chess too easy for me to win. Even the highest difficulty level on the computer wasn't a challenge. But losing in a certain number of moves was a lot more challenging, as it takes more brain power to lose a game in a certain way than to win. I had to manoeuvre the game, and I could feel how it widened my thought-pattern. After acing the target of losing in 37 moves, I smiled at Eric and complimented him on what a good match it was.

"*Well played Eric, you beat me again,*" I said. He looked back at me, but he didn't look pleased with winning the game.

"*Sabina, stop letting me win on purpose. That's not how real life works!*" Eric said

I faked my surprise and replied, "*I am not letting you win. Why would you say such a thing?*"

"*I saw you beat the AI at the holographic chessboard competition the other day. You defeated the AI at the Kasparov difficulty level, one of the most difficult chess games to ever been beaten.*" Eric revealed

I looked at Eric and decided to come out clean. I laughed and said, *"Yes, you are right. I did lose on purpose. But that's just because I enjoy spending time with you."*

"You like to spend time with me, but you are lying to me?" Eric asked indignantly.

I decided that this was far enough. I grabbed Eric's hand and looked deep into his eyes. *"I did not lie to you, I let you win to build your confidence. Unfortunately, you were too smart for me and saw through it."*

Eric sighed, and said, "Ignorance is bliss. I would rather not know that you lost to me on purpose."

"It sure is!" I replied while smiling cheekily.

I decided to change to a lighter topic and said, *"So Eric, do you want to come with me to Joshua's party on Friday night? Lindsey will be there."* I winked at Eric, and, for a moment, I could see a smile in his eyes before he fell into melancholy again.

"Did Joshua really invite me to his party? He doesn't even like me," Eric said sceptically.

"Well technically, he invited me. You are just coming as my sidekick, so I can help you get closer to Lindsey." I replied and winked.

Eric gave me a concerned look. "Thank you, Sabina. But I am worried about you. Joshua is obsessed with you. You don't want to hear the things he says about you."

"You're probably right about that," I said casually.

After a short silence, I reassured Eric that it was alright to go to Joshua's party. I smiled at him and spoke, *"Look, Eric. I am aware that Joshua is very keen to have sex with me. But I can handle myself, and I am happy that he doesn't have an emotional bond to me. I hate hurting people."* I looked at my wristwatch and spoke. "I need to go home now, but I will see you on Friday. It will be a lot of fun."

As I walked home, I thought about what Eric had said about Joshua. Should I really go to the party or not? I don't like parties nor being around young people like me, taking various recreational drugs to alter their minds and get high. I was perfectly happy with my mind, just the way it was. Drinking a cuppa tea, studying the intricate design and beauty of flowers was a lot more interesting than ingesting a variety of chemicals, hoping for acceptance from one's peers. If I wanted to experience physical closeness and fantastic sex with someone, and I am sure that I will, someday, I'd rather experience that with my full awareness.

As I came home, I told the AI in my room to turn on my favourite music album, "The Best of Chopin," and I found peace from the perfect balance and harmony, that only good music can bring.

Chapter 4: Friday Before the Party.

On the Friday night, I met up with Eric in Bondi Junction. He looked dashing, wearing a marine-blue MJ Bale suit, a white shirt, and yellow tie. This relieved me. If I were going to help my secret brother win the girl of his dream, his appearance was essential. I know what's on the inside is the most important trait in a human being, but one's appearance should never deter people from getting to know one's inner beauty. As I walked up to Eric, I studied him closely. He looked sweaty, nervous, and slightly drunk. Oh Eric, why were you making things so difficult for me?

I approached Eric with a smile and spoke. *"Hi Eric, are you ready for your big chance with Lindsey?"*

"Yes, she'll be mine for sure," Eric said with a voice echoing false confidence and pretentious arrogance. I shook my head and gave him a disapproving look.

"Eric, if you want me to help you, you'd better stop that pretentious act at once. The Eric that I know, deserves a chance at love, the Eric in front of me doesn't." I stated

My words deflated Eric's false ego, and he gave me a sad look before he replied shamefully, "But I don't know how to act to make Lindsey, or any other girl, notice me."

I looked at him with a sympathetic look and said, *"Well, I am not dragging myself to Joshua's place for you to hit on any girl, I am going there to help you out with Lindsey."*

"Okay, Lindsey is the one I want," Eric replied sheepishly.

"Good," I said and smiled. I continued with a more serious tone. *"First, I will set some ground rules. You are there to build a good foundation for the future with the person you love. If you are there just to get drunk, and get laid, I will never help you again."*

Eric looked at me with a puzzled expression and replied. *"I don't understand. What is wrong with only having sex, with no strings attached?"*

"There is nothing wrong with having casual sex, but it is nothing I am interested in helping you with." I stated.

Eric looked at me for a while, before nodding in acknowledgement. Eric said, "Okay. Let's do things your way. After all, you were the one who got me the invitation."

"Good," I replied.

We chatted and gossiped for a while, before we decided to make our way to Joshua's house. I had planned to take the bus, but Eric opted for hiring an AutoCar Deluxe. AutoCar was the most common app for self-driving electric cabs in 2037, and AutoCar Deluxe provided us with a self-driving Mercedes instead of the self-driving Toyotas that were the standard. It felt good to avoid the bus for once, and shortly afterwards, we arrived at Joshua's lavish mansion, located in Dover Heights.

Chapter 5: The Worst Party That I have Ever Been To.

We exited our AutoCar Deluxe outside Joshua's parents' mansion, and I realised that Eric had been wise spending the extra money on a luxurious car, seeing the number of expensive vehicles parked outside the premises. I saw a group of girls, dressed in short dresses and laden in heavy makeup, entering the party before us. They were all giggling and seemed to be excited. After all, they had been invited to the exclusive 18 years birthday celebration of Joshua Harkins, whose dad was one of the richest men in Sydney. It didn't impress me much.

Excessive wealth only led to corruption, and while I was confident that I could become abundantly wealthy, should I put my mind to it, I didn't really see how it would make me a happier person. I had a good life in my modest apartment, living with Mum and John. Adding 500 square metres of living area and three servants to our lifestyle wouldn't do anything to improve our circumstances, quite the opposite. Owning a mansion, we would isolate ourselves in different parts of the house and rarely speak to each other.

We walked past the security guard and realised that Joshua's parents hadn't spared any expense on getting the party as lavish as possible. There were hundreds of guests, and plenty of waiting staff had been hired to look after our needs.

Joshua spotted us and walked up to me. He spoke confidently, *"Welcome to my house, Sabina. You look smashing tonight. How do you like the party?"*

"It looks great. Both Eric and I, are thrilled to be here." I replied with faked enthusiasm.

I noticed that Joshua's face twisted for a brief moment, he clearly didn't like that I mentioned Eric. Shortly afterwards, his confident manner returned, and ignoring Eric's existence, he spoke to me again, *"Would you like a glass of Dom*

Perignon?" Eric wore a posh smile, imagining that name-dropping champagne that was selling for several hundred dollars a bottle, would impress me.

After a short pause, I replied, *"No, I would prefer a cuppa tea, Earl Grey if possible. But I am sure Eric would be thrilled to taste Dom Perignon."*

Hearing that I preferred a cup of tea, over a very dear French champagne, surprised Joshua, and he seemed a bit lost for words.

Eventually, Joshua replied, *"Are you really asking for a cup of tea, on an 18-year coming-of-age party, Sabina?"*

I ignored his sarcastic question and responded with, *"Yes, I am not interested in drinking alcohol. Thanks for offering, though."*

Josh looked dumbfounded, but eventually, he gave in. He called a waiter and spoke, *"A glass of Dom Perignon for me, a cup of Earl Grey for the breathtaking lady, and a bottle of Daft beer for Eric. I reckon the beer matches his socioeconomic status."*

I gave Joshua a short stare for his comment about Eric, but he ignored it. Instead, he spoke again, *"I must leave you, for now, as I need to attend the other guests. Please attend my speech a bit later."*

"Sure thing." I replied casually.

When Josh had left, I turned to Eric and spoke. *"What a dick that guy is, mocking us like that!"*

Eric shrugged his shoulders. *"Well, on the bright side, I do prefer beer."* Eric looked at me with a puzzled expression. *"But, Sabina, you do drink alcohol. We celebrated your birthday last month, and I saw you drinking?"*

"I know, but I am not here to lecture people on the danger of drugs and psychoactive substances. Sometimes a white lie can be useful." I replied

After we received our beverages, we set out to find Lindsey and her friends. As we found Lindsey, I walked up to her, and gently grabbed her hand. I looked her in the eyes, and spoke, "Hi Lindsey, Eric is here, and he is very excited to see you."

At first, Lindsey gave me a surprised look. But when she saw Eric, she burst out into full excitement, hugged him and said, "Hi, Eric! I am so excited to see you tonight, we are going to have such a great night."

Eric's face turned red from a mixture of happiness and shyness, and he was astonished at what he heard. But Eric found himself quickly, and soon they were involved in an exciting conversation. They seemed to have very good chemistry. I excused myself and walked off from the group. While I was excited over helping my half-brother, I was also ashamed about using my powers to influence Lindsey's mind. I was certain that they would make a great and loving couple, but was it really my place to decide what would happen in other people's lives?

I was interrupted from my philosophical thoughts when Joshua approached me, noticeably drunk. *"Sabina, I need to talk to you,"* he said.

"I am all ears," I replied.

Joshua leaned in towards me, and whispered into my ear, *"I need to talk to you in private. It's important."*

I studied Josh. I could sense his carnal desire for me. Although he could have practically any other girl at the party, he was obsessed about the one who had rejected him, i.e. me. I feared what might happen to Josh if I followed him to a private room, and I had to defend myself against him. Then I realised, that my preconceptions against Joshua might be blurring my judgement, and he deserved a chance to talk to me in private. After all, he had invited me to his party, a favour I hadn't extended him, when I turned 18. The least I could do was to let him talk. After a period of silence, I spoke. *"Okay, Joshua. Lead the way."*

I followed Joshua to a room, and I got unnerved when he closed the door after we got in and blocked the doorway with his body. Did he intend to rape me? Regardless, I would have to try as hard as I could, to avoid anybody getting hurt. Joshua gave me a menacing look and spoke, *"I don't understand why you keep rejecting me, Sabina. Everyone else thinks that I am a great catch! I just find you so mysteriously enchanting, I'm crazy about you."*

I looked at him and replied with a calm voice, *"Well, then I suggest you find someone that you like, and take her out, as I'm not interested in you like that."*

"But why do you keep rejecting me?" Josh hissed.

"Well, if you have to know. I am not looking for a partner right now, and even if I were, I wouldn't find us compatible. Now please let me leave, you are making me uncomfortable."

Josh looked at me, with evil eyes, full of desire and self-hatred. I had seen the same eyes before. The eyes of Dov Dorevitch, an enemy in my former life. *"No!"* Josh exclaimed. *"I will have you tonight, whether you want me or not. You'd better make yourself ready, Sabina!"*

In my former life, as the saintly prodigy-child Sabina, I would have been filled with grief for failing to purify Joshua's soul. But, that version of me, failed in the end, being torn to shreds by the demon Rangda, for being too naïve and good-hearted.

I had learnt my lesson. I would give Joshua one more chance to repent and save himself. Otherwise, he was solely responsible for what would happen next. *"Are you frecking kidding me, Joshua? You just threatened to rape me. Step aside and leave me alone or you'll regret it!"*

At first, it seemed like my outburst had worked. Joshua was confused and didn't know what to say. Sadly, the darkness soon returned to his eyes, and he said with a chilling voice, *"I will have you tonight Sabina. I will be the one to take your virginity, and there is nothing you can do about it."*

Having said this, Joshua jumped at me, and pinned me to the bed. I realised that there was no way I could fight him with my physical body. Joshua was, after all, a very fit and strong athlete, and physically I was just your average girl. I grabbed Joshua's arm as he was trying to pull off my pants. I stared defiantly into his eyes and spoke with a commanding voice, *"Joshua Harkins: By the power bestowed upon me by the True Maker, I command you, to let go of evil and repent for your sins!"*

The effect was instantaneous: The darkness and the desire to dominate had left Joshua's face, and the guy who was crying on the floor next to me, would almost have been pitiful, if he wasn't so explosive and unpredictable.

Most evil people won't just let go of evil. They might refrain from doing evil deeds out of fear for being punished, but the desire to harm others will always be with them. After leaving the room, I heard an anguished roar, followed by a loud sound of shattered glass. Joshua, in shock and conflicted from the forced influx of light, had broken a mirror, and turned to self-harm, or at least I assumed so, from the terrifying noises that came from the room.

I had to alert Joshua's parents. I ran up to Joshua's dad and shouted out, *"Mr Harkins! Josh has lost his mind. You must help him. He is in his bedroom."* I didn't stay to check their reactions; my body was shaky from the occurrence. I had to get home, meditate, and find my balance.

On my way out of the building, Eric spotted me, and noticed that something was wrong. *"Sabina, are you okay? What happened?"* Eric said.

"Josh ... he tried to rape me ..." I sobbed.

"Oh my god, I don't know what to say. Should I call the cops?" Eric replied with a concerned frown on his face.

"No. That won't be necessary. Josh is a lot worse off than I am." I replied calmly.

"What? What did you do to the bastard?" Eric asked in amazement.

"I didn't do anything. Joshua's conscience got hold of him, realising what he was about to do. I reckon he went insane and turned to self-harm, but I don't know the specifics as I ran away," I replied.

In the distance, I could hear the ambulance approaching, as I walked away from the house. Eric walked after me and spoke. *"Where are you going, Sabina?"*

"I am going home," I replied.

"I am coming with you. To keep you safe," Eric replied.

"But what about Lindsey?" I asked

"If Lindsey doesn't appreciate that I have to get you home safely, then she is not the right one for me," Eric replied with conviction.

"Thank you," I said as we entered the approaching AutoCar that would take me back to my cosy two-bedroom apartment in Maroubra.

Chapter 6: A Sunday Morning Jog and Reflection.

After spending the whole Saturday trying to meditate away the shock from the events the day before, I was now feeling a bit better. I tried clearing my mind with an early morning jog along the coast in the Malabar Headland National Park. I am a firm believer in moderate exercise for living a healthy life. A light morning run, some yoga, and good stretches afterwards, that is basically my fitness regime. While inactivity is bad for the body and causes premature death, so does strenuous exercise and often you see famous athletes die at an early age from the effects of overexerting their bodies.

While jogging along the oceanic coastal path, appreciating the rugged nature, and soaking up the nurturing energy of the morning sun, I was reflecting on the fate that had befallen Joshua. In his guilt-ridden insanity, Joshua had used the shard of a broken mirror to chop off his own testicles. Or so the online whispers went. He was in the hospital hoping to make a recovery, but his testicles would not. I had spent most of the Saturday pondering whether I was at fault or not. The young, innocent Sabina of my former life would have felt immensely guilty over what had happened, but I did not. While following my instincts and refusing to speak to Joshua in private would have saved him from himself, on that fateful night, it wouldn't have changed anything in the long run.

Joshua's mind was a product of his inflated ego, a product of being born with a sense of entitlement. His desire to dominate me, was the desire for what he couldn't have, and the inability to accept that he was not always liked and admired. If I hadn't come with him, he would have raped someone else eventually, someone unable to defend herself. In a world where evil existed, it was better that Joshua himself took the damage from its corrupting effects, than innocent people suffering.

Friday's occurrences made me realise, that it was time for me to do what I was born to do: To step up my search for the primordial Zeto Crystal, more commonly known as the Holy Grail.

I had been battling with the philosophical question on whether it was wise to unleash the real purifying power of the Zeto Crystal or not. Technically, the Zeto crystal, when activated from their dormant state, would inhibit mankind's free will, by limiting mankind's inclination towards evil, as things would turn good. But the concept of free will was an illusion. In this life that I am living, I couldn't hover from my location without the aid of planes, I couldn't swim underwater to the bottom of the ocean without scuba gear. I couldn't teleport to another dimension by the power of my will, I couldn't reverse time to fix my mistakes. To sum things up: there were already so many things that the laws of the universe prohibited me from doing, thus limiting individuals' inclinations towards evil deeds would just make things better.

But to be able to do good in the world, I needed to accumulate money, as travelling the world looking for the Zeto Crystal wouldn't come cheap. I thought about ways to make money, the idea gave me a sense of discomfort. The desire to make money is perfectly natural; it is, after all, challenging to live in a human society without it. But too often the desire for money leads to greed, which corrupts the soul and, in extension, humanity.

But how would I accumulate the money for my travels? I could spend years, working to make money the regular way, but it didn't seem that stimulating. Don't misunderstand me, working is great and people working together is an essential part of human society. But my goals were larger than typing on a computer all day or serving burgers at the local fast-food joint. If I wasted time doing menial tasks, humanity would have to wait longer for our golden age, and, as a result, a lot more suffering would occur.

I finished my run, and I saw an advert for a massive lottery jackpot. I thought of buying a ticket, but then I realised the pointlessness of the idea. I had many abilities, influencing people and seeing patterns among other things, but neither of those would affect the outcome of the random number generator that gave the lottery outcome.

But what could I do? I realised that online trading was my solution. I had an unparalleled ability to see patterns and predicts future events. While I worried that online trading would expose my soul to the corrupting influence of greed, I realised that I was an adult now. No matter how I choose to live my life, I would need to make money, and online trading would cause me the least mental stress.

I went home, and I checked my online banking account. I had a thousand dollars, mainly from teaching yoga classes at my local gym. *"Here goes nothing,"* I thought as I poured my money into the trading account and waited for Monday to come for the stock market to open.

Chapter 7: Convincing John to Help Me Apply for a Visa

A few days later, there was $20,000 sitting in my account; an amount which was enough to splurge on my upcoming trip to Israel, where my search for the primordial Zeto Crystal would begin. There was a slight problem that I needed to deal with. I needed to secure a visa to Israel, so I could visit Jerusalem, where I believed the primordial Zeto Crystal, also known as the Holy Grail, was located. Unfortunately, the security situation in Israel was so bad, so that the Israeli government didn't let any foreigner in unless they had a trusted person vouching for them. That's where John came in, since he was Jewish, and held an Israeli passport.

My relationship with John, who is the man who raised me, believing that I am his daughter, is not as good as it could be. This is one of my biggest regrets. John is a stable, loving, and hard-working man, and he deserves all the love in the world. Sadly, I just cannot make myself care about him. I guess the circumstances around my conception is to blame.

I was reborn, because of the spirit of the sacred Sabina Eisenstein, who fell to the evil of Xeno queen Rangda in the apocalyptic war of the 29th century. Instead of accepting defeat, the spirit of Sabina Eisenstein convinced the True Maker to turn back time to the year 2019, when compatible parents for my rebirth was available on Earth. I was reborn as a beautiful baby. I remember how the spirit of Sabina Eisenstein, my future self, or past life shall I say, made sure that my mother, Ellen, and my long dead biological father, Marvin, met and had a brief sexual encounter behind John's back. I made it happen, and my feeling of guilt towards my cuckolded "father" has always kept me distant from him. I know that John wanted more children, but since he was sterile, this never happened.

Thus, I feel guilty for deceiving John, and I am aware that the truth would destroy his happiness. So, my mother and I, kept the truth to ourselves as the truth, that I am not his daughter, would be too devastating for John to bare.

As for my mother, I feel close to her. Ellen is a good woman, and her short tryst with Marvin was purely because I influenced her mind to make it so. It was a necessity for my rebirth, but if someone is to blame, it is me, and only me.

I met with John for a quick lunch in the Central Business District. He had rump steak and chips, and I had a vegan salad with avocado, couscous and grilled tofu. I like eating vegan foods when I can, but it is not my passion, and I don't preach it as I believe preaching rigid veganism causes more damage than it solves.

John looked at me with a worried expression. *"Is everything okay Sabina? You haven't been yourself since Joshua's party. You haven't even been to school since. Did anything bad happen at the party?"*

I pondered on how to answer the question. I didn't want to lie, but I didn't want to tell him what had happened either. Eventually, I spoke. *"Yes, something bad did happen at the party, but that is not why I haven't been to school."*

"So, what is really going on?" John asked.

"I needed to make a bunch of money for an upcoming project of mine, Dad," I replied.

Hearing this, my father spat out the coffee he was drinking in surprise and yelled,

"Sabina? You're staying home from school to make money? I thought you didn't even like money or material possessions?"

"No, dad. I don't like being controlled by money or material possessions. But I do need them to live. There is a difference." I paused briefly and then I continued speaking, *"Anyways, I made the money I needed, so now I need your help."*

My father was shocked and replied, *"What? What did you do to make money? You have hardly left your room for three days. Your mother has been worried sick about you!"*

I paused for a bit, and then I smiled at him, sensing my girlish pride bubbling from within over my achievement. *"Online Trading, Dad. I have spent my time doing online trading to raise $20,000 for a trip I want to make."*

I handed John my phone with my web bank transaction details, he looked, and his chin dropped in amazement. *"Sabina, this is amazing. How did you do it?"*

I shrugged my shoulders and replied, *"Online Trading. It is just like chess. You must anticipate the opponent's move and act accordingly. But I must say there are so many more interesting activities than hoarding money."*

"But this is amazing! We could become rich!" John said in excitement, with the greed for money twisting his face into an unpleasant grimace.

"Yes ... But that wouldn't make us happier," I replied calmly. I took John's hand and used my powers to calm his excitement.

When John was calm again, I spoke. *"So, dad. I need your help. I have made the money so that I can go to Jerusalem and study your heritage."*

"Our heritage," John replied with pride in his voice.

"Okay, our heritage." I shrugged and corrected myself. I have never classified myself as belonging to any specific race or sect. I see humanity as one, but I needed to appease John, my gentle and unknowing dad, to get things my way.

John gave me an inquisitive look and spoke. *"But Sabina. You have never been interested in our heritage. You seem to be more interested in yoga, crystals, and eastern religions. What has changed?"*

"Nothing has changed. I just want to broaden my horizons." I replied.

"But Jerusalem is a perilous place these days." John objected.

"Fear shouldn't cloud our judgement and deny us of our heritage. We should face any adversity and be proud of what we are." I proclaimed with a sarcastic tone, but humorously and lovingly.

John sighed. He couldn't argue against my words, as they were his words uttered by me. "Okay." John paused for a second, looking for words. "I will vouch for your visa application, if your mother agrees to this trip."

"Thanks, dad! You're the best!" I exclaimed cheerfully and hugged him. "I need to see Mum now, see you tonight!"

"Okay see you tonight, my darling Sabina," he said gently before I ran off in excitement.

On my jog back home, I felt excited. My mum knew my secret desire to go to Jerusalem, and she wouldn't deny my wishes. She would have objections, of course, but she would realise that it was all part of a higher plan. As for John, he clearly preferred me not going, and I knew that he hoped for my mother to say no, so he wouldn't have to. But once my mum supported my idea, John would come around and help me. I knew it. In a couple of weeks, I would graduate high school, and after that, I would embark on my first great adventure.

Chapter 8: Garnering My Mum's Support.

I met my mum a few hours later, when she came home from work. She seemed distraught and was close to crying. *"I spoke to your dad,"* she said.

I looked at her with a sympathetic look and replied calmly, *"I figured as much."*

"But why do you want to go to Jerusalem and study Judaism? You don't even profess to the Jewish faith!" My mum said with a heartbroken voice, and tears running down her cheeks.

"Neither do you. You're a white South African, mum," I replied and then explained myself. *"I believe that the primordial Zeto Crystal of Earth, is in Jerusalem and that the constant death, violence and hatred in the city has corrupted its powers."*

Hearing my explanation, my mum nodded. My mother was the only one that knew my secret; that I was the reincarnation of the Chosen One, Sabina Eisenstein, who died in the 29th century, while trying to save the world.

Ellen had believed me when I told her about my purpose. After all, what other possible explanation could there be, when her newborn daughter told her this story in private, when I was two days old? Newborn babies don't talk, and they wouldn't lie, even if they did speak.

Ellen looked at me in silence, for a long time, weighing her words before she spoke. *"But why do you think the crystal, that you are looking for, is in Jerusalem? It's a dangerous place, and you are still very young. Can't you search other sites first?"*

I took my mother's hand, looked deeply into her eyes, and replied, *"Think about it, Mum. Jerusalem is the holiest place on Earth. A lot of devoutly religious people go there, hoping to find solace, peace, and harmony. And yet, even though everyone comes there searching for the same thing, many of them end up being hateful fanatics that wish to harm other people. Jerusalem has been contested and the epicentre for wars for thousands of years. No other holy place has that effect."*

My mother studied me for a long time, and eventually, she spoke, "But didn't you tell me, that Rangda has been locked up for millennia, and that she won't escape for another 800 years. How could she have corrupted the primordial Zeto Crystal?"

I pondered my mother's statement. Ellen was correct, but she was missing a crucial detail: Rangda wasn't the only source of evil in the universe. There was good and evil in every living being. What differed between different beings was the proportion of good and evil in their minds, their conscious choices, and their power to affect the world by their choices.

I looked at my mother and spoke. *"You're right. Rangda wasn't the one who corrupted the Zeto Crystal in Jerusalem. Instead, it was humans with their evil choices, who gradually weakened the good energy emitting from the Zeto Crystal. Eventually, the good energy was replaced with evil, and as things are getting worse, the corrupted Zeto Crystal will have a detrimental effect on humanity."*

"So, are you going to purify the Crystal? What if you fail?" My mother asked nervously.

"I am powerless to change the crystal on my own. Only the True Maker can purify the crystal, as it contains a shard of her soul. But if I fail, I will be changed. I will still be alive, but you won't recognise me anymore," I replied calmly.

I watched my mother cry: I knew her so well; that I knew what she was going to say before she said it. Her eyes were wandering, with tears running down her cheeks, and she cleared her throat to make a desperate plea. *"But can't you just leave the crystal where it is? Live a good life, my love. Find true love and happiness. Be happy with the life you are living now. The end of times is more than 800 years away, after all."*

I took up a napkin and gently wiped the tears from Ellen's eyes. I looked into her eyes and spoke. *"Mother, I am already living a good life with plenty of love from you and John. But restoring the crystal and stopping Rangda is my purpose in life, the very purpose that I was reborn. How can I deny myself, and humanity, of this purpose?"*

Ellen nodded in silent acknowledgement. She wasn't going to argue her point and try to stop me from going. Suddenly, she burst out with words that surprised me, *"Sabina, please take me with you on your search?"*

Although this was a natural response from a worried mother, her words baffled me, and I didn't know how to respond. My main concern was that my mother would be considered unimportant to the True Maker. Thus, she wouldn't intervene to save my mother from danger. Going to Israel had always been dangerous, and in the last few decades, things had gotten worse. The extended droughts caused by global warming had turned the entire region very dry, and highly dangerous. The region was filled with greedy paedophiles, who recruited the starving children of Israel for prostitution, and preachers filling the destitute population with false promises about the afterlife. If my mother went there, she was likely to be kidnapped, raped, or killed.

"No, Mum, I cannot let you go. I have a reason to go there, but you don't. I have foreseen my future, but I can't see what would happen, if you follow me there." I said with a grave voice.

"What did you see in your visionary connection with the True Maker?" Ellen asked

"I have seen that I will find the crystal, and that I will die in this city, on my 112th birthday, in 94 years." I replied

For the first time during the conversation, Ellen smiled a bit. *"Wow! That's an encouraging thought, my daughter will live for over a century."*

"Yes. Can you organise the practical details with Dad, please? I had a feeling he wanted you to say no to me, so he didn't have to." I replied

"Yes, I will speak to your father. I will tell him that I support your travel plans," Ellen replied.

"Thank you, Mum. Let's walk to the top of the hill. I sense that the sunset will be beautiful today." I said and smiled, while holding her hands to give her a sense of security. My mother nodded, and together we walked to the top of the hill where we watched the beautiful sunset in peace, tranquillity, and harmony. We felt complete oneness with the universe.

Chapter 9: Taking Off to Jerusalem.

A few weeks later, I had graduated high school, passing my final exams with an HSC mark of 99.95%: the highest score possible. It had been an easy task for me, as I was born with unique abilities granted by the True Maker. I was blessed with heightened intelligence, telepathy, and foresight. I would have scored 100.00%, if the computer system that generates gradings in Australia had been set up to do so. While I didn't particularly care about the result myself, I was happy that my results gave pride and joy for my humble parents.

I arrived at the airport where my mum, dad, Eric, and his girlfriend Lindsey came by to wish me safe travels to Jerusalem. In a way, it felt silly that they all came to wish me safe travels, as I only planned to stay away for a couple of weeks. But I knew the reason: they all secretly feared that I wouldn't come back. I couldn't blame them for this, going to Jerusalem was extremely dangerous, but I was glad that they kept up a happy façade. I had experienced enough emotional talk from Mum and Dad, over the last few weeks, being just a naïve and sappy 18-year old girl.

Another thing that made me happy, was that Eric and Lindsey had found each other, after the incident at Joshua's party. This was important for me, as that meant that the terrible things that happened at the party weren't for nothing. At least something good had come out of it. Eric looked happy with Lindsey, and I predicted that they will share a long and happy life together. I couldn't be certain. as there were too many variables in life. They said that the only certainty in life was death, but even that rule could be bent. I had died fighting Rangda, and yet here I was, in another era, with different people around me, who love me for who I am.

As I walked towards the passport control, my mum came after me, and hugged me with tears in her eyes. *"I wish that I could come with you,"* Ellen said.

"You can't go with me now. But let's go together next year, when the balance of the universe is restored, and peace reigns in the Holy City." I said,

Hearing this, John looked dumbfounded and spoke, *"But what can change in one year? Aren't you just going there for study and school projects?"*

"Everything!" I replied and smiled.

After that, I hugged everyone and walked past the line indicating that I was in the international terminal. There were no passport controls anymore, as everyone on Earth was linked to a global database by 2037, and every movement on every airport was followed by an extensive network of cameras, that utilised facial recognition as well as biometric data to determine the identity of everyone on the premises. While the system wasn't flawless, it was a lot safer than the previous method of passport controls, as passports were easier to forge than the global travel database was to be hacked.

I walked to my gate, and suddenly I felt a bit of shame. I had spent the last few weeks trading extensively and made a lot of money, over $200,000. I had initially set out to travel with $20,000, but now I had over $200,000 in my account, and despite having more than I needed, I felt the urge to open my trading account and do some more trades. I decided to test myself. I intentionally bought the wrong stocks and lost one thousand dollars. What did I feel about this? I didn't feel much at all. The lack of attachment to money was a relief to me, and it meant that greed hadn't taken a firm grip on me yet.

Suddenly, I was gripped by an unnerving thought: What if things went badly in Jerusalem and I needed a way out? I realised that I was better off dividing my money into several accounts in case of an emergency. The best way to ensure that I had money available for an emergency, was to open an emergency account where I stashed some of my money into a universal cryptocurrency account. After doing some research, I decided that SplitCoin was my most viable option, and I deposited half of my money into an encrypted SplitCoin account.

I turned off my phone and walked on Orbit Flight 55222 to Tel Aviv. Orbit Flight were aeroplanes that resembled spacecraft. They flew at a higher altitude than regular planes. Cruising at 30,000 metres, they faced minimal air resistance, and they could reach a top speed of Mach 5, reducing the maximum travel time to anywhere on Earth to just 6 hours. The tickets were costly compared to regular flight tickets, but with my newfound talents in trading, I could afford them. When I got on the flight, I was offered a glass of champagne, and I accepted it. *"I could always have a glass just for the occasion,"* I thought, before finishing the drink and falling asleep in the amazingly comfortable leather arm-chair that I was sitting in.

Chapter 10: A City Filled with Fear.

I woke up a few hours later, when the flight was about to land at Tel Aviv International Airport. I was immersed by the powerful sense of fear that was gripping the entire country. It broke my heart that these holy lands had fallen so far away from the paradises they were meant to be. What had happened to 'love thy neighbour'?

As I reached immigration, I was subjected to a new technology that took a 3D scan of my body, and detected my movement patterns, so that it would be possible for the AI to identify me, even if I concealed my face. While I was impressed by the technology, it also frightened me. The people in power were continually looking for new ways to control the population, and the fearmongering was getting worse. In the past, it had been enough to leave your phone and your credit cards at home if you wanted some alone time, but now, it was almost impossible. Paradoxically, the more the government could track the population, the lonelier everyone got. In a culture where no-one trusted their fellow man, no-one came out as the winner.

After having my movement patterns and body scanned for an extended period, I was brought into a room for further questioning. A stern-looking security officer studied me with his predatory eyes, and I sensed that this individual was content with the current state of affairs.

"Sabina Hines, why have you come to Israel?" The man asked with a voice filled with suspicion. The security officer's hostility frustrated me as he was acting out on his fear, which in turn made the fear spread, and society was turning more fearful and dangerous. I decided to not confront the officer for his attitude, and instead I played along with his little game.

"I have come to this Holy Land to learn more about myself and my heritage," I said with a serious and sanctimonious voice.

"Is that so?" the man asked rhetorically before continuing, *"Our sources in Sydney state that you rarely visit the synagogue, and that you work as a yoga teacher."*

I studied the man in bewilderment. I had travelled to multiple places on family holidays throughout the years, and never had a government spied on me. If my quest to Jerusalem hadn't been so important, I would have said 'thanks, but no thanks' and returned home. But my journey here was of utmost importance, and the decline of the Holy Land, proved to me, how essential it was that I found and purified the Zeto Crystal, to bring back kindness and trust into this world.

"What do you have to say for yourself?" The man's aggressive voice interrupted my thoughts. I hate it when my mind wanders, but I had to snap back to the present.

"What you say is true. I have tried different paths to spiritual awareness throughout my life. The spirituality I have tried, is not contradicting the first commandment, however, as I haven't worshipped any other gods," I said with an imploring voice.

The man studied me for a while and spoke. "Very well, because of the good standing of your father, John Hines, I will grant you entry to Israel. But we will be watching you."

The menacing security officer stamped my passport. I thanked him, and I was on my way. I felt relieved that I hadn't needed to use my powers to get past him. I needed to function as a human, and not just rely on spiritual, meditative powers every time I needed to get things my way. Besides, I could feel that the security officer's soul, was filled with xenophobic hatred and paranoia. The less I exposed myself to those kinds of feelings, the better.

I ordered an AutoCar to Jerusalem, and an hour later, I arrived at my hotel in Jerusalem. I scanned my irises at the blast-proof security checkpoint and got in. Tired from the exposure to paranoia and suspicion, I retreated to my room, where I meditated for hours to regain balance and to calm myself down, before I could finally go to sleep.

Chapter 11: The Suicide Bomber.

The following day, I woke up refreshed. The sun was shining, and there was a crisp winter breeze coming in through my window as I opened it. After eating breakfast, I set out to explore Jerusalem on foot. While most guidebooks strongly recommended guided tours with bulletproof vehicles, I felt that I didn't want to give in to fear. Besides, I was looking for clues on the whereabouts of the Zeto Crystal, and I believed that my senses would be better attuned to find them, if I were out in the open, slowly walking around the city. But Jerusalem was large, so where would I start my search? Since it was a Saturday, and I was under surveillance by the government, the natural choice would be to go to the Western Wall to pray.

I don't like praying to deities, following specific rites, and gathering at specific buildings. I see this merely as a symptom of man's vanity, to worship gods, created by men, for men. The True Maker is everywhere, she is the universe, and any place is as good as the other to connect to her. What is important is the mindset of the individual, not the location and the ritual.

Casting aside my own preferences, I approached the wall, and I sensed something magical. Could it be that the Zeto Crystal was nearby? Suddenly, the sensation was dulled by another feeling. The strong feeling of danger and fear. I turned around, and I saw a young man, around my age. His face was solemn, and he was reciting his prayers, but this was only a façade. This man was here to harm himself and others. I touched the man's hand to get a better read of his emotional state, and to get a sense of who this strange person was.

Yussuf was a seventeen-year-old Palestinian man struggling with severe depression. Unfortunately, instead of finding help to deal with his problems, he had come across evil men. Men that would manipulate him, into killing himself and others, so that perpetual vicious cycle of hate, fear, and paranoia could continue. Although I hadn't come to Jerusalem to save individuals, I had to save Yussuf from himself. My life, and the lives of countless others, depended on it.

I grabbed his hand tightly to establish a telepathic link. I didn't say anything. Partly because it would be hard to talk with him with all noise around us. But also, because I didn't want to arouse panic in the people around me. If the worshippers found out about the suicide bomber among them, they would run away in panic, and in the stampede that ensued, people could get harmed, or even die.

"Don't do it. There is still hope!" I communicated to Yussuf telepathically. Yussuf stared at me in awe and replied. *"Who are you? How can you get inside my mind?"*

"It doesn't matter. All that matters are that everyone here can go home unharmed, and I can help you build a better life." I replied

I saw tears running down Yussuf's cheeks, and he replied telepathically. "I believe you, but it is too late. I had already activated the bomb when you contacted me!"

Yussuf stood up, shouted out *"Allah Akbar*!" and shortly afterwards, I saw the bright flash from the detonation followed by Yussuf's body disintegrating into blood and flesh from the terrible force of the bomb.

The shockwave from the bomb knocked me unconscious, and my mind was transported to the Divine Dimension. There I saw the True Maker, taking the form of my first mother, Keila Eisenstein. She spoke with an urging voice, *"Sabina! You must be careful. You cannot fall here. Get up!"*

I woke up, and I studied the carnage around me. My head was pounding, my ears were ringing, my eyes were blinded by the flash, and I was covered in blood. How severely wounded was I?

I got up on my feet and concluded that I wasn't that I was unhurt. But dead and wounded people covered the ground around me, and I could hear people's scream in pain and terror. I desperately needed to find inner peace, so I walked towards my hotel to have a purifying shower. I got to my hotel room and entered the shower. The warm water washed away the blood, and the shock and terror slowly receded from my body. I didn't have the time to find inner peace though, as heavily armed police raided the room shortly afterwards, bringing me with them.

Chapter 12: Meeting up with the Namesake of a Future Enemy

I was locked up in a police interrogation room. It had been several hours; my head was pounding, and worst of all, I suffered from a terrible thirst, as no-one had acknowledged my pleas for a glass of water. The door opened, and in came the same security officer that had questioned me at the airport the day before. I stared at him in disbelief; why had the immigration officer from the airport come to question me? The man sensed my confusion and stretched out a hand to greet me. "Miss Sabina Hines, we meet again. I didn't introduce myself the last time we met. I am Special Agent Dov Dorevitch, from the Mossad Spy Agency."

Dov Dorevitch! The name gave me shivers. It was the name of the genocidal dictator on Mars, who I had defeated as a 7-year-old in 2882, eight and a half centuries into the future. Could this be the same person, or was it just a coincidence that they had the same name? I studied the man in front of me. Clearly, it wasn't the same soul, nor the same appearance, and it was just the stress that caused my mind to play tricks on me.

Dov spoke again. *"So, Miss Hines, security footage shows that you are holding the hand of the suicide bomber and looking him in the eyes, just moments before the explosion went off. Do you care to elaborate?"*

I realised that I would have to use my divine powers to get out of this mess. Dov was difficult enough at the airport without a terrorist attack taking place. I wanted to try talking first; however, so I responded. "Yes, he seemed to be agitated, so I tried to calm him down. Sadly, I couldn't do it."

Dov studied me in silence for a while. I didn't know if he was thinking of anything or if silence and observation were his interrogation approach. Eventually, he spoke. *"The terrorist was carrying a bomb belt with a dozen bombs filled with shrapnel. Nine of these bombs went off, killing and maiming a lot of innocent people. The three that didn't go off, were the ones facing you. I want you to tell me why these three bombs didn't explode?"* Dov's tone and implied accusations made me upset. I had survived a tragedy, and instead of receiving treatment and proper care, I was exposed to toxic accusations by the man in front of me.

I snapped at Dov and yelled out. *"I don't know why those bombs didn't go off. Maybe Yussuf defused them."*

I bit my tongue and realised my mistake. I hadn't spoken to Yussuf, and yet I knew his name. This wouldn't help to prove my innocence, and I would have to use my powers to get out of this mess. As anticipated Dov noticed this detail, and he screamed back at me. *"How do you know the name of the terrorist? You arrived yesterday, and you are not seen talking to him before the explosion."*

I froze. I needed to come up with something to convince Dov of my innocence, but would I make up a story about how I knew Yussuf's name, or should I address the elephant in the room: How Yussuf got past the security checkpoints? I decided to go with the latter.

I grabbed Dov's hand and focused my empath ability to influence his mind. *"What you should really focus on,"* I paused, trying to come up with the words before continuing, *"...is how Yussuf got past the security checkpoints unnoticed on his way to the Western Wall."*

I studied Dov as his facial expression was changing. I had managed to influence him in the right direction, and hopefully, the input would lead him to the real villains behind this heinous crime. With a concerned expression on his face, Dov replied. "I believe you, Sabina. Our efforts need to be put towards finding the ones responsible for letting Yussuf through our security checkpoints."

After this, Dov pressed a button and leaned towards me, whispering in my ear. *"I have turned off the recording. I sense that you are special. Please help me find the ones responsible for this crime."*

Dov's request surprised me. I had hoped that he would believe me and let me go. But asking me, an outsider, to help with his investigation? Had he sensed my powers or was he testing me? I took a tighter grip of Dov's hand and established a telepathic connection with him. *"Why do you need my help, Dov?"* I asked.

"I knew it! You're an empath! I will get you out of here, just follow my lead." Dov replied, and before I knew it, he was leading me out of the room.

Dov grabbed me by the arm and was intercepted by one of his colleagues. *"Where are you taking that girl? She is still a suspect."* Dov's colleague remarked.

"I am taking her back to the hotel. She is innocent and had a plausible explanation on how she knew the terrorist's name!" Dov snarked. Before his colleague had the time to answer, Dov dragged me into the elevator, and we ended up in the basement of the building.

Dov led me to his car. *"Get in the car!"* he commanded.

"I'd rather just catch a taxi back to the hotel." I replied.

Dov opened his coat displaying the pistol he had holstered. *"Get in the car now, I don't like asking twice."* Dov hissed at me.

I nodded and got in the car. Dov got in the driver's seat and drove away from the garage quickly. I sat in the car and pondered what I would do. Dov drove fast, too quick for the conditions as it was heavy rain and there were thunderstorms in the sky. I realised that I had been too careless, when Dov turned off from the main road and turned onto a small gravel road with no streetlights. I was alone with an armed and unstable man. I hoped that he would be a friend and not a foe.

After driving for ten more minutes, we arrived at a small, seemingly abandoned shed. *"Get out!"* Dov hissed, and I exited the car. The frigid winter rain chilled through my bones, and the coldness amplified the fear I felt being at this spooky location. Suddenly, I heard gunfire, and I took cover on the ground.

Chapter 13: Saved by the Lightning.

I lay in a puddle while the shooting took place. With my hands firmly grounded to the Earth, I could feel the planet speaking to me, and I momentarily lost track of time and place. As the shooting ended, I saw Dov lying on the other side of the car. It seemed like he was dead. I got up, and I saw that Dov's colleague from the police station was approaching me. I felt a sense of relief.

"You saved me! That deluded man brought me here at gunpoint, talking about conspiracies and stuff." I said timidly.

"Silly girl!" The man exclaimed. *"Dov was correct. There is a conspiracy within the security agency, that allows the operation and funding of terrorist attacks,"* he continued.

"So, I guess you are not here to save me then?" I replied.

The man laughed menacingly and replied, *"You are catching on fine. Dov Dorevitch was kidnapped and murdered by the foreign terrorist, Sabina Hines. I, Special Agent Jakub Kluger, intercepted the terrorist and killed her when she tried to get away."* The man replied with an evil grin on his face. I studied him carefully, planning my next move, but I didn't say anything.

Jakub raised his gun and aimed it at me. *"Any last words?"* He asked with a mocking tone. I could feel his aura. I knew that the sociopath in front of me wanted me to beg for my life, to make himself feel powerful, but I wouldn't succumb to it. Instead, I replied defiantly.

"Any last words? I have another 94 years to think about that. I warn you, however, put that gun down and surrender, or things will end badly for you!"

I could sense a moment of hesitation reaching Jakub's mind. I expected him to be man killing from behind his desk, by ordering others to do his dirty deeds. To murder an innocent girl while staring into her eyes wouldn't be as easy for him, especially not when the innocent girl was me, a girl with powers bestowed upon me by the True Maker.

A dozen of very tense seconds ensued. Suddenly, I could sense that Jakub was going to shoot me. Being able to sense his thought pattern in advance, I managed to time my action perfectly. I jumped away, avoiding the bullet, and landing on the ground, in the split second it took for Jakub's mind to send the signal to his finger to pull the trigger. The shot missed, as I landed safely into a muddy puddle. From my position, I could see that Jakub changed his aim to take another shot at me, and there was no way I could avoid this shot.

The shot never happened, as Jakub was struck by a bright lightning flash from the sky, caused by the raging thunderstorms. His metallic pistol had acted as a lightning rod, drawing electricity towards him. Thus, Jakub's decision to kill an innocent girl to cover up his heinous crimes, ended up being his undoing.

I got up on my feet, and I studied the two men on the ground. I wanted to save Dov, now that Jakub had told me the truth, but it was too late as he was already dead. Jakub was still alive, but unconscious, and dying from the lightning strike. I could save him, but did he deserve to live? If he was brought back to life, there was no evidence against him except for my words, and if things came to worst, I would become the scapegoat for Jakub and the people that he worked for. If Jakub survived, the conspiracy could keep killing and hurting the innocent, so they could retain their power through intimidation and fear.

I studied Jakub's pistol that was lying on the ground next to him. I felt enticed to pick it up. If people were out to kill me, I needed to protect myself. I shook my head at the notion. I didn't have the right to take people's lives, that was not the mandate I was given. If I took up a gun to take another person's life, I would have fallen. Killing people was not the path I wanted to take.

I decided to leave Jakub to die, as I didn't feel compelled to save the man who had tried to murder me. I entered Dov's car and drove back to the main road. Once I got close to the main road, I got out of the car and ordered an AutoCar using Dov's phone, as it would be unwise to drive around in a car stolen from a murder victim. I directed the AutoCar to drive me to a discreet building, where I had paid for a room using cryptocurrency. I knew that the Mossad still had my phone and my passport, which was a complication, but I had to settle for what I had.

Chapter 14: Limping and Incognito.

I woke up the following morning in the worn-down room, when there was a knock on my door. I opened the door, and in front of me was a handsome-looking woman around my age. She was slim, tall, and had a boyish haircut. She was dressed like a computer hacker, equipped with a cool-looking laptop, and headphones with loud music banging. She delivered my package and left without saying a word. I opened the package, and I was grateful that I had found a good dark web shop, which delivered the promised goods instead of robbing me of my cryptocurrency or tracing me, to turn me over to the authorities. The package contained a set of clothes, a laptop, a cell phone, a fake ID, a prepaid credit card and a pair of sunglasses.

I put on the clothes and realised that it was used clothes. The same could be said for the phone and the laptop. But there wasn't much to say about it. After all, beggars couldn't be choosers, and I was happy that they had delivered my package at all. I checked the internet, to see how I could outsmart the security cameras that were located everywhere. Apparently, a hoodie and sunglasses were a good start, but since the security cameras also detected a person's movement pattern, I needed a more radical change to fool them.

I concluded that I had twisted my ankle the previous night, when I avoided Jakub's bullet. If I sustained a slight injury on my shoulder, my walking movements would not be recognised by the AI as it would think I was someone else. I wasn't a fan of self-inflicted damage, but I realised that I was here on a mission, so I had no other choice. I deliberately slammed my shoulder forcefully into the wall, dropping to the floor in agony and pain. Hating what I would have to do next, I kicked the wall with my bare foot, causing my ankle to twist even more.

Once the pain had receded, I got up. I studied myself in the mirror. I realised that the pain had caused me to stand and walk differently, although not for the better! I put on my hoodie and my sunnies, and I went out to commence my search for the Zeto Crystal.

As I exited the room, I damned myself for my immoral cowardice the night before. By letting Jakub die, I also killed off the trail to the conspiracy that was holding Jerusalem and its inhabitants' hostage. What if the conspiracy was somehow linked to the Zeto Crystal? I hadn't thought about it in my agitated state the previous night, but now the question overwhelmed me with relentless force.

I realised that the moral dilemma was irrelevant now. I was here on a mission. My mission was to find and cleanse the Zeto Crystal to make Earth a better place. I wasn't here to save the lives of cold-blooded murderers who had tried to kill me.

But how would I find the Zeto Crystal, and where would I begin my search? I realised that I had felt a tingling sensation at the Western Wall, just before Yussuf and his suicide-homicidal plans had shattered the peace. But the Western Wall precinct was probably in lockdown after the previous day's terrorist attack. I decided to explore the remaining parts of the Old Town on foot, as it wasn't very suitable for traversing in a driverless cab. It was painful walking on my rolled ankle, but it was, unfortunately, the only way to cheat the automated AI cameras. I just hoped that my injured state wouldn't attract the attention of the local police.

I walked around in the local quarters for an hour, sensing that the Zeto Crystal was somewhat near, but not close enough for me to pinpoint its location. I froze as someone screamed at me from behind. "עצור, משטרה!" It meant nothing to me, as I don't speak Hebrew, but I turned around and much to my dismay, I was facing a police officer in combat gear.

"*I don't understand,*" I said, as the police officer faced me.

"*Take off your sunglasses and show me your ID!*" the police officer stated with an assertive voice.

I froze for a moment, angled myself away from the facial recognition security cameras, hoping that the police officer wouldn't recognise me. After that, I took off my sunglasses and showed him my fake ID.

The police officer studied my fake ID and my face for a while. He nodded, forced a smile, and spoke. "*Thank you, Miss Keila Eisenstein. Do you need medical assistance with your limp?*"

I smiled back and replied. "*No, it's just a minor sporting injury. I should be fine in due time.*"

"Very well, carry on then, civilian." The police officer said and walked away from me.

I was relieved that I didn't need to use my powers to get out of the situation. I was also comforted that there evidently wasn't a warrant for my arrest. Otherwise the police officer would have studied my ID more closely. I walked into a small alleyway and went into a small coffee shop. I ordered some peppermint tea, to calm my very tense nerves.

Chapter 15: Meeting with the Templars.

As I was enjoying my peppermint tea and trying to relax, I was approached by a group of three shady-looking characters. They wore white Middle Eastern robes and Turbans that covered most of their faces. I freaked out at first, had the conspirators within the Mossad sent assassins, as Jakub had failed to kill me? I was relieved when the leader of the three men removed his turban and spoke. *"Keila Eisenstein, we have been looking for you."*

I studied the man. He was in his fifties and looked strangely out of place in the surroundings. The other two men were of Middle Eastern appearance, while he was tall, blonde, had sharp icy blue eyes, and very distinct North European ancestry. But, why was he looking for my mother from the future, Keila Eisenstein, and should I play along with the ploy? I decided to do so.

"Yes, I am Keila Eisenstein," I replied before continuing. *"Who am I speaking to?"*

The mysterious man bowed to me and replied. *"I am Martin Al-Sham. I have been looking for you for almost twenty years."*

I gave him a puzzled look and replied, "But I am only eighteen years old, surely you must have mistaken me for another person?"

"You think I might be mistaken, but I'm sure that you are the one that I'm looking for. You are the Keila Eisenstein that I have seen in my visions, you are the one that Brahma told me to find." Martin replied solemnly. It was as if, he had waited for years to come to this epiphanic moment.

As confusing as the man's statement was, it all made sense to me. I was struggling with the mission that the True Maker had assigned to me. I realised that the appearance of these strange men must be the intervention of the True Maker herself. I looked Martin Al-Sham deeply into his icy blue eyes and spoke. "If that is so, Martin. Then how can I be of assistance?"

Martin nodded at me and pulled up his sleeve. He revealed a strangely glowing tattoo on his right arm. *"I was meant to show you this tattoo, which I* received in a sleepless dream. In the tattoo, there are strange codes and intelligent markings. I have failed to decipher them for the last decades, and so has everyone I've ever known. But you will understand them, as you are the Chosen One." he said with a solemn voice.

I watched the strangely captivating and illuminating tattoo. The markings and codes looked strange and alien in origin, but they didn't mean anything to me. In a way, this made sense, as I wasn't Keila Eisenstein, after all. I tried touching the tattoo, and I could feel a deep psionic message, and yet I couldn't understand it.

"There is a message conveyed in those intelligent markings. Yet I cannot understand it," I said.

"But you have to understand it. You are the only one that could open the portal to another dimension," the man said. I could spot the desperation and plea in his wise eyes. Martin continued speaking. "I joined with the Templars after an incident 20 years ago. 20 years ago, I travelled to the Divine Dimension and met with the Zetans. They urged me to find Keila Eisenstein and gave me these undecipherable markings on my arm."

I froze as I heard this, and I realised that this man must be crucial to the success of my mission. "Zeto Crystal, I am looking for the primordial Zeto Crystal," I said.

Martin nodded in acknowledgement and replied. "Yes, I know what you are talking about. I once bought a tiny azure crystal in a shady Egyptian market, just days before I entered a portal to another dimension. After the incident, I have travelled the world looking for alien artefacts. I joined the Middle Eastern Templars as I realised that we were looking for the same thing. The Holy Grail, or as you call it, the primordial Zeto Crystal."

I felt excited hearing this good news, but also a hint of apprehension. Who were these mysterious men, and why were they looking for the primordial Zeto Crystal? While it was a good sign that they were also in Jerusalem, it could also be a sign of immediate danger. I realised that I could use my empath powers to read Martin's mind, but before I had the chance, there was a loud banging on the door. "This is the police, open the door now!"

Upon hearing this, Martin got up and said, "Quickly, get into that ventilation shaft over there. We'll delay them."

I realised that time was short, but before I escaped, I took a picture of Martin's tattoos so that I could decipher them later. I got into the ventilation shaft, but my curiosity got the better of me, so I felt compelled to stay hidden and see how things would unfold.

Chapter 16: A Mysterious Enemy.

I overlooked the small café from the ventilation shaft. I saw Martin open the door for the police officers. A few police officers dressed in combat gear, entered the room with drawn weapons. They were followed by a mysterious man, who I assumed was their leader. The leader was dressed in a long coat, wearing a monocle and a top hat. He looked very much out of place, both in time and location. I could sense a strong evil aura from the man, and it terrified me. *"Where is the girl?"* the man hissed to Martin.

Martin: *"What girl? I don't know what you are talking about?"*

Stranger: *"You know exactly which girl I am talking about: Keila Eisenstein. That is why you came here, isn't it?"*

Martin: *"Perhaps, but, alas, I didn't find her."*

Stranger: *"You need to be careful with your words, Martin. Accidents happen so easily."*

Martin: *"What is this girl to you anyway? Why is she a person of interest to you, Ben Yehuda?"*

Ben Yehuda: *"She is the key to finding the Holy Grail. The Holy Grail is destined to change mankind as we know it. I cannot let that happen."*

Martin: *"What if she can change it for the better?"*

Ben Yehuda: *"Bah, we are living at the best of times, and my masters are close to achieving their goal of world dominance. I am giving you one last chance to save your life. Where is the girl going?"*

Martin: *"Perhaps she is going to the Templar Tunnels under the Great Temple of Solomon."*

Ben Yehuda: *"Yes, perhaps. In any case, you have outlived your usefulness, Martin. Greet your heathen gods from me!"*

Having said this, Ben Yehuda aimed his gun at Martin's chest and shot him with several bullets. Ben's accomplices followed suit and killed the other two Arabic templars.

Hiding in the ventilation shaft just above them, I was petrified from witnessing the murders. But I kept my calm, and I crawled silently away from the scene.

I needed to find a new hiding place and a new identity, as Keila Eisenstein was clearly not a good name to use to avoid attention. I logged into my Split-Coin account and ordered the closest available safe house. I followed the ventilation shaft to its exit at the main street. After that, I followed the instructions on my phone to make my way to the safe hiding place. I made my way to the abandoned house, where I collapsed in tears as soon as I had locked the door behind me.

Chapter 17: Traumatised in the Safehouse.

I woke up the following day, traumatised and unable to get out of the lice-ridden bed. I was shaking from the shock, and I had lost all resolve to get on with life. Here I was, a fugitive in a foreign land, having witnessed several murders and barely survived the ordeal. All I wanted to do was to be held in my present mother's arms and be comforted, like when I was a child. I had felt a similar sense of apathy after Joshua tried to rape me, but at that time it was easier. Back then, I had been in a safe place, and Joshua had never posed any real threat to me. Although it did hurt my spirit, knowing the damage that my self-defence had caused him.

I looked at my encrypted phone. All I wanted was to call my mother and speak to her. I knew that she would be worried sick, as I had promised to call her every night and I had failed that promise. But then I stopped myself. My phone and personal belongings were in the Mossad's possession, which meant that they knew who my mother was, and they were certainly monitoring any calls or electronic communications that were made in her direction. If I called my mum, then the Mossad would know. They would track my location and come after me. But what if I called Lindsey, instead? She was not closely aligned to me, but she could still let my mother know that I was alive.

I dialled Lindsey's number, and a few signals later she picked up the phone. *"Hello, Lindsey speaking, who is this?"*

"It's me, Sabina. I need you to tell my parents that I am alive." I said.

"Oh, has something happened? Show yourself in hologram mode." Lindsey replied

"I cannot show myself; they would find me. I need to go." I stated as I hung up the phone abruptly.

I collapsed on the bed, and I dreamt terrifying dreams about the murders that I had witnessed. I woke up with a twist, realising something strange. There was no blood in the visions where Martin and his fellow Templars were murdered. Did this mean that the murders were staged, or was my mind playing tricks on me? I needed to find out, and to be safe, I ordered a new ID, new clothes, a new phone, and some cash, as I reckoned cash was less traceable than a prepaid credit card. I checked my SplitCoin account. Buying things illegally wasn't cheap, and I hoped I wouldn't run out of money.

A few hours later, the same young hacker girl delivered my package, and just as before she didn't say anything. She just delivered the parcel and left. I studied my ID card. Hopefully, 'Eleonore Smith' wouldn't attract as much unwanted attention as the name 'Keila Eisenstein' had done. I got dressed and set out to investigate the crime scene I had witnessed the day before.

Chapter 18: A Dead End and a Clue.

A short walk later, I arrived at the coffee shop where I had witnessed the murders the day before. Or rather, I arrived at the location where the coffee shop had been, as the building was razed overnight. Razing a building where a triple murder took place wasn't the normal police procedure, so clearly something was amiss.

I knocked on the neighbour's door, and she reluctantly came out to answer the knock. *"What happened here?"* I asked the neighbour.

"Why should you know?" she snarled at me.

"I am not from here, but I can make it worth your while," I replied as I pulled out a bunch of 100-Shekel-bills.

I could sense the internal dilemma the woman was facing, on the one hand, she was a poor Palestinian, who really needed the money, on the other hand, helping a foreigner the day after the neighbouring property was destroyed was risky. I reached out, grabbed her hand, and looked into her eyes. *"Please help me, it's important."* I said.

The woman's face changed, and she became friendlier. *"Come in,"* she said, and I entered the small house.

I handed her the pile of notes, and she invited me to sit down by a small table. *"So, what happened next door?"* I asked.

"There was gunfire, and a while later, six men left the building. Shortly afterwards a missile hit the building, and it collapsed." The woman revealed

"What about the other customers in the cafeteria?" I asked.

"Cafeteria? It was just a home, not a place of business," the woman replied, with a puzzled look on her face.

I tried to recall what had occurred on the day before. Had I really walked into someone's home, believing that it was a coffee shop, and ordered tea? It wasn't impossible, I had been quite riled up the previous day.

"The men that left, can you describe them?" I asked the woman.

"Yes, there were six of them. Two police officers in combat gear, one man in a brown trench coat, and three tall hooded men in white robes," the woman replied. This confirmed my suspicion, that the murders that I thought I witnessed yesterday was fake and staged by a group of high-level conspirators. But why would they do such a thing? What should I do?

"Is there anything else you can tell me?" I asked the woman.

"These are dangerous questions. A poor woman like me, should never reveal too much, or else the authorities will shoot me," the woman replied nervously. I reached in my pocket for another pile of bank notes, but before I had reached them, the woman spoke again. *"I found this outside the house, one of the men must have dropped it."* The woman handed me a police ID. I took the ID, and I gave her another 100 Shekel bill as gratitude.

I put the ID in my pocket and spoke again. *"Is there anything else that you can tell me?"*

"Please don't ask any more questions. I have children to look after." The woman stammered, and she was close to tears.

"I understand. Thank you for your assistance. I will pray for you." I said reassuringly.

Knowing that I couldn't get any more information from this terrified Palestinian woman, I made my way back to the safehouse. I knew exactly who I would ask for help in this tricky situation.

Chapter 19: Seeking Help from the Young Hacker Girl.

As I came back to my hideout, I visited the same site on the dark web that I had ordered from twice before. I didn't need to buy anything, but I needed to meet with the young hacker girl that had delivered my last two deliveries. I put through an order, and I waited eagerly for the delivery, hoping that the same girl would deliver it.

While I was waiting, I realised that I was starving. With all the stress from the last few days' events, I had forgotten to eat. I decided to order the food from the same website, as I didn't want to be away from the room, when the girl came with the delivery. I hoped that the food would be worth the hefty price tag, but I had no illusions. The prices were steep because of the secrecy of the platform, not because of the quality of the food.

A few hours later, the young hacker girl delivered the goods But this time, I wouldn't let her leave without saying a word. I grabbed her hand and said. *"Hey, wait. We need to talk. I don't know your name yet."*

I sensed anxiety from the lanky, boyish girl, and I tried to send her a calming emotion. This was a lot harder than it usually was, as the events that I had witnessed, had upset my inner peace, but eventually, she seemed a bit calmer.

"What do you want to talk about?" the girl said carefully, staring at the floor.

"You don't need to be afraid of me." I said, and I put a reassuring hand on her shoulder. The girl looked up, and I saw her eyes. She had beautiful features, hidden by her boyish and alternative looks.

She talked softly and replied, "Perhaps not, but someone who spends nearly 100,000 Shekel on discreet accommodation, clothing necessities, laptops and fake ID's, must be up to something?"

I nodded and replied. *"Yes, I am here on a mission. But first, what do you know about the conspiracy within the Mossad?"*

The girl shook her head and replied. *"There are many conspiracies in the world. But the only way for someone like me to survive, is to stay off the grid, and don't put my nose where it doesn't belong."*

I pondered on what the girl had said. She was doing the right thing by staying out of trouble, but I really needed her help. Then again, what moral rights did I have to risk her life and well-being to pursue my own goals? I closed my eyes, and I could hear the voice of the True Maker. *"Human lives are finite; the future is what matters."*

I felt relieved that I had gotten the True Maker's approval, but I was still uncomfortable with what I had to do. I looked the girl into her eyes and hypnotised her with my soft and yet commanding voice. I said, *"Listen. I really need your help. It's important, for all of us, for the future of humankind."*

Upon hearing these words, the girl relaxed, and she entered my room, closing the door behind her.

"Okay, Sabina Hines. I will help you," she said.

"How do you know my name?" I asked.

"I wouldn't last long, if I didn't know how to research my potential customers," the girl replied. I nodded in acknowledgement; this hacker girl clearly knew what she was doing.

"So, you know everything about me, but I don't even know your name?" I said.

"Simona, Simona Fischbein is my name." Simona replied

"Is that your real name?" I asked.

"Well, names are just imaginary, a human construct that doesn't exist in nature. Simona Fischbein is not the name that my parents chose for me, but it's the name I am using now." Simona replied.

I nodded. While Simona had used a lengthy way of telling me that she was using a fake name, I understood her predicament, and I didn't want to push the issue further.

"You are very beautiful, Sabina," Simona said, while looking nervously at the floor. *"Do you feel the same way about me?"* She continued.

Hearing this, I was a bit lost for words. Was Simona sexually attracted to me, or was she just a lonely girl that needed a compliment?

"What matters is the beauty of the soul, and I don't know you well enough to determine the beauty of your soul." I replied, and then quickly added in. *"But I am very grateful for your compliment, and that you're helping me out."*

Simona seemed hesitant and indecisive, but eventually, she spoke. *"But have you been with a girl before?"*

Ouch, this was awkward. Being a divine reincarnation of the Chosen One, Sabina Eisenstein, I don't focus on sex and physical attraction. I do know, however, that my physical body is attracted to boys my age. I had felt very attracted to a guy called Alexander O'Neill at my school, but I had never pursued that attraction. I felt no spiritual connection to him; purely physical attraction, and I hadn't figured out whether I should pursue the desire of the flesh or if I should wait for the individual that would fulfil me both physically and spiritually.

Things were getting more awkward as Simona was interpreting my silence as a signal to seduce me, and I could feel an unpleasant shiver when her hand stroke the side of my breast. *"I am not comfortable being touched that way,"* I said with a meek voice.

"Am I too ugly for you?" Simona said, with a shivering voice.

"No, you're beautiful. But I am not into girls," I replied.

Simona crashed onto the bed, with tears running down her cheeks. *"Do you know how hard it is for me, being a lesbian in a country where my desires are shunned upon, and I can't live openly?"* Simona said.

I grabbed Simona's hand, and I spoke to her. *"Simona, the increasing oppression in this region is terrible, and I am here to help. But to do that, I'll need your help,"*

Simona dried her tears with the bed sheet and replied. *"But I need you right now."*

"Well, you cannot have me without disrespecting my physical integrity. Surely you wouldn't want to do that?" I replied

"But I thought we had such a strong connection," Simona said.

"What you believed to be physical attraction, was actually me trying to connect telepathically with you. I am an empath, not a lesbian." I replied calmly.

After a moment of tranquil silence, I telepathically soothed Simona's struggling mind, and Simona finally came to peace. *"So, why are you here, and how can I help you?"* Simona asked. I exhaled, relieved that I was no longer an object of Simona's unrequited attraction and replied. *"I am here because I need to find something. I need to find the primordial Zeto Crystal, commonly known as the Holy Grail."*

Simona studied me for a while. Then then she nodded and replied. *"So, you are a young white girl, travelling on her own, to seek a mythological Arthurian treasure?"* Simona said.

"Yes, that's right." I said with a light-hearted tone hoping to ease up the tension

For the first time, I saw Simona smile. Simona had a beautiful warm smile, and she replied. *"You are crazy. We must be soulmates."*

"Perhaps spiritually, but not physically!" I replied.

"I guess that's better than nothing." Simona replied, and we both laughed at the funniness of the awkward friendship-budding situation.

"So, tell me. How can I help you?" Simona said with a more serious tone.

"I was shown this strange-looking tattoo by a mysterious man, Martin Al-Sham. Martin then pretended to be murdered by a group of Mossad agents. One of the agents dropped his ID card at the scene." I said. I showed Simona the picture of the tattoo that I had on my cell phone, and I handed her the ID card of the mysterious Mossad agent, Ben Yehuda,

Simona studied the pictures and the ID card carefully. She opened her laptop and searched on the dark web, looking for answers on a discreet hacker forum. Eventually, she spoke. *"I have made some queries on the dark web. I think you might be onto something thrilling."*

I could feel my pulse rise in anticipation, and I replied. *"Please tell me what you know, Simona."*

"Martin Al-Sham is a prominent member of the Templar Order. If he is in Jerusalem, that must mean that they have resumed an archaic project," Simona said.

"Which project?" I asked.

Simona hesitated for a bit, looked around in the room, and then spoke again. *"In 1099, the Templars invaded Jerusalem during the first crusade. They located their headquarters at the Temple of Solomon and immediately started to dig under the Temple. Rumours have it, they found magnificent treasures under the temple."*

"What did they find, and why did they stop digging?" I asked eagerly.

"No-one knows, but rumour has it, that they found the Holy Grail. They disappeared with all their treasures in 1307, and the Templar Order hasn't been seen since," Simona stated.

"Except that Martin Al-Sham introduced himself as a Templar, so they are not seeking secrecy anymore," I said.

Simona paced back and forth nervously in the room before she finally spoke again. *"Yes, they are getting bolder. That must mean they have found what they are looking for. The first place to look would be in the tunnels under the Solomon Temple."*

"I assume they are not organising tours down there?" I said innocently.

Simona smiled and replied. *"Not exactly, but that's where you are lucky to have met me. I can make you a fake ID that will give you easy access."* Simona smirked and looked at me wittily.

"Except that, your services are not cheap, and I have run out of SplitCoin." I replied shortly.

Simona bit her fingernails and stared at the floor in silence. I could sense that she was conflicted and didn't know what to do. I thought of influencing her but decided not to. This was her choice to make. Eventually, Simona spoke to me with righteous conviction. *"I'll help you for free on one condition: That you are taking me with you."*

"You want to come with me to the tunnels under the Solomon Temple?" I asked with a confused voice and then added in, *"But why?"*

Simona looked at me with a serious face and spoke. *"This Mossad agent you came across. His name is Ben Yehuda, and he murdered a dear friend of mine. Whatever he is after, I intend to stop him!"*

"You'll be up against some very dangerous men, I am not sure I can keep you safe," I said with a grave voice.

Simona looked at me with a confused expression and replied. *"So, you are worried about me, but not about yourself?"*

I nodded and replied. *"Yes, I can foresee my future and I know the date of my death. 20th October 2131, about 94 years from now. I haven't seen your destiny though, as it is outside the scope of my powers."*

Simona shook her head, laughed, and spoke. *"You are crazy, Sabina, do you know that?"*

I smiled at her and replied. *"Yes, I have been told."*

"Well, at least we are on the same page. So, am I coming with you?" Simona asked.

"Sure, I need all the help I can get." I replied.

"Great, I am heading home, to gather our equipment and make fake ID's for both of us. I will be back in a couple of hours." Simona said. Then she took off before waiting for my answer.

After Simona had left, I felt melancholy gripping my body. Simona was young, lively, had a pure soul, and we could become good friends. But I was certain, that she wouldn't make it through this ordeal alive.

Chapter 20: Fake ID's and Cover Stories.

A few hours later, Simona returned with new ID's. I was now Madeline Berkley, and I was a 28-year-old professor in archaeology, who was here to study the Solomon Temple. I studied the credentials carefully, and while they wouldn't get through a thorough examination, I could always use my powers to influence if things were getting hairy.

"I brought some makeup," Simona said. Her statement confused me; we were going on a dangerous undercover mission to recover ancient artefacts. Why did I need makeup? Simona explained herself before I had the chance to say anything *"Makeup to make us look older."*

"Oh, good point." I said sheepishly, embarrassed that I hadn't understood Simona's intention straight away.

As Simona carefully applied my makeup, I realised how similar we were. She was also very multi-talented, and I asked myself if she had also been sent by a higher power to help me with the mission. I didn't think about it for long, as Simona finished quickly. I studied my new face. I certainly looked older, and the tinted lenses and the wig helped as well.

Hopefully, I would be able to impersonate the real Madeline Berkley. To do that, I would need to learn a lot about archaeology quickly. I accessed the internet and utilised my photographic memory to accumulate lots of archaeological knowledge. It was an interesting subject, but I only needed to know the basics for my cover to work, so I logged off the internet and turned to Simona. *"Now, I know everything I need to know, to blend in as an archaeologist."* I said

Simona stared at me in disbelief. *"Was that what you just did when you quickly scrolled through that text?"* Simona said.

"Yes." I replied.

"It took me years of elementary school to learn all that stuff," Simona said.

"Some people never learn, even though they have years of schooling," I replied.

Simona smiled at me and spoke. *"So, Miss Madeline Berkley, are you ready to see the catacombs of the Solomon Temple?"*

To which I replied, *"Yes, Miss Arya Simon, I am very grateful for you showing them to me."* After that, we left the safehouse and headed in the direction of the Solomon Temple.

Chapter 21: Influencing the Guard.

A short walk later, we arrived at the Solomon Temple. The sun was setting, and most of the visitors were heading home, but we had other plans. We walked towards the tunnel entrance and were approached by a guard.

Simona spoke Hebrew to the guard for a while, and then the attendant turned towards me. *"So, Madeline Berkley from Australia, why are you here?"* he asked.

"I am here to get a private academic tour of the Solomon Temple catacombs, with my fellow researcher from Jerusalem University, Miss Arya Simon," I replied.

"That won't be possible." The guard replied with a stern voice.

"But, why am I not allowed to go in? I have travelled so far to study these catacombs with my own eyes," I replied.

"The catacombs are closed on orders from the Israeli government. It is a matter of national security," the guard replied, with a hint of insecurity in his voice.

I studied the man. He was guarding alone, and I could sense that he was easy to influence. He would most certainly be in trouble later, if he let us through, but it was imperative for me to get through and uncover the secret that lay in those catacombs. This was the constant dilemma in life. There were rarely any clear cuts solutions between right and wrong. While I needed to get down in the tunnels, I didn't like the prospect of having this innocent employee punished. I shrugged off my moral objections, grabbed the man by the arm and looked into his eyes reassuringly. *"We need to get down to those catacombs tonight. Strange things are taking place down there, and we must stop the perpetrators from causing more damage to the people of Jerusalem, and to humanity as a whole,"* I said.

The guard shuddered and stuttered out a reply. *"But they know that I am working by myself tonight, if I let you past this entrance, they will come after my family."*

"Who are they?" I asked.

"The mighty men in Templar robes, working with that authoritative and wicked government official, Ben Yehuda," the guard replied.

I gave the man a concerned look, but I could feel the excitement growing within me. We were close to something. *"I am going to be honest to you,"* I started. The guard looked attentively at me as I continued speaking. *"We are not really university scholars. We are here to save humanity from enslavement and fear."*

I realised from the fear in the guard's eyes that I had made a crucial mistake. I should had kept up my façade, but now there was only one way to go, to move forward. I focused my psychic energy, grabbed the guard tighter by the arm, and knocked him unconscious with a psionic shock that I sent with my mind.

"What did you do?" Simona exclaimed in awe.

"I knocked him unconscious, he wasn't going to cooperate, it was the only way," I replied.

"But, how did you do it?" Simona asked.

"With my powers. I don't have time to explain. We need to move!" I urged Simona. She nodded, and together we rushed down the stairs to the catacombs below, leaving the unconscious guard where he was.

Chapter 22: Searching the Tunnels and Avoiding the Enemy

As we reached the tunnels below, I realised that expelling the psionic shock to knock the guard unconscious had jumbled up my memory, and I no longer knew the layout of the tunnels. But I could sense the Zeto Crystal, and it gave me a general sense of direction on where we were headed. We moved as fast and silently as we could, until a discomforting feeling overtook my senses. The feeling that we were not alone. I sensed four males just ahead of us, and, as we got closer, I could hear them.

I recognised the voices of Martin Al-Sham and Ben Yehuda, although I couldn't make out what they were saying. I was annoyed at myself for not learning the local language before I set out on my mission. I was convinced, that my heightened intelligence, would enable me to learn any language in less than a month, and yet I had been too careless to learn Hebrew before setting out on my mission.

I turned to Simona and whispered. *"What are they saying?"*

She responded, "I am not sure. They seem to be speaking in riddles. One of the men is speaking in bad Hebrew," she replied.

"But why are they speaking in Hebrew if they are not good at it?" I asked.

"Maybe they know that you are listening, and they don't want you to know what they are talking about." Simona replied.

Simona's words struck me to the core of my being. Maybe she was right, and I was the one being played by my opponents. I didn't have much time contemplating this option, as I could hear the men approaching our position. We snuck into a small side tunnel, which was a dead end but hidden from the main tunnel. I really hoped that they wouldn't find us there, or we were done for. On the bright side, why would they come looking for us there?

I spotted Ben Yehuda, Martin Al-Sham and the two other Templars walking straight past us, through the main tunnel. I let out a sigh of relief, and when the coast was clear, I led Simona in the direction where I could sense that the Zeto Crystal was located. Eventually, we made our way to a tiny room, illuminated with glowing markings on the wall, full of strange alien symbols.

Chapter 23: Unlocking the Door and Finding the Primordial Zeto Crystal

As we entered the dark and mystical room, the alien symbols suddenly lit up in an opaque, dimly lit, and soothing neon-bluish colour. I recognised the symbols from the tattoo on Martin Al-Sham's arm, but I couldn't make out the pattern. Staring at the pattern caused me migraine, as there were simply too many extra-terrestrial symbols, and too many possible combinations for my head to compute. The harder I tried to figure it out, the worse my migraine became. After a minute of pushing my brain to decipher the illuminating encryptions, I was lying on the floor in terrible pain, suppressing my screams to avoid getting the attention of Ben Yehuda and the Templars.

Simona kneeled next to me as I was lying on the floor and spoke. *"What's the matter, Sabina?"* I coughed up some blood, and Simona stared at me in horror and spoke. *"Sabina! You are bleeding from your mouth, your nose, your ears, and your eyes! What's going on?"*

"I can't decipher the encryptions, and my brain is overloading from thinking too much." I said with a weak voice. I felt like I was close to fainting.

"Well, then stop thinking!" Simona exclaimed.

Hearing this brought me back to my senses, and I felt slightly rejuvenated. Thinking hard wasn't the solution to the mystery. Good feelings and karmic intuition were. The riddle was meant to be deciphered by my mother from the future, Keila Eisenstein, and not by me. While I was the thinking kind, possibly the most intelligent human ever alive, Keila Eisenstein, my true mother from the future, had something that perhaps was more important to break the codes, telepathy, and premonition. While I also had these supernatural talents, thinking too much and not following my intuition, had dulled my other senses, and stopped me from deciphering the alien codes.

I got up, wiped the blood off my face with my jumper, and spoke. *"Thank you, Simona. For showing me the way."*

I closed my eyes, zoned out from this world, and got dream-like visions from the True Maker. In the visions, I saw Keila Eisenstein deciphering the code and opening the door. Blessed with a photographic memory, I replicated all the steps I had seen Keila take in my vision. When I finished, the entire wall lit up, and a huge rock moved to reveal a secret passageway.

"Follow me," I whispered, and we ran towards the newly revealed room. Inside the room, sitting on the top of a medieval plinth from the Arthurian era, I could see the primordial Zeto Crystal, glowing ever so slightly, with a faint soothing light. I ran towards it, but before I could touch it, I heard an acrimonious man's voice, the voice of Ben Yehuda. "Not so fast, or your friend will die!" Ben said menacingly. As I turned around, I saw Ben Yehuda accompanied by the Templars, and Martin Al-Sham, aiming their pistols at Simona.

Chapter 24: A Terrifying Sacrifice

"Thank you for opening that secret door, we have spent a decade trying to open it." Ben Yehuda spoke with a maliciously grim voice. *"Martin Al-Sham was right all along, finding Keila Eisenstein was the key to opening the door."* Ben Yehuda continued, looked at Martin and nodded malevolently.

"Is that so?" I asked rhetorically before continuing, *"You see, I am not Keila Eisenstein."*

Martin Al-Sham interjected, *"Bull! Your ID card said that your name was Keila Eisenstein, and you look exactly like the girl from my visions."*

"I was using a fake ID; my real name is Sabina Hines." I replied.

"Stop it!" Ben Yehuda shouted. *"Your real identity is of no concern to me. All that matter is that you led us to the Holy Grail. With it in my possession, I will conquer these lands and control our people."* Ben Yehuda said maliciously

"And how do you intend to do that?" I shouted.

"Oh, I am sure you know about the powers bestowed in this extremely valuable hidden treasure. Why else would you be after it?" Ben Yehuda said and smiled cunningly.

"I know the powers of the Zeto Crystal. What I don't know is how you intend to use it?" I replied with a calmer voice.

"And why would I tell you?" Ben Yehuda scoffed at me.

"I am just trying to make up my mind on whether I should stop you or not," I replied.

Ben Yehuda was flabbergasted by my answer, but after a period of silence, he decided to answer. *"Very well, I'll tell you my plan. I intend to use this crystal to fulfil my God-given duty to unite my people, and to claim this land for our master race. This land was given to us, and we shall not share it with anyone."*

"Although the crystal could also be used to end the discord. To bring peace and unity to humankind," I replied.

"Perhaps, but I care little for utopian dreaming and teenage fantasies," Ben Yehuda responded nonchalantly.

I realised that I had to stop Ben Yehuda. It saddened me that I saw no way to save Simona, who was held captive and was kneeling while having four pistols aimed at her. I looked at Simona and exclaimed, *"I am sorry for failing you Simona, but the True Maker has her own reasons to make me do this."*

Having said this, I quickly turned around, leapt towards the archaic plinth that held the Zeto Crystal in place, and grabbed the crystal while in mid-air, landing just behind the plinth. I heard several shots, and I knew what that meant; Simona was no longer with us.

Once I had the crystal in my hand, I studied the Zeto Crystal. It was the size of a tennis ball, and it shone with a bright blue light, giving me a sense of peace and harmony. The visions were so beautiful that my mind entered a state of pure bliss, and I forgot about the perilous situation I was in.

I was brought back to reality, as I heard another shot and felt a sharp sensation of excruciating pain in my abdomen. I looked up, and I clutched the Zeto Crystal closely to my chest, as Ben Yehuda unleashed a dozen pistol shots into my body, causing me excruciating agony on every impact.

I heard Ben Yehuda scream, "Why won't you die? This is impossible?" Ben Yehuda reloaded his pistol, and I knew I was going to die, and there was nothing I could do about it. Oh, why have you abandoned me, I wailed, but there was no response from the True Maker. I closed my eyes, held the Crystal tight, and prepared myself for dying. Suddenly, I heard several gunshots followed by several thumps, and I saw Ben Yehuda drop dead to the ground.

Chapter 25: An Unlikely Hero.

I looked up and saw Martin Al-Sham dropping his smoking pistol to the ground. Next to him were the bodies of the two other Templars and the body of Ben Yehuda. Suddenly, Martin kneeled to the ground and started to cry.

"Michael and James were good friends, and yet I killed them." he said.

"Why did you choose to save me, if I may ask?" I inquired.

"Well, I guess I just wasn't a major fan of unity through genocide. My main reason for staying in the Templar Order for twenty-odd-years was to find Keila Eisenstein and to show her the tattoo that I was bestowed by the Zetans." Martin replied and kneeled beside me. *"How did you survive getting shot multiple times?"* Martin asked.

I got up on my feet and studied the enchanting and mystical alien crystal. It had stopped glowing, and it looked dull, like a regular uncut sapphire. *"I must have been saved by the healing powers of this Zeto crystal,"* I replied.

"The crystal seems to be drained of its energy," Martin replied with a hint of disappointment in his voice.

"It will re-energise in due time, at least we saved it from being stolen by evil men today," I replied.

"Yes, that's the main thing. Do you need help removing those bullets?" Martin replied.

I studied my torso. All the bullets had penetrated one centimetre deep with the back of them hanging out from my body. They would leave me scarred as a reminder, but I would survive. *"I'd rather remove them in a medical centre. Removing the bullets here, without the chance of getting immediate stitches and disinfection, could be lethal,"* I said.

"There is medical equipment in the Templar safehouse, that I can use to stitch you up." Martin replied.

I contemplated my options. Martin Al-Sham was a murderer, and there was no guarantee that he wouldn't try to kill me to steal the Zeto Crystal for himself. Then again, if that was his goal, why wouldn't he try now? I decided that seeking his help was my best option and spoke. *"Thank you, Martin. Can I borrow your robe? I don't want to walk there looking like a messy pinboard, riddled in holes and bullets.".*

"Sure, here you go," Martin said and handed me his robe.

Before we left, I sat down next to Simona's dead body and whispered softly to her. "I am so sorry for dragging you into this. I am sorry for failing you and causing your death. I am sorry that I couldn't be the lover you needed," I said grievingly.

It might have been my mind playing tricks on me, but when I studied her beautiful face, I could see a hint of a peaceful smile, as if she was happy with her end on Earth. After this, I got up and left the room without looking back.

Chapter 26: Getting Stitched Up and Learning About Martin Al-Sham's Motivations.

A short while later, I was in the Templar safehouse where Martin and his templar associates had been based during their stay in Jerusalem. I needed to get medical treatment, and while I would have preferred to visit a proper hospital, it would have been a nightmare explaining how I survived getting shot thirteen times.

"Would you like some pain killers?" Martin asked.

"No, I don't believe in using drugs to dull my senses. Whatever I will feel, is what I am meant to feel," I replied.

"Are you sure?" Martin asked while shaking his head.

"Yes, I am sure." I replied

"Okay. This will hurt a lot!" Martin said as he began to pull out the bullets and disinfect the bullet wounds.

I would lie if I said it was a pleasant experience, but the pain I felt from causing Simona's death was worse than the physical pain that I experienced. I let down my guard, and I started crying like a baby. *"Are you sure that you want me to continue?"* Martin asked with a concerned voice.

"Yes, this needs to be done." I replied, while grimacing in pain. After a while, the pain receded, and I got back to my senses. I decided to find out more about Martin, so I spoke to him. *"So, why did you team up with Ben Yehuda and the Mossad when you didn't agree with their views?"*

Martin looked around the room before he answered my question.

"Well, you would think I am crazy if I told you." Martin said.

I smiled warmly at Martin and spoke to him gently. *"Would it comfort you, if I told you that I have lived once before, in the distant future, and that I asked the True Maker to reverse the time so that I could be reborn in this timeline. Furthermore, I intend to find a genetically compatible sexual partner, so that I can give birth to my future mother and raise her as my daughter, to bring her into this timeline. Would you believe what I just said?"*

Hearing this, Martin smiled a broad smile and spoke. *"Okay, you definitely win in the crazy story competition!"*

"Exactly, so what is your story?" I asked.

Martin nodded and replied. *"My story is that I visited Egypt in 2019. I found a mysterious crystal at an Egyptian bazaar, it looked like a miniature version of the one we found today, and I went to the Cheops Pyramid for a tour the next day. Unbeknownst to me, that crystal that I had hidden in my pocket emitted an unusual extra-terrestrial energy, which opened a portal to another dimension. I stepped into the portal, and there I met some Zetan extra-terrestrial beings, who claimed to be humanity's deities. They gave me this glowing tattoo and urged me to show it to Keila Eisenstein. I woke up in a hospital a few days later, knowing that I have a crucial mission in life from thereon. I joined with the Templar Order a few years later when I realised that we were looking for the same thing."*

"And what about now?" I asked.

"Well, my time is over," Martin replied.

Martin sighed heavily before he spoke again. *"The others will come after me, and so will the Mossad and the police when they find out what I have done. All that matters now is to get you and the Zeto Crystal to safety."*

"Is that something you can help me with?" I asked.

"Yes, you are in luck." Martin replied.

"Why is that?" I asked.

"Ben Yehuda took your confiscated passport and belongings from the Mossad. He also secretly deleted your records. He wanted you to lead him to the Zeto Crystal without telling the others. If I can take back your belongings from his house, it will be easy for you to leave Israel." Martin said confidently.

"Okay, let's go. The sooner that I get out of here, the better," I said, while feeling hopeful and excited. Martin nodded and, we left the house to take back my belongings from Ben Yehuda's house.

Chapter 27: A Shootout and a Narrow Escape.

An hour later, I was waiting nervously in a dark alleyway outside Ben Yehuda's house. Suddenly, I heard an explosion, and I saw Martin running towards me.

"What did you do?" I asked.

"Isn't it obvious, I took back your passport and possessions so that you could leave the country. But I also set an explosion, to get rid of the evidence." Martin answered.

I didn't have the time to answer, as a bullet grazed my ear and I had to take cover. Martin fired back at the attackers, and after a brief shootout, he dropped to the ground with a bullet wound in the side of his body. "Take this bag and run, they are coming!" Martin shouted.

I grabbed the bag, and I ran for my life, leaving Martin where he was. I ran as fast as I could, but with the injuries I had sustained earlier during the evening, I couldn't run particularly fast, and the Mossad Agents were closing in on me, with bullets hailing around me.

"The Zeto Crystal!" I shouted to myself. I took it out of my pocket, and I squeezed it with my hand trying to extract energy. The power that was still in the crystal, guided my way, and I managed to outpace the Mossad agents to the relative safety of a nearby nightclub. From the nightclub, I quickly ordered an AutoCar while hiding at the back, and as it arrived, I sprinted through the kitchen, reaching the driverless taxi unnoticed. I stayed down and crouched out of sight until the cab had taken me to the airport.

Once I was at the airport, I passed the border control officers, grateful that Martin had been right. Ben Yehuda had indeed deleted my records. I was no longer perceived as a criminal in this country and was able to travel as myself, Sabina Hines. I boarded the next flight departing Jerusalem, and 20 hours later, I arrived in Australia unharmed.

Chapter 28: Back in Sydney.

As I arrived back home, my present mother, Ellen Hines, hugged me tightly and cried with relief. I had been impossible to contact for the last week, and my parents had feared for the worst, hearing about the recent terrorist attack at the Western Wall in Jerusalem.

"What happened? You were uncontactable for a whole week! I was worried sick about you." Ellen asked me with a worried voice.

"I ran into some serious trouble, Mum, but I'm okay now," I replied.

"What kind of trouble?" Ellen asked. I hesitated for a while. For my mother's safety, it would be better if I told her a lie, but she was my best friend, and I couldn't keep what had happened to myself.

I decided to tell her the truth, on the condition that she wouldn't tell anyone. After telling Ellen what had really happened, we agreed to make the official story that I was injured in the terrorist attack. This would explain the many scars I had on my body. Rumours tended to spread quickly, and I didn't want the Templars or the Mossad to find out the truth about what I had done, or that I was in possession of the Zeto Crystal.

After speaking to my mum, I went back to my room. John was on a business trip, but I was sure that my mum would call him to come home. Then I would have to tell him the lie about being injured in the terrorist attack, causing me to be in the intensive care for a week. It was just as well; I had never been close to him.

I contemplated what my future would hold. I had the Zeto Crystal, but it was drained from saving my life from certain death. It would recharge eventually, but I wanted to be proactive and do something useful in the meantime. I realised that I shouldn't be afraid of making money. Money was a great tool to make the world a better place, and I could do a lot of good, if I utilised my talents for trading, to support charitable projects

I thought about Simona, and I had another epiphany: It was time for me to experience sex! When Simona had tried to seduce me, I had felt discomfort as I wasn't a lesbian, but it had also awoken my dormant attraction to my former classmate, Alexander. While Alexander wasn't meant to be the father of my future daughter, he was smoking hot, and I realised it was time for me to lose my "holier than thou" mentality, lose my virginity, and pursue my sexual desires, as any 18-year-old woman would.

I called Alexander on his mobile, and he replied. *"Hi Sabina, what's up?"*

I said to him straight up, *"I want to have sex with you, are you free today?"*

"Is this a joke?" Alex asked with a sceptical tone, but he seemed pleased at the same time.

"No, are you at home?" I asked.

"Yep," Alex replied.

"See you in an hour, we'll have lots of fun," I said and hung up the phone.

As I left my house, my mum asked me where I was going. *"I am going to my former classmate, Alex,"* I replied.

"Alex? What are you going to do there?" my mum asked with a confused voice.

"Well, after saving the world from an evil underground conspiracy, it's time for me to do something long overdue!" I replied.

"And what is that, sweetheart?" Ellen asked.

"To experience sex and be a normal 18-year-old girl," I replied cheerfully, and took off before my mum had the time to say anything, leaving her speechless.

Chapter 29: Sabina, You're Hurt!

I was with Alexander in his room, and we were kissing passionately. For the first time in my life, I was giving in to my carnal desires, and it felt amazing. I was so excited about leaving my terrifying Jerusalem trip behind me, pursuing the sensual passion that was shared among most humans, which is crucial for our survival.

I could feel my excitement rising, as Alex pulled off my T-shirt, but then… he just stopped and looked silently at me. *"Sabina darling, what happened to you?"* Alex asked with a concerned voice, deep and rusty, but gentle. At first, I didn't catch on. I was so aroused, and it made me mad that he just stopped what he was about to do. I looked at him pleadingly and replied, *"But I want you, Alex, why did you stop…?"*

He grabbed my hand and looked deep into my eyes. *"Sabina…",* he started to speak, searching for words. *"Your beautiful torso is full of fresh scars and stitches. What happened to you?"* I realised that Alex was right. I should be in severe pain, as I had arrived from Israel not too long ago and was still dealing with the injuries that I had sustained. My brain had disconnected from the physical pain as a coping mechanism to my 18-year-old tight and luscious body. I could feel my bottled-up feelings getting the better of me, and tears flooded down my cheeks.

"I almost died in Israel, "I replied weakly.

"Tell me what happened?" Alex replied. I hesitated. Should I tell him the truth that only my present mother, Ellen Hines, knew? That I came from the future; that I was kidnapped and shot multiple times by the Mossad conspirators; and that I was saved by the magic power of the Zeto Crystal? Or, should I tell Alex that I got injured at the suicide bombing incident that happened at the Western Wall? I decided to do the latter and told Alex, that I was at the hospital in Jerusalem for the rest of my dreadful holiday. If I couldn't trust my secret with the man who brought me up, I couldn't share it with Alex, not at

this stage at least. *"I was wounded in the terrorist attack at the Western Wall. I got back from Jerusalem yesterday,"* I said plainly.

"Oh, this is terrible. First the rape incident with Joshua Harkins, and now this. You have been through a lot, Sabina," Alex replied sympathetically. Hearing Joshua's name made me froze. The last thing I needed was more bad reminders. Alex noticed my reaction and hurried to add in: *"I am so sorry; I shouldn't have brought it up."*

I nodded, forced a smile, and asked. *"How did you know about Josh?"*

Alex hesitated, cleared his throat, and spoke: *"I saw Eric Orchard kissing Lindsey McGowan at Joshua's party. I thought that you should know, so I was looking for you. When I found you, I saw you go upstairs with Joshua. Shortly after you left, there was a big commotion with an ambulance picking up Joshua. I heard that he almost raped you. After that, he had a mental breakdown, broke the mirrors, and cut himself with them. What really happened between the two of you?"*

I decided to answer Alex's question, but I left out the part about my powers, as he did not know I was an incredibly special girl. *"Joshua said he needed to talk with me in private that night. We went up to his room, and he threatened to rape me. I pleaded for Joshua to let me go, but he wouldn't. Suddenly he turned insane, kicked the mirror, and shattered it. Joshua turned to self-harm by cutting himself with the shattered pieces of glass. That's when I ran away and alerted his parents, who then called the ambulance."*

Alex nodded and let it all sink in. *"Wow... Well, I guess we are lucky that he turned to self-harm instead of harming you"*, Alex said with an afterthought. I shook my head and replied:

"No. There is no luck in someone turning to self-harm and ending up in a psychiatric ward. There is not always a silver lining to everything. "

I noticed that my words came out as intimidating to Alex, and I decided to speak a bit softer to him: *"But yes. I'd rather Josh hurts himself, than him hurting other unknowing girls."* Alex nodded, and I decided to change the topic. *"How come you were looking for me on that evening, why did you think I needed to know about Eric kissing Lindsey?"* I asked.

"I... I was perplexed. I thought the two of you were a couple, Eric, and you. I was angry that he cheated on you, but then I saw that you went up to Josh's room. I was so confused; I didn't know what to do." Alex replied nervously.

I nodded towards Alex. I realised that Alex could not have been the only one believing that Eric was my boyfriend. We were always best of mates; we must have appeared to be a crazy fun couple. Alex had always adored everything that I did, and to see Eric kissing Lindsey, well, that would have made him mad, as he would have hated to see me hurt emotionally. To Alex, hurting me, or lying to me, was the epitome of betrayal, and he would never have let anyone harm the girl he had always adored. I realised that a lot of things in life was very dependent on different perspectives, as I had not seen it from his point of view, until I came back from my crazy adventure in Jerusalem, realising how much I had missed Alex, who I was kissing moments earlier.

"Eric, and I have been close for years, but we were never romantically involved. In fact, I was the one who introduced him to Lindsey, as Eric had told me he had liked Lindsey for years," I told Alex.

Hearing this made Alex relieved, and he spoke: *"I feel a bit silly now. I have had a crush on you for years, but you never even looked twice at me, and I thought Eric was your boyfriend."*

I was unprepared to hear this. I had liked Alex for years as well, but I had never thought of being in a relationship with him, or any guy for that matter, as I thought it would clash with my real purpose in life. *"How could you hide it from me for years? What about all the other girls you go out with, don't they ever interest you too?"* I asked. Alex shrugged his shoulders and looked away. He replied with a controlled voice while looking out through the window. *"Those girls, they were only interested in me for my good looks and money."*

I reflected on Alex's statement and replied: *"And why do you think that I am different from them?"*

"Maybe I am just dreaming, but I think I have seen the real you. I have seen the gorgeous girl, who could be so popular in class, but instead shows empathy and kindness towards the unpopular kids." Alex replied solemnly.

I nodded and replied: *"I guess you are right; popularity and vanity have never interested me. Being kind and doing the right thing is what matters. But you were popular in class, Alex. You are good-looking and good in basketball; you could have gotten any girl you want?"*

"I guess appearances can be deceiving. My mother died when I was young, and my father spends most of his time to make lots of money. I guess I am just a lonely kid stuck in an unfulfilling hedonistic lifestyle. I really liked your personality, and

I have hoped for many years that you'd pay special interest in me, and be there for me, but you never were." Alex replied.

"Well, I am here now, am I not?" I replied and looked at him sweetly.

"Yes... You finally are. Come with me and enjoy the sunset. There is a perfect spot nearby, where my mum used to take me." Alex said. I nodded and I felt a warm fuzzy feeling spreading through my body as he took my hand. We walked to a picturesque garden, on the top of a hill, where we could witness the beauty of the sun setting over the Sydney Harbour.

Chapter 30: Feelings of Sadness and Remorse.

Later the same night, I lay alone in my bed and felt miserable. I touched and studied the Zeto Crystal, but there was nothing that distinguished it from a typical blue sapphire. I felt remorseful, depressed, and full of angst. My innocence had been torn away in the last few months. It had started with Joshua's damn party. I ignored my gut feeling that told me I shouldn't go, and I went anyway. I ignored my gut feeling, when I followed the drunken Joshua into his room to 'talk in private'. He had tried to force himself on me, and I had unleashed my supernatural powers on him, causing havoc on his sanity and leaving him as a self-mutilated mental wreck.

But had it been justified of me to turn him mental, which led him to cut himself, and had him admitted to a psychiatric ward? I felt a rush of guilt surging through me. I quickly shook off the feeling. Regardless of Joshua's emotional state, he didn't have the right to rape me! Josh was just a rude, selfish prick. Alex, on the other hand, had been infatuated with me for many years, yet he refused to have sex with me unless I was mentally ready. Alex was always so kind and observant of my feelings, I knew that he would never take advantage of me.

My thoughts wandered to Yussuf, the suicide bomber, who had killed dozens of people and would have killed me, if it wasn't for divine intervention. Could things have been different, if I had used my superpowers and blasted Yussuf unconscious with a psionic blast, as soon as I sensed his agitated state of mind? There was no way for me to know, and it didn't make sense to knock him unconscious pre-emptively. Yet the thought wouldn't leave my mind.

I thought of Jakub Kluger, the Mossad agent who had murdered Dov in front of my eyes and was about to kill me, when lightning struck him. I could have saved him and yet I left him to die. I decided that his outcome was due to his own actions, but did I have the right to leave evil people to suffer and die?

Most of all, I thought of Simona Fischbein. I had dragged her into a dangerous situation, when I brought her to the Templar Tunnels at the Solomon

Temple. There was no reason for her to come with me, and in the end, her contribution didn't matter. Yet, I had willingly risked her life, bringing her to the Tunnels. Although it was Ben Yehuda that had ended her life, I was complicit in her death, and it was something I would have to live with.

I looked at the selfie we took together, while posing as happy tourists outside the Solomon Temple. She looked so beautiful, youthful, and innocent in that picture, and yet, less than an hour later, the Mossad killed her. As I cried myself to sleep, I promised myself to never again let an innocent die because of me.

Chapter 31: An Uplifting Meeting with Eric Orchard.

A few days later, I felt a bit better, and I met up with my best friend and half-brother, Eric Orchard. Most of my classmates thought that we were a couple, as no one knew that we were related besides my present mother, Ellen and I. Eric's late father Marvin Orchard, was my biological father, as he had an impromptu affair with my mother, under the influence of The True Maker. Not knowing of this secret, Eric thought of me as his best friend, and I had played along.

Before I left the house, I did something I usually don't; I applied simple but sweet make-up to my face. I had spent the last few days in sadness, crying a lot, and hardly sleeping. I realised that it was a natural response for someone who had lived a safe and sheltered life, to react this way after witnessing all this death and bloodshed in Israel, but I didn't want to bring it up anymore.

I met up with Eric at an expensive sushi restaurant, close to the chess club where we used to hang out after school. As we got seated, Eric looked at me and spoke: *"Wow, I never thought I would see you wearing thick makeup Sabina... You look like a charming clown!"* He smirked and looked at me, cheekily.

"Shh. I am going on a date with Alex later today, and I want to look stunning for the occasion," I replied, slightly annoyed at Eric's brotherly joke.

"Alex? Who's Alex?" Eric asked with a confused voice.

"Alexander O'Neill from 12C" I replied and smiled.

"I see. I have heard that Alex is immensely popular with a lot of girls." Eric said tentatively.

"Well, he has professed his adoration to me. Now that I finally see him eye to eye, I would love to date him officially," I replied confidently and added in, *"And regardless if he is the one or not, I cannot live my life as a prudish virgin anymore. I want to lose my virginity to him."* I replied

"Okay, I just wanted you to be aware of it," Eric said.

"I am, and it doesn't bother me that I am not his first time," I replied. I called a waiter to attend our table, and I ordered, *"An extra-large Sushi Canapé platter for two, a teapot of Earl Grey and Hibiscus tea, and a pack of beer."*

"Wow, that will be over $200, Sabina," Eric said in amazement. I shrugged my shoulders and replied.

"I just want to taste everything the restaurant has to offer. Money comes easy to me these days. Remember how we used to walk past this place, on our way to the chess club, amazed at how expensive it was?

"Yes, Sabina. That's just a couple of months ago!" Eric replied.

"It feels like a lifetime ago. You know, I went through a near-death experience while I was in Jerusalem. I died for a fleeting moment during the suicide bombing attack. I remember that the True Maker told me it wasn't time for me to go yet. And I woke up. Dying and coming back changed my perspective on life. And that's why I am eating expensive sushi and going on a date with Alex."

"I understand," Eric replied. But Eric couldn't understand, not entirely, as Eric was just a regular dude, while I wasn't. I was a unique girl, packed with supernatural powers of empathy and mind-altering abilities.

Our Sushi tasting platter came in, and it was delicious. My younger and innocent self would have objected to killing animals for food, but I was more preoccupied with my deeper senses of guilt. As I had some more Sushi and Nigiri rolls, I felt my melancholy coming back. While the taste of the fresh Sashimi stimulated my taste buds, it didn't satisfy my soul. My soul needed a purpose to be happy, and I struggled to find a fulfilling purpose after what I had experienced.

Eric noticed that something bothered me and brought it up: *"What's bothering you? Don't you like the food?"*

I shrugged my shoulders, looked away, and replied: *"The food is delectable, I guess. It's just nothing."*

Eric grabbed my hand and sought eyes contact. He looked into my eyes and spoke: *"Sabina, I have known you for many years. I can tell when something is bothering you."*

I nodded and replied: *"It's just... It's just I am an adult now, and I want to make the world a better place, but I don't know what to do?"*

Eric gave me a reassuring smile and replied: *"But you are making the world a better place! You are making it better for me, your parents, and everyone around you."*

"Thank you, Eric. It's just that I want to make a lasting impact and make humanity better as a whole." I replied quietly.

My statement silenced Eric for a while, and he looked like he was thinking intensively about something. Eventually, he spoke: *"How about you use your talents for online trading to do good?"*

I shook my head and replied: *"Nothing good comes of trading, it's just a system created by the rich to maintain the status quo. Regardless of how much money I make from trading, I haven't contributed to society."*

"Don't be so small-minded, Sabina. The world is unfair because the wealthy are too powerful. Revolution doesn't work, but what if you beat them at their own game?"

Eric's reply lifted my spirits. I had been depressed for the last few days because I realised that retrieving the Zeto Crystal hadn't led to anything, and I had lost my innocence, witnessing all the death and suffering in Jerusalem. But Eric had given me an idea about how I could use my abilities to make the world a better place. A lot of projects could improve the future of humanity, but they didn't get funding because they weren't profitable. If I could make a lot of money from trading, I could spend them on philanthropy, and projects that would make the world a better place.

"Eric...Thank you for lifting my spirits. That's a great plan!" I exclaimed happily.

"Uhm, you're welcome, Sabina," Eric replied, amazed at how quickly my mood improved.

"I got to go, time to make some money," I said happily. I left a few hundred dollars for the bill, and I took off with the flabbergasted Eric sitting there, unsure of how he was going to eat all the Sushi platters left.

Chapter 32: Getting Alex Involved in My Project.

A few weeks later, after losing my virginity to Alex, I was looking at my cute boyfriend, sleeping next to me, looking so handsome and sweet. He had a rocking chiselled body and sharp facial features that reminded me of a Roman soldier, especially with his strong jawline and sporty broad shoulders. Whenever he smiled with his white straight-teeth and big bright smile, feelings of excitement bubbled within me, with girlish squirms that I felt silly for experiencing.

Losing my virginity to Alex had been pleasant and sweet, but it wasn't as amazing as I had hoped sex would be. After my physical wounds had healed, and my mental scars from the ordeal in Jerusalem were slowly fading away, it had seemed like the natural step to progress our relationship. When I was a virgin, I never understood why people were so pre-occupied with sex, and now that I no longer am a virgin, I still didn't know why it was such a big deal.

To me, physical connection can never surpass emotional and intellectual connections. While an orgasm is great and amazing, it is just a short-term fleeting moment of spikes in serotonin levels. Mental and emotional experiences, on the other hand, can fill me up with a long-lasting sense of joy and tranquillity. Sex is crucial to keep our species around. But compared to the perfect geometry of the Golden Ratio and the Fibonacci Sequence, or the sweet harmony of a well-composed musical work, such as Bach's, it's insignificant.

Since my ordeal in Israel, something had changed inside of me. Before I turned 18, I spent most of my time pursuing spiritual perfection: singing, making music, and forming friendly and emotional connections with people. While these pursuits were fulfilling and gave me great satisfaction, they did not change the world around me, or served to further my goals. Now, that I had matured into adulthood, I believed that I could fulfil my desire to make the world a better place, using my superpowers and high intellect.

I studied Alexander closely. Except for the scarring from a broken arm from when he was a kid, there was nothing that indicated that he had lived a difficult life. Indeed, staying in his father's extravagant Vaucluse house, Alex was better off than most kids growing up. Yet there was something about him losing his mother at an early age. Growing up with a cold and distant father that made me feel connected with him. I trusted him completely, and Alex fulfilled my needs physically. I realised that Alex was someone I could trust and love as well. But would he satisfy me, intellectually? I decided that now was the time to find out.

I opened my online trading app, where I now had a balance in the millions of dollars. A drastic change from the $1,000 I started out with, just two months earlier. I had been trading obsessively for the last few months. While I realised, that it wasn't healthy to stay fixated for days on end on the online trading sites, sometimes forgetting to eat or sleep, it had been my coping mechanism.

I nudged Alex and he woke up. He yawned, gave me a sweet look, and said: *"Baby.... What an amazing night we have had. What are you looking at?"*

"I was simply curious about your opinion on something. Should I put or call on this $10,000 investment option on the Euro currency exchange rate?" I asked. With my heightened intelligence and my premonition, I knew which direction the floating currency was heading, but I was still curious about how Alex would respond to my question.

Alex shook his head and replied: *"Just turn off your phone, Sabina. It's not good for your sanity to use internet devices, day and night."* I realised that Alex thought I was playing a virtual game on my phone instead of making a real financial stock market investment. *"But you do know that pressing the right button on this phone will have a tremendous impact on my bank account? I can make or lose several years of a high-paying salary at the click of a button."* I stated.

"Okay, show me this game you are playing," Alex said, and had a closer look at my phone.

"It's not a game, it's my actual trading account," I stated proudly.

"Oh my God! There are millions of dollars in there, is this real money?" Alex asked in shock.

"Yes," I replied.

"But you have never mentioned this before, and I have seen your family and your apartment. They are not wealthy?" Alex asked in bewilderment.

"I only became a millionaire a couple of days ago, and I reckoned we had better things to talk about. More important things," I replied.

Alex was silent for a while, struggling to process the news of my sudden wealth. Eventually, he asked tentatively *"So, how are you going to spend the money?"*

I smiled at him and replied: *"I haven't decided yet. How would you spend the money?"*

He thought for a while and replied. *"Hmm, I would like to contribute to cleaning up the oceans."*

I was happy with Alex's answer, cleaning up the oceans from plastic waste was one of the many projects. that I was interested in supporting. That he had thought of a charitable cause, instead of luxury, showed me that we were in harmony. Although admittedly, I would get myself some luxury as well. I was not the saintly prodigy child, that I was in my former life. *"Great, Alex. I would like to clean up the oceans as well. Tomorrow I'll donate $250,000 to the Ocean Clean-Up charity."*

After making the trade, I turned off my phone, so it wouldn't disrupt my sleep. As I put it away, Alex winked at me and spoke: *"I thought we could do something else before we go back to sleep..."*

I smiled back and replied: *"Great idea, I was thinking the same thing"*

Chapter 33: An Unexpected Reproach from Eric.

A few days later, I met up with Eric for lunch. He didn't look happy when he approached me, and he addressed me in a quite angry tone: *"I heard you donated $250,000 to the ocean clean-up charity, have you gone mad?"* Eric's reaction bewildered me. This was my money, and as far as I knew, he wasn't against cleaning up the oceans. Disliking his snappish tone, I snapped back at him: *"Yes, I did. I like to support charitable organisations, and besides, you have no reason snooping around in my business!"* Having said this, I immediately realised the hypocrisy in my statement, as I tended to meddle in other peoples' dealings.

Instead of shouting back at me, Eric leaned in to whisper in my ear. *"Calm down, and I will tell you why I am worried."*

I did as Eric asked, and once he noticed that my mood had stabilised, he spoke to me again: *"I have no problem with you donating money to charities. But you must realise, for every cent you make on online trading, someone else loses it. "*

"I don't follow you, Eric. What does that have to do with my donations to charities?" I asked tentatively.

Eric fixed up the collar on his newly purchased Gucci shirt, fixed his sunglasses, and replied: *"You want to change the world to the better, right?"*

"Yes, I do," I replied, wondering what Eric was getting at.

"Well, if you truly want to change the world, a few millions won't do anything. You might get lucky now, but you must watch out for those who are going to cause you trouble!" Eric stated.

"Well, if that's what it takes, that's what I will do," I replied confidently and added in. *"But you still haven't told me why you are upset."*

"I am not upset; I am just giving you a heads up. If you make millions from trading, that means someone else is losing millions. Some of the companies that have lost money due to your trading skills would act against you, if they found out who you are. If the people that are willing to dupe governments, cause war and

famine, find out that they have lost billions to you, they won't play it nice. You could be the next Julian Assange." Eric said with a concerned voice.

I realised that Eric was right. If I really wanted to change the world, I would need to do so anonymously. The money I had donated this far, wouldn't cause many questions. But once I started spending more money, I would get unwanted attention from the people that were manipulating the world to enrichen themselves. Acting anonymously would protect me from potential threats, accusations, or lawsuits.

"So, what do you suggest that I do?" I asked.

*"Well, if you really want to beat the dark forces at their own game, you'll have to remain anonymous like they do. You'll have to start using fake companies, proxies, and hidden accounts all over the world, "*Eric explained.

I hugged Eric and said. *"Thank you, Eric. You are really the smartest person that I know."*

Eric smiled back and replied. *"Thanks! That means a lot coming from the girl who beat the Chess Clubs' A.I. on Kasparov level, and made $8million from online trading in a couple of months!"*

"Well, it's the truth. Let's eat, I am starving!" I exclaimed, and I called the waiter over. As I ate the delicious Italian spaghetti meatballs, while discussing strategies with Eric at the local Italian restaurant, I realised something. That being wealthy wasn't bad at all.

Chapter 34: 'Building a Better World Pty Ltd.

A few months later, my mission to improve the world was up and running. To make everything look legit, I set up a charity in the Central Business District of Sydney and called it 'Building a Better World Pty Ltd'. As a non-profit organisation, and a privately funded charity, it could receive donations, from my anonymous trading activities. While nothing was 100 per cent foolproof, it was a lot better than donating millions to projects under my own name.

I employed Eric, Alexander, and Eric's girlfriend Lindsey, to run the charity, and I tasked them with finding worthwhile projects all over the world. It was good to have an inner circle that I could trust and share ideas with, and I was confident that I could trust them.

My certainty was because I used my empath powers to read their minds, to know what they were thinking and influence them covertly. While it wasn't morally right to spy on my friends and my boyfriend, it was a temptation that was too hard to resist. Everyone has doubts about people around them, and if you can use your powers to calm your doubts, and to get people to do things your way, it is hard to not use those powers.

I decided to make Alex the CEO, and the face of the charity. He was the best-looking in the group, and the one with the most natural charisma and leadership. While my empath powers made better at influencing people in actual meetings, it didn't make me the better option for speaking in advertising videos and giving speeches at large conferences.

Due to the almost unlimited advertising budget and Alexander's natural charisma, Building a Better World Pty Ltd soon became the largest charity in the world. Money started to stream in from other sources, although my anonymous contributions were the largest source of income for the charity.

Chapter 35: Proposing to Alex.

Just a year later, life progressed well, and I could see the positive results of our many charitable projects. The Zeto Crystal was still dull and out of its true iridescence power, and I realised that I couldn't fulfil my real mission until it was fully charged.

My real mission was to stop the wicked Xeno Queen Rangda Kaliankan from conquering and destroying the Milky Way Galaxy. As I failed on my first attempt, the True Maker allowed me to be born in the past to try again before Rangda was too powerful. I needed to stop Rangda during my lifetime to stop her from destroying the future, as Rangda would collect and corrupt all the Zeto Crystals by 2887, making her unstoppable.

With the current world improving for the better, I realised that I could focus on another life goal. I wanted to give birth to Keila Eisenstein, my mother in my former life.

Unfortunately, Alex's DNA was incompatible with becoming Keila Eisenstein's father, but I realised something. My current body didn't have the same genetic combinations as I had in my former life, so even if Alex couldn't father the biological Keila Eisenstein, he could still give me a normal child with her spirit.

I have never been very traditional, but thinking about motherhood, I realised that I wanted to be married to the person I love. Alex would make a great father, and although the constitution of marriage was just a tradition, it was a beautiful tradition and one I wanted to pursue.

I studied Alex as he was watching a soccer game on television. I approached him and spoke: *"Hey babe, I brought you a beer."*

Alex looked at me, positively surprised and smiled. *"You are bringing me a beer to drink? What about the lectures regarding the danger of alcohol, drugs, and other psychoactive substances?"* Alex teased me gently.

"Well, I wanted to get you in the mood for some positive news," I said confidently and smiled.

"Well, you certainly have my attention now," Alex said in excitement.

We snuggled comfortably on the sofa, and I continued to speak: *"The last year with you have been amazing. I want the following 90 odd years to be equally great, together with you. Do you want to marry me?"*

"Ha-ha. You're silly, babe. Spending the next 90 years with you is not long enough, I won't settle for less than a century," Alex said cheekily, smiled at my confusion and continued, *"Of course I will marry you, Sabina. You are the greatest woman I have ever met."*

"Well, I don't have a hundred years left in me though," I replied and winked at Alex.

"You drive a tough bargain!" Alex laughed and continued: *"Okay, we'll get married. Deal."*

He grabbed me with his firm, sexy hands, and we kissed passionately.

Before we went to sleep, I decided to settle a detail with Alex. *"Hey babe, do you care about details like the flower arrangement, or the font on the wedding invite?"* I teased him.

"Of course. I want the day to be perfect for you," he replied diplomatically.

"Well I don't care, so how about we leave all those pointless details with the wedding planner?" I replied sweetly.

"I can live with that," Alex stated and laughed a burst of kind-spirited laughter.

"Good, then I'll have enough time to work on my secret wedding gift to you," I said happily.

"Oh, a secret wedding gift! What am I getting?" Alex asked happily.

"Shh. It wouldn't be a secret if I told you. Now sleep, future husband. We need to get our beauty sleep for the fundraising charity event tomorrow", I teased back.

"Yes, my princess!" Alex said with a broad smile. Shortly afterwards, we both fell asleep.

Chapter 36: Pre-wedding Jitters.

A few months later, I was sitting in the green room of a beautiful wedding venue in Rose Bay, overlooking the Sydney Harbour. I was stressed and frustrated with my wedding planner, but not for the usual reasons. My frustration was because my wedding planner kept bugging me with insignificant details for months on end. The banquet menu, wedding decors, which companies we should buy the wedding flowers from, where to get the cake, etc. I had assumed that hiring a wedding planner and giving her a million-dollar budget would be enough to run a smooth wedding, but I was mistaken.

What frustrated me more than my finicky wedding planner, was that I couldn't get my wedding gift for Alex to work. I knew that by the 23rd century, the oceans would be cleaned up by self-replicating fusion-powered marine robots, but I couldn't get the team of engineers that I had hired, to build a working prototype. The technology simply didn't exist yet.

But I wanted to give Alex something meaningful as a gift, as I knew that he really wanted the oceans to be clean of plastic and polluted water, so I had settled for constructing a solar-powered marine prototype. The machine couldn't self-replicate but was achievable with the current technology. The machines wouldn't be enough to clean up the oceans, but at least they would be a start that inspired hope.

There was a knock on the door, and much to my dismay, it wasn't the delivery of my prototype, but my wedding planner. I could tell from the anxious look on her face that something had happened. *"Sabina, I have unwelcome news,* "she started.

I struggled to hide my irritation and gave her an empathic answer: *"Tell me, Amanda."*

"The Florist crashed her van, and the wedding flowers were destroyed," Amanda replied.

"Oh no! Is Jenny okay?" I asked.

"She got some bruises and a minor concussion," Amanda replied, close to tears.

"Okay. I am glad that it is not any worse. You can go see Jenny in the hospital if you want. Tell her I can't make it today, I have to be at the wedding venue, "I said and tried to lighten up the mood with a smile.

"But... What about the flowers?" Amanda asked with a shrilling and panicky voice.

I decided to use my empath powers to calm Amanda down. I had my own worries, and I couldn't afford to focus on minor things such as Jenny's minor injuries, or the absence of flowers at my wedding ceremony. I grabbed Amanda's hand and looked into her eyes. Then I spoke soothingly to her: *"Do not worry about the flowers. We'll be fine without them. Now visit Jenny in the hospital and come back when you are feeling better."*

I noticed how Amanda's facial expression changed, and she looked more at peace than I had ever seen her before. *"Okay, I'll visit Jenny in the hospital,"* Amanda replied, and wiped her crocodile tears.

"Good. Tell Jenny to focus on her recovery. I'll pay for the flowers regardless, so she doesn't need to worry about that," I replied.

"Thank you, Sabina. I'll go see her at once," Amanda said, and she left the room.

After Amanda had left the room, I wondered why I hadn't used my powers to calm her down a long time ago. My last few months would have been a lot easier if I didn't have to deal with her panicky and stressful nature. But then I realised that I wasn't bestowed with these supernatural powers to stay clear of every inconvenience in my daily life. The True Maker gave me these powers to fulfil a purpose, not to always have smooth sailing through life.

There was a knock on the door again, and this time, it was better news. My chief scientist had arrived with a prototype for my ocean clean-up project. I looked at the prototype. *"Dr Tony Phillips, is the prototype working now?"* I asked him.

"Yes, but it is still in the pilot stages," He replied.

"That's fine. Have you prepared the presentation slides and speech notes?" I asked him with a concerned voice

"Yes, but shouldn't you be the one who present the subject, as you are giving this as a present to Alex? I just built the prototype you asked for. I'm not a good public speaker," Tony responded nervously.

"Well, it lends more credibility when a senior Marine Scientist presents the topic to the public, rather than me presenting it. Besides, I am the bride at the wedding. People expect me to be beautiful and prepped up. I'm not going to present on a serious topic wearing a wedding dress. Sometimes you'll have to give society what they expect" I replied calmly.

"Wait, so the wedding is today? "Tony asked in bewilderment.

I smiled, realising how much I had baffled Tony. *"Yes, the Ocean Clean-Up Project is my wedding gift to Alex, and I would like you to present it to all of the guests."* I replied

As the confused Dr Tony Phillips left the room, I was filled with excitement. This would be a wedding to remember, and today would be an important turning point for our beautiful marine life.

Chapter 37: A Beautiful Flowerless Wedding.

A few hours later, I was dressed up and prepared for my wedding. We had decided to have a non-religious wedding, as we prefer to keep things simple rather than religiously dogmatic. Sectarian behaviour had caused endless segregation, and conflicts throughout the history of humanity. Thus, we didn't want to involve any religious matter on our wedding day.

Besides, although I have long heard the True Maker inside my head, I had another reason for not marrying Alex under a Terran religion. The deity, who had rebirthed me, was the True Maker, the creator of the Universe. But no religion on Earth acknowledged the True Maker, so it didn't make sense to marry under any Terran religious beliefs.

We exchanged our wedding vows in front of 500 people at the beautiful and serene Lyne Park on a sunny March day. The sun reflected beautifully on the crystal-clear water of Sydney Harbour, and it was just the perfect temperature for a nice event. I wondered if the True Maker was looking over me to make my wedding memorable. I concluded that wasn't the case. The almighty creator of the Universe had better things to do than manipulating the weather for my enjoyment, or so I thought.

"I do," I replied to the marriage celebrant. Then I turned to Alex and kissed him.

As we walked around among scenic locations for the wedding photos, Alex turned to me and smiled. *"You look stunning today,"* he said.

"I better; otherwise three hours of makeup and wearing this impractical white dress would be for nothing," I responded, and winked at Alex.

"I can't wait to help you take it off!" He responded cheekily, purring under his breath.

"That makes it two of us. But believe it or not, I have an even better present for you tonight!" I announced.

"Ah, do you perhaps have a twin sister?" Alex asked jokingly.

I gave Alex an angry stare, and he quickly backed down. *"Just kidding, Boss!"* he apologised, sporting a big silly grin on his face.

"Good. I wouldn't like sharing you with anyone else. But I will share your wedding present with the world. Let's go to the reception, it is starting soon." I replied.

The wedding reception went smoothly. The food and drink were all delectable, but unfortunately, I didn't get to enjoy much of it, as I wanted to avoid going to the bathroom with my impractical dress. After the main course, we danced the wedding waltz, which we had practised a lot. Dancing was one of the better ways for a couple to stay fit together, while also building a closer bond.

After the wedding waltz, came the highlight of the wedding, which was the wonderful speeches. I had prepared the speeches to get media attention, and I had invited several reporters to my wedding. I had realised that revealing my plans to clean up the oceans on my wedding day would be unique and would give the topic a lot more attention than if I called in a separate press conference. I went up to the podium and spoke: *"Dear friends and family. Thank you for attending our big day. First of all; this wasn't meant to be a flowerless wedding; we do apologise for it. Our florist had a minor accident and is now recovering in a hospital. I would appreciate if all of you can send her your best wishes on social media, whenever time suits."* I looked at Alex, we looked at each other with a beautiful and warm gaze. I continued my speech and said, *"To you, Alex, you are the love of my life. While I could spend the next 45 minutes talking about how much you mean to me, I want to show you, and everyone here, how much you mean to me. Behold, your wish comes true, I have organised for projects on the first step to cleaning up the oceans. May I introduce, Dr Tony Phillips, who will lead our ocean preservation projects."*

As I finished speaking, Dr Tony Phillips walked in with a marine prototype built like a vacuum suction, packed with tentacles like underwater tubes. He gave a presentation on how the machines would slowly clean up the oceans, through sucking up plastic and rubbish, to protect marine life. After the performance, we drank and celebrated all night, before we finally took a limousine to the hotel suite we had reserved for the night.

As we got to our hotel room, Alex looked at me drunkenly and spoke. *"Hey babe, you don't intend to use this dress again, do you?"*

"No, of course not, I'm never going to get married again, you silly darling. Why do you ask?" I replied with a laugh and a quick pash.

"Because today is our special day. I feel like a young kid who just got his first bike. I want to tear the wrapping off my present," Alex replied cheekily while kissing me gently.

I nodded and smiled at Alex and said, *"Go ahead, husband, enjoy your present."*

"With pleasure, my beautiful wife," he replied.

After that, we had a long and passionate night. We rejoiced that the peer pressure of pleasing everybody on our wedding day was over, so we could enjoy each other's company without interruption!

Chapter 38: Finding a New Enemy.

A month later, we came back from our honeymoon. We had been island-hopping on the Pacific Ocean and pursued one of Alex's biggest passions, scuba diving. I also loved scuba diving, but it made me sad knowing that all the beautiful reefs of the 20th century had died off, due to global warming and plastic pollution.

Altogether It had been a wonderful trip; we were young, rich, and free, and we could do whatever we wanted, just the two of us. A part of me wanted this life to never end, and I could choose to live that way if I wanted to. But I felt that I had an obligation to the world. I wasn't reborn to live a hedonistic lifestyle with my incredibly handsome partner. I was reborn, so I could change the world for the better.

I opened the safe in my home office to inspect the Zeto Crystal. It didn't glow, and I wondered if it would ever be useful again. At the moment, it looked like a dull blue sapphire, albeit it was massive, the size of a tennis ball. Next to the Zeto Crystal, there was an old cell phone. I recognised it, but I couldn't remember putting it in the safe. It was the encrypted phone that I bought from the Dark Net that Simona had delivered to me, when I was in Israel, two and a half years earlier. For some reason, I felt compelled to start the phone, so I plugged it into a charger.

Initially, nothing happened. Suddenly, there was a loud beep and a message showed up on the phone. The message was from over two years ago and meant for Simona. She was part of the revolution on the dark web against the Mossad, called A Better World, written in Hebrew. I hesitated for a bit. Did I have the right to read the message intended for my dead friend?

But then again, why had I suddenly opened the phone several years later if I wasn't meant to read it? Unable to control my curiosity, I read the message. It read: *"Simona, I am worried about you. I haven't been able to reach you for several weeks. Did the Mossad capture you? Anyways, I have found out who is funding the conspiracy within the Mossad. It's funded by the leader of the World Bank, Pierre Beaumont. I have attached all the proof on our Dark Net servers. Please contact me, I am worried about you. //Joanne"*

This message confused me and filled me with so many puzzling questions. I wanted to see the proof for the Mossad conspiracy that Simona's friend was talking about. But I didn't know what encryption programs Simona had used, so finding the encrypted server on the Dark Net was like looking for a needle in a haystack. But what else could I do? I could contact Joanne, but how would she react? She must know that Simona was dead by now, so why would she trust me if I tried to contact her with Simona's phone several years later? And worst of all, what if the message was a trap set by the Mossad? They didn't know about my real identity, since Martin Al-Sham destroyed my files at Ben Yehuda's house. Sending this message could be their way to lure me out.

I turned off Simona's encrypted phone and put it back in the safe. I needed to act, but what could I do? I decided to do some research on the World Bank on my own. Initially, I got a lot of positive reactions. I expected this to be the case for a large organisation like the World Bank. Such an organisation could pay Google and other search engines for Search Engine Optimisation and make sure to censor opinions about them. I had done the same for Building a Better World Pty Ltd.

I realised that I had to dig deeper. I found out that most of the countries that the World Bank 'helped' ended up worse off, with the ownership of their natural resources transferred to various shady organisations.

While this didn't prove anything, as the World Bank perhaps operated under misguided humanitarian acts, I realised that they didn't improve the world. But should I go after them or were there bigger fish to fry? I did an online search on Pierre Beaumont, and I realised that he was visiting Sydney for a global economic forum in the coming week. That kind of meeting was inaccessible to your average woman, but not for me. I was after all one of the wealthiest persons in Sydney after making billions on the stock market and other financial markets.

I accessed the Global Economic Forum website, and I bought VIP tickets for Alex and me to have lunch with Pierre Beaumont the following week.

Chapter 39: Lunch with Pierre Beaumont.

The following week, I was heading to the Global Economic Forum with Alexander in tow. He wasn't happy with me, and he voiced his concerns: *"Why did you spend $100,000 for us to have lunch with Pierre Beaumont? That money could have been used to improve thousands of lives."* Alex claimed in anger.

I struggled to come up with a proper response. I wanted to meet Pierre Beaumont, so that I could use my empath powers to find out about his true intentions for the world. But I had never told Alex about my empath powers. I was worried that he would see me differently, if he knew that I could enter and alter his mind when I touched him. No-one wanted to be a slave to someone else, even if it was for good intentions.

"Well, I think if we can get Pierre Beaumont on our side, then we can convince him to eradicate poverty. That's how powerful he is." I stated.

Alex shook his head and replied: *"Bah, get these people on our side? Those plutocrats only care about benefitting themselves. Why else do we still have poverty on our planet?"*

I nodded and replied thoughtfully: *"Regardless, I think it helps us, if we meet these people and get to know how they think."*

"Well, I assume the ticket are non-refundable, so we might as well go. I just wished you would have asked me first!" Alex grumbled.

I looked away and didn't say anything. There was nothing more to say, and I knew that Alex would calm down once we arrived at the meeting. I thought of saying that I was sorry for not consulting with him first. But I wasn't sorry, and I didn't want to lie, so I kept quiet for the rest of the drive to the International Convention Centre, where the meeting took place.

We arrived at the ICC, and we attended the conference in the morning. It was interesting, but without any revolutionary innovative ideas. During lunchtime, we got our money's worth, a private lunch with Pierre Beaumont in a small meeting room.

As I entered the room, I felt that something was amiss. Pierre Beaumont turned out to be a balding man in his fifties with a strange monocle, the same type of monocle that Ben Yehuda had worn. While I could not read his mind without touching him, I could sense the dark aura of evil and greed in the room. This was a man who had died on the inside a long time ago.

"Please, do sit down, I've only got 10 minutes." Pierre Beaumont urged us, and we took a seat. Pierre spoke again: *"As you know, my time is valuable, but I will make an exception and let you make your case, for whatever you seek the World Bank's assistance with."* Alex looked at me, and I nodded to encourage him.

Alex cleared his throat and spoke: *"As you know, we have developed automated marine prototype vessels that will clean up the oceans from plastic waste."*

"Don't be too confident, there are many worthy projects out there. But yes, I have heard about your utopian project, and if you are asking for the World Bank's support on this matter, the bank's answer is a NO." Pierre replied with an arrogant and firm tone.

"But why? It could save a lot of marine life at a low cost, and it is a green and earth-friendly project" Alex pleaded.

"We do not prioritise preserving marine life, and the World Bank has a lot of missions on its hand," Pierre replied coldly.

"Geez! we paid $100,000 to see you, the least you can do is to answer the question properly, that answer is not good enough!" I proclaimed in anger.

Pierre brushed off some imaginary dust from his suit, nodded and replied. *"Okay, Miss Hines. I will be as forthcoming as possible. Cleaning up the oceans and saving marine life are worthwhile goals. But the ocean is for everyone, it is not an investment asset that we can capitalise on, so it does not have any value to us. The World Bank doesn't deal with utilitarian social aims, we deal in financial and investment assets."*

"But you said that you wanted to create a better world?" I asked.

"Everything good has a monetary value. Cleaner oceans don't have a monetary value. Thus, it isn't for us to pursue," Pierre replied.

"Money isn't everything in the world!" I responded angrily.

"Well, that is where the bank has to disagree with you. Money doesn't exist to serve humans. Humans exist to serve money. In the absence of deities, money becomes the new god, the raison d'être for humanity." Pierre stated in a malicious manner, while rubbing his hands together.

I pondered the ugly old man's statement for a few seconds. I wondered what made him so mean and wicked. I responded with a sad, pitiful smile. *"Do you know what you need? You need a hug. You must never have been loved or loved anyone before."* I said and hugged Pierre before he had the time to answer.

I didn't hug Pierre because I liked him, although I did pity him for being so greedy and wicked. I needed to get physical contact with Pierre to use my psionic powers to reach his mind. Much to my dismay, I couldn't access Pierre's mind. I didn't know what to do. as I hadn't expected this. An unnerving thought reached my mind: What if Pierre was also an empath, and was reading my mind?

Suddenly, I heard Pierre's voice: *"Humph!! Miss Hines, this hugging is not part of the lunch meeting. Ugh, now that you have succeeded in making me feel miserable for a few seconds, would you please stand back and let me continue my duties?"* I stepped back and felt like an idiot for doing such a silly thing. Pierre spoke again: *"Humph! I didn't like that at all. What a waste of time! I am afraid our time is up, Miss Hines and Mr O'Neill. I am a terribly busy and important man, and I have many dignitaries to meet in Australia. Godspeed. "*

A few of Pierre's bodyguards approached us, so we took the hint and left the room. When we got out of sight from the room, Alex scolded me: *"What was that all about? Why awkwardly hugging the leader of the World Bank in front of your husband?"*

"I needed to feel his aura. Now I have, and I realised something eerie about him and his shady corporation." I replied with a worried voice.

"And what is that?" Alex asked irritably.

"We must focus our efforts on taking down the World Bank's evil operations. As long as they are around, they will keep funding evil corporations, supplying weapons for wars, drilling more holes in the Earth, polluting the oceans, and killing our trees. We can never get the world we desire, as long as the World Bank's exists", I stated with tears in my eyes.

"Unbelievable. How could you come up with that, after randomly hugging the CEO? I am going home." Alex growled.

I thought of saying something or using my powers, but I decided against it. I understood where Alex was coming from, and while I was determined to take down the World Bank, I didn't know how to handle my husband's short fuse. I felt sad and helpless, and there was only one person I could confide in, my sweet mother, Ellen.

Chapter 40: Confiding in My Mother.

A few hours later, I snuggled up in the couch with a blanket, drinking a nice cuppa in my parents' cute 2-bedroom apartment in Maroubra. It felt ridiculous having a blanket as Sydney was still warm in March, but it was one of the things I did when I felt vulnerable. My mother Ellen brought in a cup of yummy chicken and ham soup. Then she gently wiped the tears off my cheeks with a handkerchief.

Ellen held my hand, looked at me, and spoke gently to me: *"Sabina, darling. Tell me what happened?"*

"I had a fight with Alex, and I don't know what to do." I sobbed.

"A fight with Alex? But I thought you guys were so good together. What did he do?" Ellen asked.

"He didn't do anything. It's all my fault," I said quietly.

"Now, now, Sabina. Just tell me what happened." Ellen responded in a very understanding tone.

"I haven't told him, mum. I haven't told Alex about my empath powers. You are the only one that know." I said, staring out in the distance while sipping on the delicious soup.

My mum sighed and looked for the right words. After some silence, she replied: *"I see, that is an important thing to hide from your husband. Why haven't you told him?"*

"I love him, but I am afraid that he would distrust me if he knew that I have the powers to read and change his mind", I replied.

"Well, would you do that to him? As in, manipulate his thinking to suit yours?", Ellen asked gently.

I knew there was no reason to lie to my mother. She was the one who knew me the best, and the only person I had told about my secret. But as much as it pained me to tell her the truth, the truth was even more painful to myself. The fact was, that I had used my supernatural powers to dupe and manipulate Alex, into becoming the person I wanted him to be. *"Yes, I have done it to him..."* I replied with a faint and guilty voice.

Ellen nodded gently at me and let it all sink in. Eventually, she responded, *"Hmmm. I suspected as much. It must be difficult to have such powers and not use it for your own sake."*

"Yes, exceedingly difficult. I am happy with Alex, but I feel guilty knowing that I am overstepping my boundaries..." I replied.

"I guess the best thing would be, if you owned up to what you did, and told him everything," Ellen stated with a reassuring voice.

"But, what if he leaves me?" I said with a concerned voice.

"Well, Sabina. I believe that you will be happier on your own, rather than living in a marriage based on a lie," Ellen replied with a heavy heart.

"Would you have been happier, if you had ended up marrying the guy who fathered me, Ma?" I asked.

I saw my mum's face changed; I had reminded her of the guilt that had lingered for all those years. I was the product of her short tryst in Egypt with Marvin Orchard, while she was married to John, my "dad", who never found out that he was sterile, thus unable to father any children. *"I am sorry, Ma. I shouldn't have brought it up."* I bit my lip and said this quietly.

"It's okay, darling. You're grown up now. It's something I thought about many times throughout the years. I might have been happier ending my marriage, but you needed John to be your father. When you have a child of your own, you'll understand this," Ellen responded.

"Thank you, mum," I replied, and kissed Ellen gently on the cheek.

We sat silent for a while, hugging each other, slowly sipping the tea, and drinking the soup. Eventually, Ellen spoke: *"So what was Alex upset about today? What did you do?"*

"He was upset that I spent a lot of the charity's money on organising a meeting with Pierre Beaumont, the CEO of the World Bank", I replied.

"Was the money well-spent?" Ellen asked with an inquisitive voice.

"Well, yes and no. Now I know that Pierre Beaumont is evil, and that I need to stop him and the World Bank. But it caused that stir between Alex and me, so in that way, it wasn't." I stated with a calm and confident voice.

"Good luck, super-girl. Dealing with the World Bank is long overdue!" Ellen said, winked at me, and smiled in a motherly manner.

After this, we sat quietly for some time, hugging each other, and listening to soothing meditative music. Eventually, I realised that I had to meet Alex and tell him about my powers. He was my dear husband, and I could not keep him in the dark any longer.

Chapter 41: Telling Alex About My Empath Powers.

Ten minutes later, I arrived at my south Coogee six-bedroom house, overlooking the cliffs and beautiful streaks of the blue ocean below. The weather had turned bad, and it was a rainy and stormy evening. As I entered my house, I felt that it was too large for just the two of us, and I missed the cosy apartment where I had grown up. My mother had made a smart choice by choosing to live simple in a clean little apartment.

I walked upstairs and found Alex in the home office. He looked up and spoke to me: *"Where have you been Sabina, I tried to call you several times. I got worried when you didn't pick up the phone."*

"I went to my mother to have a nice long comforting chat. I needed to talk to her and find some inner peace after our fight today." I replied while looking deeply into Alex's eyes.

Alex looked back at me gently and spoke: *"I am sorry about that fight, Sabina. It's my fault. I shouldn't dictate what you spend money on. You are the charity's biggest contributor, after all."*

I smiled at Alex replied: *"I am happy you say that. But to be fair, we are both at fault, I should have consulted you before I decided to pay the money to see Pierre."*

"Great. Let's put this behind us. I know we will easily make the money back, given your special abilities to make the right choices in the stock market. Would my lady want a deep-tissue massage before we go to bed?" Alex said. He looked relieved and smiled at me.

Alex's bright smile and the offered massage were so enticing, so I almost forget the important matter I had to discuss with him. I forced my smile away and instead looked at Alex with a serious face. *"Alex...There is something else that I need to tell you. Something I should have told you a long time ago,"* I said cautiously.

Alex's smile disappeared, and he responded with a worried voice: *"What is it, Sabina?"*

"I... I haven't been honest with who I am. What I am," I said quietly.

"What on Earth are you talking about? We grew up together. We went to school together. I know who you are, Sabina," Alex responded in confusion.

"Well, the first time you met me, I was sixteen. But there was something remarkable that happened to me before that age, that I haven't told you," I responded cautiously.

"So, what is it that you haven't told me?" Alex asked.

Now, here is the dilemma. How do you tell your loving husband, who you have known since your teenage years, that you are the future saviour of humankind, reborn into the present day by the supreme deity? How do I tell someone I love this crazy story that I have psionic powers, enabling me to read and influence minds? I decided to tackle the issue head-on.

"I have lived before, in another life," I stated.

Alex stared at me in disbelief, unsure whether I was joking or not. Eventually, he spoke: *"Hmm. I think you are serious here, Sabina. Well, I have heard of people claiming to have lived before, and you are hardly the only person in the world that believes in reincarnation. But it puzzles me that you haven't told me about it until now."*

"Well, those people are usually just imagining, but I am different. I am the reincarnation of Sabina Eisenstein, The Chosen One, from the 29th Century. Although I feel that I have become increasingly human when living during this era," I stated.

Alex looked at me for a while, and then he broke out in thundering laughter. He laughed so hard, he was struggling to breathe and was rolling around on the floor. When he had calmed down, he replied. *"What a prank, Sabina. You really got me with that one. "*

I smiled back at Alex. I couldn't resist being pulled into his mindset as he was a very handsome and charismatic man. Eventually, I managed to be serious again. *"I am not joking, Alex. I was reborn in our age, given psionic powers, premonition, and heightened intelligence by the True Maker."*

Alex, still in a good mood since his fit of laughter, replied playfully. *"So, tell me, my love, except for being stunningly beautiful and making billions of dollars, what power did your deity give you?"*

"Well, he allowed me to survive a dozen bullets. I also survived standing next to a suicide bomber. More importantly, he gave me the power to read and influence minds."

Alex, still in an upbeat mood, laughed it off and responded: *"Are you sure there is only normal tea in your mother's tea kettle? I want to come by and drink tea with you guys someday, if this is the effect I'm getting."*

"It's definitely just tea. I'll prove it to you. Think of three random letters." I said.

"Sure, surprise me," Alex said and laughed.

"You were thinking of E, S, X" I stated confidently.

"You got the order wrong, but yes" Alex teased back.

"Umm... Okay. The night your mother died; you wore a pink t-shirt with a pony cartoon!" I stated.

"What? How would you know? It's totally uncool to bring up my mother's death, Sabina! But how on earth would you know?" Alex replied in surprise.

"I told you already, Alex. I am an empath, I can read people's minds" I replied.

"That's enough, Sabina. Why did you bother finding out my embarrassing childhood secrets? And why did you bring up my dead mother?" Alex asked. He looked angry, and his face turned red. Clearly Alex's mother's death, was an unhealed wound.

I hugged Alex and whispered. *"I am sorry, Alex. I just needed to show you my abilities. Now, I want you to be happy again."*

At the end of that sentence, Alex smiled at me. *"Yes, I am happy. But why, just a second ago I was feeling sorrow and rage. What is happening?"* he asked, genuinely surprised.

"I am an empath. I was influencing your mind to feel a certain way," I replied plainly.

My response scared Alex, and he backed away from me. *"Why are you doing this to me? Are you playing me around like a fool?"*

"I am sorry, Alex; I didn't know what else to do. Originally, I intended to carry out my purpose on my own. But when I got close to you, I realised that I needed you. That I had to be with you to be happy. I had my powers; I just couldn't stop

myself from using them to make us happy." I said this with tears running down my cheeks.

"*So our relationship is a big lie? You used supernatural powers to manipulate my feelings, so I don't even know what is the real me anymore?*" Alex asked in disbelief and anger.

"*I hope that you believe me when I say, that I want us to be happy. I know we are both happy together.*" I replied reassuringly, hoping to calm Alex down.

"*But how can I know?*" Alex asked.

"*I... don't know*" I stuttered.

We sat silent for a while. Eventually, Alex spoke: "*So, why did you tell me now?*"

"*I have struggled with my conscience. I know I shouldn't spy on you, but I just couldn't help myself. It's a complicated ability to have and not use. Like seeing things in front of your eyes, without seeing it*", I replied with a sincere voice.

Alex sat silent for a long time. Eventually, he spoke. "*Sabina, I have some cousins in Queensland that I haven't seen for years. I will visit them on my own and consider our relationship. I'll leave this evening.*"

I realised that Alex was doing the right thing. The only thing that he could do after my confession, was to stay away from me for a while, and decide whether he wanted to stay in the relationship. The prospect of losing him petrified me, so I cried out. "*I understand. Please come back. Consider how happy we have been and all the good that we can do together.*"

Alex nodded and replied. "*I know. I just need to figure out whether this is something I really want, or if it's just what you want me to desire.*" Having said this, he opened the door and walked off, leaving me to feel sad and lonely in my big empty mansion.

I thought of going back to my mother and seek her sympathy, but I realised that Alex left because of my own actions. I was no longer a little girl; I was a strong woman. With or without Alex, I had a goal to achieve; to make the world a better place.

I went to my home office and started trading. I had a new target. I wanted to beat Pierre Beaumont and the World Bank at their own game, to stop their nefarious influence on the world.

Chapter 42: Almost Dying and Finding the Zeto Crystal Energised

72 hours later, while sitting in front of my computer desk, I collapsed to the floor. I had been so absorbed by my mission to take down the World Bank, that I hadn't left the computer for the whole time. While I had taken billions of dollars off the World Bank, it was still only the tip of the iceberg, and I felt devastated. I had hoped that Alex would come back, or at least call me, but I hadn't heard anything from him in the last three days. Without Alex in my life, there was nothing that balanced my addiction to trading, and kept me grounded in life.

I realised that I had neither slept nor drunk any water in the last 72 hours, both life-threatening conditions, I got up from my chair to fulfil my physiological needs. I didn't get far though, as my knees were so weak that I slipped, and hit my head, knocking me unconscious.

Suddenly, my mind was in the Divine Dimension, and I spoke to the True Maker, who had taken the form of Keila Eisenstein, my first human mother of the 29th century.

"Why are you doing this, Sabina? Why are you forsaking the physiological needs of your body?" Keila Eisenstein asked.

"I am really depressed, mother. I lost Alex, and I have nothing but my goal to live for," I replied weakly.

"You haven't lost Alex, darling. He loves you, and he will come back when he is ready. But if you forsake your body, there won't be anything for him to come back to." Keila said with a weighty voice.

"But it has been 72 hours, and I haven't heard anything from him?" I said with tears running down my cheeks.

"Sabina, you have to let go of things you are not meant to control. But don't forsake your body. You are dying Sabina, and that is why you are here, speaking with me. Your spirit has left your body." Keila replied.

"Am I dead?" I asked in amazement.

"Yes, and no. Unlike other humans, you have my spirit and the option to come back. This has already saved your life on several occasions," Keila said.

"I know, and I am grateful for that, mother," I replied.

The True Maker nodded and smiled at me. *"Great, when your mission is over, I will let you live out your life as a regular human. Now return to life. Your physical body is fragile. Make your way to the safe. I have energised the Zeto Crystal for you. Grab the Zeto Crystal and hold it tightly. It will grant you the energy to make your way to the water tap so you can drink some electrolytes to fix your severe dehydration. Then, go straight to bed, Sabina."*

I woke up at my home office. I was in severe pain affecting my head and my knees, as I took a deep painful breath of air. I remembered my conversation with The True Maker, and I summoned my energy to crawl the painful metres to the safe. Once I reached the safe, I realised that I had forgotten the access code to the safe. "My birthday," I heard Keila whisper in my ears, and I entered 22-03-2850 onto the display.

The safe opened, and I grabbed the Zeto Crystal that was now energised. As I grabbed the crystal, I felt energised and got up on my feet, feeling fitter than ever. I remembered what The True Maker had told me and made sure to drink plenty of water with added electrolytes before I made my way to bed. As I reached the bed, I passed out for some much-needed dreamless sleep.

Chapter 43: Having Brazilian BBQ With Ellen.

I woke up 24 hours later, and I felt hungrier than I had ever felt in my life. I checked my fridge but much to my dismay, all the food had gone bad during my obsessive trading frenzy, as I hadn't bothered eating or cooking anything since Alex left. Besides, the food in the refrigerator was not what I craved. I usually ate a mostly vegan diet because I didn't want animals to suffer, but this morning, I was craving for meat, lots, and lots of meat. I realised that the Brazilian BBQ in Darling Harbour would do the trick to satisfy my raging hunger.

I called my mother Ellen, who was pleasantly surprised by my suggestion and she agreed to meet up. Two hours later, we met up at the buffet for a delicious lunch. Ellen looked at me with a shocked face and spoke: *"Oh my god. Sabina, you're so pale! You don't look well at all. Is everything alright? "*

"Not really, but it will be," I replied and forced a smile.

"Tell me what happened," Ellen urged.

" I told Alex the truth, and he took off. I didn't want to seek help for my emotional suffering, so I focused my energy on obsessive trading instead. After 72 hours without drinking or sleeping, I collapsed to the floor." I replied.

"72 hours without drinking any water?!" Ellen exclaimed and continued, *"That is extremely dangerous Sabina. You have to look after yourself!"*

"I know, that's what she told me" I replied in resignation.

"Who is she?" Ellen asked.

"The True Maker, taking the form of Keila Eisenstein. I died, my spirit left my body, but she brought me back to life." I said with a tired voice, before continuing with a more cheerful tone: *"On the bright side, she also told me that Alex still loves me. Alex will come back when he is ready."*

Ellen looked at me for a long time. I knew the struggle she was going through. It wasn't easy seeing a loved one suffer. Eventually, Ellen spoke: *"I un-*

derstand. Why don't you come home and sleep in your old bedroom for a couple of days? Separating from a loved one is never easy."

"Yes, I guess you're right. I'll pack my bag and come by tonight." I said. I was relieved that I no longer needed to force myself to be stronger than I was.

A waiter came by our table, and he was shocked when he heard my order, *"12 chorizos, a kilo of beef tenderloin and a kilo of chicken breast."*

"Miss, do you expect other guests? I can move you to a bigger table if you want?" the waiter asked with a surprised voice.

"No, this table is perfect. It's only my mother and me today" I replied, smiled, and gave the baffled waiter a big tip.

An hour of massive eating later, I was feeling very full, and I checked my phone. I had received a message in my encrypted email that both scared and interested me. It was from Martin Al-Sham, who was in Sydney and needed to meet me.

I felt very hesitant and anxious. How could Martin Al-Sham have survived and escaped the Mossad agents in Jerusalem? The last time I saw him, he was shot, and I was running away from pursuing agents. Then again. Could I deny meeting the man who had betrayed his group and saved me from certain death, when Ben Yehuda had tried to murder me?

I looked at my Zeto Crystal, and I felt it's energy vibrating when I touched it. Martin Al-Sham appearing now, just days after my Zeto Crystal was charged? This could not be a coincidence. "Meet me at Barangaroo Wharf in one hour," I replied, and I turned off my phone. I got up from my table Ellen looked at me in surprise and spoke: *"Where are you going, Sabina?"*

"I need to meet someone, someone who saved my life once," I replied.

"Martin Al-Sham?" Ellen asked.

"Yes", I replied.

"Bring me with you, I want to thank him for saving your life," Ellen said

I considered Ellen's request. I didn't like it. Martin Al-Sham was a murderer, and I feared that danger was ahead of me. The powered Zeto Crystal and the True Maker would protect me, but there was no-one to protect my dear mother. But on the other hand, I didn't want to bereave my mother the opportunity to meet and thank Martin Al-Sham if he had come in peace. I decided to settle for a compromise.

"Ellen, Martin might be dangerous. If you want to meet him, please stay in the background, go, and have a cuppa and cake at the coffee shop. I'll introduce him to you if everything is safe," I said to her anxiously.

"Sabina! Don't meet this man if he is dangerous," Ellen urged me.

"I have to meet him; his return can't be a coincidence. Besides, the True Maker and the Zeto Crystal will protect me," I stated.

Ellen realised that there was no point in arguing with me when I was this determined, and replied, *"Oh, okay, I'll stay in the background. Be safe, Sabina."*

"Thanks mum, you too," I replied.

After this, we paid our bill and headed for the meeting point at Barangaroo Wharf.

Chapter 44: Meeting with Martin Al-Sham and Getting Attacked by Mossad Agents.

An hour later, I was waiting cautiously at Barangaroo Wharf when Martin Al-Sham approached me. He was limping, he had aged a lot, and he wore a thick jacket, which seemed strange considering that it was a warm and humid April day. He smiled bitter-sweetly as he approached me and spoke: *"Thank you for seeing me, Sabina."*

"It's the least I could do. You saved my life, and you helped me escape Israel. I thought you died. The last time I saw you, you were shot, and I was running away from the Mossad agents. How did you survive and escape? "I asked curiously.

"It's pretty straightforward. I survived the bullet wound and an ambulance picked me up. I was brought to court once I recovered. For some reason, I was never charged with murdering Ben Yehuda and the Templars. Getting shot is not a crime, and the Mossad agents that shot me didn't press any charges. All I got was a year in prison for the illegal possession of a firearm," Martin Al-Sham responded.

I was sceptical, to say the least. It seemed highly unlikely that no-one had found the bodies in the secret room, as we had left the doorway open at the Templar Tunnels. Unless Martin had accomplices that disposed of the bodies to cover up the murders, there was no way the Mossad would let him go. But why had Martin appeared now, almost three years later? I decided to tackle this question first.

"So, why have you come to visit me after such a long time, Martin? If your story holds up, you were released from prison over a year ago?" I asked sceptically.

"I saw you in a dream a couple of nights ago. You were dying and you were saved by the power of the Zeto Crystal. I felt compelled to meet you as quickly as possible, so I booked the next flight from Sweden to Australia." Martin stated with urgency.

"What were you doing in Sweden? I asked.

Martin responded: *"Well. Sweden is my home country, and as soon as I had served my one-year prison term, Israel deported me. Regardless, I had fulfilled my mission, so I felt no need to stay there any longer."*

I decided to use my empath powers to read Martin's aura. I held his hand and looked into his eyes, and I felt a powerful sense of familiarity, stronger than I had ever felt to John, who had raised me. I felt that he was a kind and trust-worthy person, a gentle but bitter-sweet soul who had gone through many years of wars and pain. But why did I feel this way about this mysterious middle-aged man, that I had only met a few times in my life?

I couldn't answer this question, but I concluded that Martin was a trust-worthy friend, and that I should introduce him to my mother, Ellen. *"Come Martin. My mother Ellen would like to meet you and thank you for saving my life,"* I said and pointed in my mother's direction as she was observing us from a nearby coffee shop. *"Is the blonde woman in the red jacket your mother?"* Martin asked and looked like he was thinking about something.

"Yes, have the two of you met before?" I asked.

Martin didn't have the time to answer my question, as we were interrupted. *"We finally meet, Miss Keila Eisenstein!"* I heard a voice, with a thick Israeli ac-cent, saying to me from behind. I turned around, and I saw a man with a mon-ocle, accompanied by three shady looking characters, all wearing dark suits and sunglasses.

"Ben Yehuda, is that you?" I asked in amazement.

The man shook his head and smirked at me. *"No. Ben Yehuda is dead, mur-dered by that traitor standing next to you, Martin Al-Sham. I am Szymon Yehu-da, Ben's younger brother."*

"Wow, just the man I have been waiting to meet," I replied sarcastically.

"I am sure you have..." Szymon replied, paused, and then continued talking. *"Fortunately, today is your lucky day. I am not here to avenge my brother. I am here to retrieve the crystal that you stole from the Templar Tunnels. Aid me in this quest, and you might even get out of this alive."* Szymon gave me a menacing and sadistic smile, and I realised that his vague promise was nothing but a lie.

"Oh, do you mean this Crystal?" I said defiantly and pulled out the energised Zeto Crystal from my pocket, showing the glowing orb in front of Szymon's face.

"Yes, hand it over to me, Keila, so I can use it for its intended purpose," Szymon said with a chilling voice.

"What is that? To murder and eliminate everyone that stand against you?" I asked defiantly.

"No… To perform Yahweh's plan for the Holy Land. I want to kill all the Palestinians in Israel and win the wars of our holy people!" Szymon replied wickedly and self-righteously.

I trembled with fear and anger over what Szymon had said. I squeezed the Zeto Crystal with my right hand, while I clenched my left fist and responded. *"I have decided…."* I paused for a second and then continued *"…to not give you the Zeto Crystal"*. Having said this, I punched Szymon with a surprising amount of speed, and broke his nose. I then backflipped down into the water and swam towards the bottom to be safe. The assassins started shooting after me, but they couldn't hit me, as I was underwater, the water was a bit murky, and the bullets slowed down in the water.

I panicked when I realised that I couldn't stay underwater for long. I squeezed the Zeto Crystal and prayed to the True Maker. To my great relief, I no longer needed to breathe, and I felt one with the water, like if I was an aquatic creature. The shooting ended, and I saw blood flowing down in the water. I didn't dare to swim up to the surface to check what had happened, and instead, I chose to swim away as fast as I could.

An hour later, I surfaced at Farm Cove, in the Royal Botanical Gardens, a 5-kilometre swim. My phone was broken, and my clothes were soaked. I realised that I had to get home and get my stuff. The Mossad clearly didn't know my real identity and had followed Martin Al-Sham to find me. Thus, my home was my safest bet, but how would I get there? While I wanted to seek help from the authorities, I worried that they might have been compromised. I decided to run the 6-kilometres home and I powered my fitness level with the Zeto Crystal. It wasn't the wisest way to spend its limited energy, but I was afraid, and I wanted to seclude myself from the outside world.

With the energy from the crystal, I ran home in less than 20 minutes. I scanned my fingerprint on the entrance scanner to enter my mansion. Once inside, I made my way to the bathroom, and I collapsed into a warm bath. I instructed the A.I. housekeeping robot to bring me tea, and to keep the bath water warm. Exhausted from the physical strain, I dozed off in the bath. When I woke up, I saw a face I had longed to see for the last few days; my sweet and handsome Alexander looking kindly at me.

Chapter 45: Reconciling with Alex and Finding Out What Happened at the Pier

"*I came back as quickly as I could, when your mother told me the news,*" Alex said, shocked but relieved to find me. Before I had the time to answer, he spoke again: "*At the airport, I thought I had lost you, but I realised that if you survived the ordeal, you'd try to make your way home where you would feel the safest.*" Seeing Alex released all my emotional baggage from my latest near-death experience, and I started crying. "*I thought I had lost you. I thought that you didn't want to see me again*", I sobbed while feeling very relieved at the same time.

Alex took my hand, smiled at me with his glittering white teeth, and looked at me with his lively green eyes. "*Sabina, you are the love of my life. Why would you believe such a thing?*"

"*Well, you were very upset when you left, and then you didn't call me,*" I sobbed.

Alex replied with a soft and sincere voice, "*I am sorry, Sabina. I was vindictive and foolish. I realised on the second night that you made me whole, and a better person than I ever could hope to be on my own. But I wanted to make you realise that you had done wrong, so I stayed away for a few more days. But I could never imagine that you'd take my absence so hard. Your mother told me that you didn't drink or sleep for three days straight and collapsed.*"

"*Yes... It wasn't just your absence that hurt me. I also felt that I wasn't worthy of sympathy, and I tried to work my way out of the situation*", I replied.

Alex stroke my wet hair away from my teary eyes, and gently wiped my tears with a towel. "*Don't wallow in guilt, Sabina. You simply have unique abilities that others don't. As much as I am upset that you spied on me, I would have done the same if I had your abilities.*" Alex told me with a gentle and deep soothing voice.

Alex's reassuring words made me feel better. He always did, he was the rock that I needed to give me stability and purpose to my human side.

"Thank you for coming back!", I said.

"What happened at Barangaroo Wharf? After I jumped into the water?" I asked.

"You really don't know?" Alex asked in amazement.

"No, the power of the Zeto Crystal allowed me to swim underwater without breathing. I didn't dare to swim up to the surface until I had swum to the other end of the city."

Alex looked at me in confusion and replied: *"I don't know what to say about that. I am just happy that you are okay. Anyways, after you broke the nose of one of the agents and jumped into the water, the other agents started shooting after you. Suddenly, your mysterious friend, grabbed one of the agent's pistol and shot the other agents."*

"Did Martin get out there alive?" I asked, surprised that I suddenly felt so worried about him.

"Yes, your mother said he ran off. You should contact the police. Your mother didn't reveal your identity to them, but they will figure it out soon.", Alex urged.

I knew that Alex's request was sensible, but I couldn't follow it. I had made billions from trading against the World Bank in a few days, and suddenly Martin Al-Sham and the Mossad assassins had come after me. The Mossad still believed that I was Keila Eisenstein, but if I spoke to the police, I would reveal my real identity. While I wished that I could trust the New South Wales Police Force, I simply could not, considering that my adversary was the World Bank, one of the most influential organisations in the world.

"No, I will not speak to the police," I stated firmly.

Alex was surprised by my position, and his body language showed disapproval. *"Why not, Sabina? They'll have to investigate when unknown assassins try to murder you. They can protect you."* Alex urged me.

"The World Bank has infiltrated the Australian government. Speaking to the police will reveal my identity, and they will know that Keila Eisenstein is not the person they are after. Besides, I have an important task ahead of me!" I asserted.

"Sabina, you just survived an attempt on your life. You need to rest and recover from the ordeal", Alex pleaded.

"No, I don't have time to rest! There is something I must do!" I said in anger, making Alex take a step back. I continued speaking, *"I need to go to Mexico and activate the portal in the Pyramid of the Sun."*

"*And why is that?*" Alex asked cautiously.

"*Because the purpose of my reincarnation was to secure the Terran Zeto Crystal and to stop Rangda from conquering the Milky Way Galaxy. I have the Terran Zeto Crystal, and it is charged. I cannot let anything stop me from achieving my goal.* "

Alex studied me for a while and then responded with a determined voice: "*I am coming with you.*"

"*No, Alex. It is going to be extremely dangerous. I don't want to put you at risk,*" I said to him.

"*We are a team. Never again will I leave your side. We will face adversity together.* "Alex said proudly.

I was happy to hear about Alex's faith and love to me. I decided to not argue with him anymore. He had come back for me, and we were clearly meant to fulfil our purpose together.

"*Alex, pack a bag and find our passports. I'll call our private jet and tell them to prepare for departure.*" I said.

"*We don't have a private jet?*" Alex asked in bewilderment.

"*Yes, we do. I bought one the other day from some of the money I made from trading against the World Bank*", I responded.

Alex smiled at me and responded in amazement: "*You never cease to amaze me, Boss. I'll get us ready to go shortly.*"

"*Good, we have no time to waste!*" I urged. I got out of the bath, put on my clothes, and called the private airline.

Chapter 46: Worrying Premonitions.

Just two hours later, I was sitting on the private jet next to Alex, drinking champagne to calm my nerves. I was apprehensive. We would have to land in Fiji and Hawaii to refuel the plane, but this was not what worried me. I was wealthy and could pay a premium to have professionals deal with the flight-paths and permissions. What bothered me were my premonitions. I had tried to see different potential outcomes for Alex, and no matter what I did, my premonitions told me that Alex would die in the next few days. If I insisted on leaving him behind in Sydney, the unholy alliance of Templars, Mossad agents and World Bank operatives would murder him when they couldn't find me. If he came with me to Mexico, he would die on the dangerous journey ahead of us.

I grabbed Alex's hand tightly. He gave me a sympathetic look and spoke softly to me: *"Are you worried about the flight?"*

I nodded and replied quietly: *"Yes, but that's not my main concern."*

"So what is really bothering you?" Alex asked with a soft, soothing voice.

I was stuck in inner conflict. I didn't want to hide things from Alex anymore, but I just couldn't bring myself to tell him about his impending death. Eventually, I settled for an answer that wasn't a lie, but it wasn't my main concern either: *"I am just so worried about my mother. Martin Al-Sham saw her from a distance, and he recognised her."*

"Have you called her and told her about your concerns?" Alex asked.

"Yes, but she didn't pick up the phone, and I don't know what to do", I replied.

"I'll call Eric for you. He can visit your parent's place and take them somewhere safe for a while." Alex said confidently.

"Yes, please do," I replied.

Alex called Eric, and they agreed that Eric would visit my parent's place and urge them to go away for a couple of days. It was an unusual request, but my mother would know why, and they would comply. I felt slightly better but not relieved of my greatest woe: the knowledge of Alex's imminent death. I decided to do everything I could to keep him safe. I had suffered a lot after Simona's death, and she was just a stranger to me. Losing the love of my life would destroy me.

Alex seemed keen to change the subject and spoke to me. *"So why are we going to Mexico, Sabina? Could we have gone somewhere else to achieve your goal?"*

I decided to give Alex an honest answer and replied: *"My powered Zeto Crystal has the power to unlock portals to another dimension. The portals are located four different pyramids. The Great Pyramid of Giza, The Great Pyramid of China, The Sunken Pyramid of Kiribati, and the Sun Pyramid in Mexico."*

"Wait a second! I have never heard about the Sunken Pyramid of Kiribati?" Alex interrupted.

"That's because it hasn't been found yet. In our time it's located over 100 metres under sea level." I replied.

Alex acknowledged my answer with a nod but said nothing.

I continued my explanation: *"The Great Pyramid of Giza is in Egypt, and that place is bound to be swarming with Mossad Agents and Templars when we get there. When it comes to China, the Australian government's bad relations with the Chinese government makes travelling there difficult. The Sunken Pyramid is found 100 metres below the sea level and is inaccessible. Our only choice, for now, is The Sun Pyramid in Mexico."*

Alex looked at me in disbelief and seemed to keep an objection to himself. *"What is it that you want to say, Alex?"* I asked curiously.

"I am glad you asked," Alex replied.

I nodded, and Alex spoke again: *"You believe that we are pursued by the Templars, the Mossad and the World Bank, right?"*

"Yes, those are the ones I am certain of. But there might be others", I said with an afterthought.

"Well, the problem is that Mexico is swarming with World Bank operatives. The current Presa Del Muerto project in Mexico is one of the World Bank's largest projects.", Alex said with a worried voice.

This revelation shocked me, and I was angry with myself for not doing my due research. I realised that my high intelligence sometimes made me arrogant and blind. But what would I do? Stay somewhere in the Pacific a few days while waiting for a visa to China? Somehow get a submarine, find the Kiribati Pyramid, and activate the portal underwater while swimming in the dark abyss, 100 metres below the sea level?

I decided to stick with my plan and go to the Sun Pyramid in Mexico. For all I knew, The World Bank wasn't even aware of my existence. *"I'll stick with my plan. We'll go to Mexico. I have already organised a tour guide there. We will be safe, pretending to be normal tourists."* I stated.

"As you wish, darling. We better get some sleep. It's a long flight ahead of us." Alex said and closed his eyes.

I couldn't sleep though, as I saw gruesome images swirling in my head, every time I closed my eyes. Images of Alex's death kept showing up in my premonitions. Despite my promise to not hide things from Alex, I couldn't be honest, and I certainly hoped that my premonitions were wrong.

Chapter 47: In Trouble with Jesus.

Many hours later, our plane landed in Mexico City. I woke up and realised that I had slept soundly. This relieved me, as my angst was less apparent now that I had rested. My relief didn't last for long, as armed men surrounded us, as we left the aeroplane. While I don't speak Spanish, I quickly realised that these were not government officials.

They threatened us with their guns and instructed us to enter a military truck. After that, we were blindfolded and gagged. I cried, and my only relief was that I could feel Alex's warm hand holding my hand. This didn't help, as I could feel Alex's emotions, and he was as fearful as I was.

Eventually, the truck stopped, and the men led us to their leader. I recognised him as Jesus Ortega, the infamous drug kingpin. He was fiddling with his gun, sitting by a table filled with banknotes. He smiled at me, displaying several golden teeth, and a missing buck tooth.

"Miss Hines and Mr O'Neill. Welcome to my humble estate!" Jesus said with fake pretence.

"I'd feel more welcome if you extended us a formal invitation, instead of kidnapping us at the airport," I said with a ferociousness, that surprised everyone in the room including myself.

Jesus laughed loudly, looked at Alex, and replied. *"Ha-ha. You sure have a fiery wife, Mr O'Neil. She must be good in bed. I might try her myself."*

"Stay away from Sabina! Tell us what you want!?" Alex responded. While he tried to sound firm, I could sense that he was terrified, and his voice trembled as he uttered the words.

Jesus shrugged his shoulders and replied nonchalantly: *"Very well. You can keep your pale skinny bitch. I get enough action anyways. I brought you here so you can endorse my campaign to become Mexico's new leader. "*

"No way! Mexico already has a president, and you are nothing but a murderous drug lord." I replied defiantly.

"Is that so? And yet your husband is already funding our little rebellion. Tell your wife, Alexander," Jesus said and smirked.

"I don't know what you are talking about?" Alex replied in confusion.

A beautiful Latin American woman entered the room. Jesus Ortega stood up and bowed theatrically. *"Miss Sabina Hines, may I introduce you to Sandra Santiago from the Escuela Mexico foundation,"* Jesus said and smiled a crooked smile.

"It is so nice to see you again, Alex. And this must be your wife? You make up such a lovely couple," Sandra said with a big seductive smile.

"Alex? You know this woman?" I hissed, and I gave him a furious stare.

"I didn't do anything like that," Alex said defensively. *"I just donated some money to her organisation. She approached me and asked for funding for her projects to provide education to the poor in Mexico,"* Alex continued.

"A very generous donation. How unfortunate that you were so mesmerised by Sandra, so you forgot to run a background check on her charity program!" Jesus said with a big grin.

"Let me guess, the charity funded your rebellion instead of providing schools for the poor" I replied sarcastically.

"You are a smart woman, much smarter than your doofus husband" Jesus replied.

I felt the anger bubbling inside of me. Alex had made a big fuzz about me paying to meet the World Bank CEO without consulting with him first. And now it turned out, that he had donated a lot of money to a terrorist group, just because he couldn't see past the superficial charm and beauty of this Mexican bimbo!

I was interrupted in my thoughts when Jesus spoke again: *"Don't look so sour, Miss Hines. Your clueless husband might just have saved your lives."*

"And why is that?" I asked in bewilderment.

"Well, Pierre Beaumont and the World Bank wants you dead. I can give you to them, but I am not their lapdog. I might find you more useful alive!" Jesus said and smiled callously.

"Why is that?" I asked.

"Well, you can give me legitimacy. I made a sample video with some of the money I made from the bogus charity. I want you to feature in videos as Building A Better World's CEO, where you praise the work we are doing," Jesus said.

"What if we refuse?" I responded, while holding in my anger.

"I have some ravenous hungry attack dogs in the basement. I am sure Pierre Beaumont would love to see the video of those ravaging dogs sharing the same meal: you're the menu of the day" Jesus responded and laughed sadistically.

"Vamos guardias," Jesus shouted out. The guards grabbed us and led us to the basement, where we sat in a damp underground cell, surrounded by starving wolf-like dogs ready to eat us alive if we tried to get out.

Chapter 48: Sandra Helps Us Escape.

As the guards left and locked the door behind them, I evaluated the situation. I wasn't particularly afraid. In my visions of Alex's death, he was shot, not eaten by dogs. Personally, I knew that I would die peacefully when I turned 112, which was a long way to go. I was an empath and animals were easy to influence, but what would I do? Turn the dogs against our captors, or give in to their demands and endorse their fake charity, which was funding war and terrorism?

Suddenly, I felt anger rushing in, and I slapped Alex in the face. *"Why didn't you tell me about this Mexican woman, and the money you donated to her charity?"* I asked in an accusatory manner. *"Sorry, Sabina. I just forgot,"* he replied weakly.

I looked at Alex. He was terrified, and this situation was uncomfortable for him as he suffered from claustrophobia, and he is afraid of dogs. I knew that I should take it easy with him, but I couldn't, my jealousy was driving me nuts. *"You forgot about meeting one of our biggest donation recipients and giving her a lot of money? What else did you forget about?"* I spat out in a furious rant. *"I donated to a charity, which I believed was funding schools for the poor in Mexico. I got duped,"* Alex replied anxiously.

I realised I had gone overboard with my useless jealousy. There was a time and a place for everything. Arguing with my partner over this Mexican woman, Sandra Santiago, when we were locked up in the basement of a sociopathic drug lord, didn't make any sense.

"I am sorry. I am just stressed," I told Alex, and I hugged him tightly to let him know that I was no longer mad at him. Alex smiled at me and replied: *"Well, even though you accused me of being dishonest, I will keep my promise to stay with you until death does us apart."*

"I'll hold you to that promise for many years to come. We are not dead yet," I replied bravely. *"We need to find a way to escape."* I continued.

The door suddenly opened, and I could hear Sandra's voice: *"Maybe I can help the two of you with that!"* Sandra winked and smiled.

"Sandra? Are you going to help us?" Alex asked in disbelief.

"Yes, I cannot let Jesus and his goons hurt you. Sabina, you have a wonderful husband. I am so jealous of what you have," Sandra said.

"So why are you involved with Jesus Ortega, if you know he is bad?" I asked.

"It's not a matter of choice. I love my family and my people. The only way to keep them safe is to accompany Ortega to bed and keep him happy. He is a terrible man when he is angry," Sandra said and shivered.

"But he won't be pleased if he finds out that you helped us escape?" I asked.

"It's too late to explain everything now. Jesus has a lot of his followers hidden in the favelas around the capital. He is planning to assassinate the Mexican president Esmeralda Ruiz today! We need to get out of here, and hopefully he won't notice in the middle of this chaos", Sandra said with a grave voice.

Suddenly, a massive explosion shook the entire building and knocked me to the ground. As I got up, I exclaimed: *"What was that??"*

"A nearby explosion from an artillery shell. I tipped off the government that Jesus Ortega was here, and the members of the SWAT team are approaching", Sandra replied.

I closed my eyes, and I had a premonition. I had an idea. I intended to release the ravaging attack dogs and use my empath powers to manipulate the dogs to attack Jesus. I knew that this action was outside of my divine mandate, but I had to save myself and Alex from Jesus, regardless of morality.

"Open the dog cages, Sandra!" I shouted.

"Are you insane?? They'll attack us and eat us!" Sandra remarked.

"Sandra, Believe in Sabina! She can control these dogs using her empathic powers" Alex added in.

Reluctantly, Sandra opened the cages. The attack dogs ignored her. Instead they ran swiftly and hungrily upstairs, to where Jesus Ortega was located.

"Lead the way, Sandra." I urged.

"Follow me to my car, and hide in the backseat!", Sandra replied.

We ran up the stairs, and I saw two of Jesus' men on the ground, having bled to death from the attack dogs' vicious bites. I had expanded the minds of the dogs. Now they were no longer primitive hungry beasts, they had turned into lethal and intelligent silent killers. I felt sickened by the scene and quickly made my way out of the room. The shockwave from another explosion shook the building and brought me back to my senses.

"Hurry up!" Sandra rushed us. I got back on my feet and ran after her. We got to her car, and Alex and I hid in the backseat. Suddenly, we heard agitated screaming and gunfire, and I knew what that meant. Jesus' men had shot at my attack dogs. I hoped that they would reach Jesus before they were shot, but it was no longer in my hands.

Sandra drove up to the unguarded backyard exit gate. She geared on full speed, drove straight through the exit gate, destroying both the metal gate and the roof of her car, instantly turning it into a makeshift convertible!

"That will surely grab their attention!" I exclaimed.

"As will the dogs that you released!" Sandra replied and continued. *"But they got other things to worry about."* Sandra pointed to the sky, and there were several Mexican government military helicopters on the way.

To avoid the army's attention, Sandra turned the car to drive into the nearby rainforest onto a very narrow and dark road. We stopped at a small hut, perfect as a hiding spot. *"Where do you need to go?"* Sandra asked.

"We need to go to the Pyramid of the Sun. We have a crucial mission." Alex replied.

"Hmm... The Sun Pyramid is several hours drive away from our location. We are going to need a new car," Sandra explained.

"Money is not a problem." Alex replied.

"Good, I will make some calls," Sandra responded and left us outside the small hut, in the hot and humid afternoon.

Chapter 49: A Lethal Confrontation.

I was sitting with Alex next to the smashed car, outside Sandra's small hideout in the jungle. I could hear gunfire and explosions in the distance, and the tiny hideout was located next to a mosquito-infested swamp. My conscience and my paranoia gave me terrible thoughts.

I couldn't feel any remorse over influencing the attack dogs to turn against and kill Jesus' men. I was now a murderer with empath powers, responsible for several homicides. The men were my captors, and they had intended to murder Alex, the love of my life, but I had still willingly traded several of their lives to save my own and his. This new, dark side of my personality terrified me.

Apart from my inner conscience, there was something else bothering me. My distrust for Sandra, the Mexican drug lord's girlfriend. I knew that she had saved us, but her reasons didn't hold up. There was something fishy with her behaviour, and I wanted to get as far away as I could from her. But it was too late, Alex had already revealed our destination to her: The Sun Pyramid.

Obsessively, I looked through the wrecked remains of Sandra's makeshift convertible, and I found something chilling in the glove box. I found a futuristic-looking monocle, the same monocle that Pierre Beaumont, Ben Yehuda and Szymon Yehuda had worn. I was alarmed when I saw it. Sandra was part of the conspiracy against us, and Alex had told her where we needed to go, so running away from her wouldn't help.

Alex noticed that I was terrified and tried to comfort me. *"It'll be okay, Sabina. Sandra will find us a transport, so we can fulfil our mission in Mexico, leaving this wretched place and go back to Sydney,"* Alex said softly.

"I don't think Sandra is planning to help us," I replied. I showed Alex the monocle that I had found inside the glove box.

"A monocle? I don't understand the significance. What is so special about it?" Alex replied.

"Ben Yehuda, Szymon Yehuda and Pierre Beaumont all wore the exact same model of monocle. I remember this clearly as I have a photographic memory. Monocles are rarely seen among people of our times, so it must be a secret code for something," I stated.

"Hmm... Or, it could be a high-technology device for top-secret communications." Alex speculated.

Alex was right. It could be advanced technology, way ahead of our times, hidden in plain sight as a meagre sheeny monocle. Being reborn in this time, I had not seen it before, and my premonitions had not told me anything about the monocles. I put on the monocle on my right eye, hoping to get some clues from it. I was amazed when the device suddenly elevated in the air, glowing immensely, expelling some type of spider web-like silky nets from the rims and attached itself straight into the optical nerves on my right eye. This surprised me and caused me anguish.

After regaining my composure, I saw an enhanced and detailed view of my surroundings. The futuristic monocle device was highlighting objects of interest in glowing red and enemies or targets in neon green. I could also see other nearby users, and I realised that Pierre Beaumont was in Mexico!

Suddenly, the device started beeping, and an error message came up in view. UNAUTHORISED ACCESS, Preparing to Terminate the User.' I felt immense pain and screamed in agony, as a needle-thin puncturing device appeared from the centre of the monocle and was pushing further and further into my right eye, moving deeper and deeper to enter my brain and kill me. Alex panicked and screamed, and forcefully pulled the monocle away from my right eye with no luck. This blinded me even further and caused excruciating pain.

I screamed my lungs out in extreme agony, and I pulled the horrid device out with all my might. I managed to pull it out, gouging out my own right eye in the process. I threw away the monocle, leaving my poor eye on the ground. I put my hand in my inner pocket and pulled up my lifesaving Zeto Crystal. I held it to my hollowed eye socket. Like magic, my right eye instantly grew back, and I looked in horror at the discarded monocle which contained the bloodied tissue and sad remains of my eyeball.

My agonizing screams alerted Sandra, and she came out of the hut wielding a tiny pistol. *"Damn, you weren't meant to see that device. I must have forgotten to hide it",* Sandra said with a sarcastic tone. Sandra studied the discarded monocle and turned her gaze back to my face. Suddenly, her arrogance turned into fear. *"What is happening. You are not a normal girl. You just lost an eye-ball, and yet you have two healthy eyes, you look unhurt."* Sandra said in awe.

"I am sent by the True Maker to save the future of humankind. There is still time for you to repent and change your evil ways, Sandra. Now tell me everything you know." I replied with conviction.

"No, no, no, this cannot be!" Sandra stuttered nervously.

"There is still hope for you, Sandra. Tell me what you know." I said gently.

"No! I cannot abandon my mission just because I witnessed a miracle," Sandra shouted and fired her gun to the sky, to make her point clear. She continued her rant: *"Pierre Beaumont and the others are on their way. They'll know what to do with you."*

"Sandra, this is your last chance. Help us and save yourself" Alex said.

Sandra fired her pistol at me and shot me in the knee cap. I screamed in pain as I collapsed to the ground, tightly hugging my left leg. A second later, there was an artillery projectile shooting from above, and Alex was knocked to the ground from a shockwave of its explosive blast. As I looked up, there was now a crater where Sandra had stood, and not much remained of Sandra. The True Maker had intervened and caused one of the army men to misfire an artillery shell, hitting Sandra.

I put the Zeto Crystal on my kneecap, and it instantly healed. I looked at the lifesaving Zeto crystal. It emitted a dimmed light now, much fainter than it had done just a few days ago. I realised that we had to hurry up and avoid more mishaps before the Zeto crystal became de-energised.

Alex got up on his feet and spoke: *"What do we do now?"*

"We drive to the Sun Pyramid, using Sandra's car" I replied.

"With that broken car?" Alex asked in disbelief.

"That car will take us to the closest town. From there, we can take a cab.", I replied.

After that, we hurried into the sub-par convertible to get away from the unpleasant jungle hut, out of the battle zone that we were in.

Chapter 50: Arriving at The Sun Pyramid.

We arrived at the Sun Pyramid a few hours later, just before the sunset. It was an incredibly beautiful sight, as this ancient pyramid, which was one the largest artefacts ever built in Mesoamerica, was erected in astrophysical alignments of the sunrise and the sunset in the Teotihuacan region. As we arrived at the gate, the guards approached us.

"Está cerrado. Vuelve mañana" the guard said in Spanish, indicating that the pyramid was closed.

"Traje dinero, I'll pay you" I replied and took out a hefty sum of cash, trying to give him a bribe.

"Oh Gringos," the attendant replied happily and continued speaking. *"For that amount, we will give you a private tour."*

"Excellent, bring us to the Royal Tomb," I said confidently.

"Señora, the Royal Tomb is sealed off for visitors," the attendant remarked in bad English.

"Please, it is very important", Alex pleaded and brought forth another wad of Mexican pesos. All the guards stared at the money in excitement and nodded eagerly.

"This money very good. I am Javier, and I can be your guide. Follow me, Señor and Señora.", Javier urged us.

I smiled in relief. I had thought of using my psionic powers to convince the guards to let us through, but then I realised that bribes were a much better way. My Zeto Crystal was losing its energy, but my bank account wasn't, so it was better to let the guards share some money, instead of using my empath powers to alter their minds.

I studied the Pyramid and the rest of the Teotihuacan complex. It was a beautiful place, and I could have found solace and meditative inner peace here, under other circumstances. But there was no time to waste. Pierre Beaumont was on his way here, and he would definitely not come on his own. I needed to get to the Royal Tomb, unleash the power of my Zeto crystal, and open the portal to the Divine Dimension before he reached me.

But what would happen after that? Would we ever get back to Sydney again, or would we be stuck inside the Sun pyramid, unable to go back? I had always envisioned myself to enter the portal on my own, but now that Alex was by my side, I could not leave him behind in this important quest of saving the future of humankind. If I did, Pierre Beaumont and the other conspirators would come after him to find me.

As we traversed and zig-zagged our way to the inner temple complex, heading towards the innermost part of the Sun Pyramid, Javier, the tour guide kept chattering about different objects and artefacts along the route. I lost my temper. *"Just hurry up and take us to the Royal Tomb, we don't have time to lose!"* I said loudly. Hearing this, Javier looked at me with scared puppy eyes and continued straight towards the Royal Tomb.

We entered the part of the hidden Tombs, and Javier pointed me to a dark tunnel with a 'STAFF ONLY' signboard. *"It's very slippery and dangerous in the dark tunnel to the Royal Tomb, you'll see much better things up here, from the top of the hole."* Javier urged, while showing us a giant viewing hole that led to underground tombs.

Alex tapped Javier on the shoulder and spoke: *"Look. It's our anniversary, and my wife has this thing for Royal Tombs. Just lead us there, wait outside for a while, and it'll be worth your while."*

Javier nodded, turned on a flashlight, and we squatted and crawled down the tunnels below, leading to the hidden tomb. After crawling in the dark and damp tunnels for 100 meters, Javier showed us the door to the Royal Tomb. *"The Royal Tomb is inside, Señor and Señora. I'll wait here, don't take too long!"* Javier said nervously.

"We'll take our time, but don't worry, we'll make it worth your Pesos," Alex responded, and we entered the dark chamber, closing the door behind us.

Chapter 51: Interrupted by Pierre Beaumont.

"*What a wonderful place to celebrate our wedding anniversary!*" Alex scoffed and remarked sarcastically, as we looked around in the empty cavern that formed the Royal Tomb of the Sun Pyramid.

I laughed a little, ignored Alex's snide remark, and looked around the massive tomb. I needed to find some encryptions or code that I could decipher to open the portal, but no matter how hard I tried, I saw nothing but a plain and cold empty tomb that once housed the mummified Teotihuacan King.

"It must be here, but I can't see anything!" I shouted out in frustration.

"*What exactly are we looking for?*" Alex asked.

"*Inscriptions or something. Something like this image*" I said. I took up my phone and showed Alex the picture I had of Martin Al-sham's tattoo, which I took, when I was in Jerusalem.

Alex shook his head and replied. "*It's definitely not here. If it were, we would see it, the tattoo ink on the hologram is luminescent, and I see nothing glowing in here.*"

I felt devastated. The portal had to be here, and besides, we had the villain Pierre Beaumont and his accomplices coming after us. "*So, what do I do?*" I shouted out in panic.

"*Why don't you try your magical Zeto Crystal?*" Alex suggested.

I realised that it was my only option. I closed my eyes and clutched the Zeto Crystal to my chest. Suddenly, it gave me a flashback in a vision. It showed an image of what the dark room had looked like, centuries ago, before lava had flowed in to form tubes and destroyed the subterranean parts of the pyramid. I could clearly see the inscriptions on the wall. "*True Maker, please reveal the code of the ancient Zetan civilisation*", I thought. When I opened my eyes, the dark room had suddenly transformed to the way it originally was, a beautiful and undamaged majestic royal palace filled with golden walls and gemstones!

"*Wow!! I don't believe it!*" Alex exclaimed, and I could only agree. What a beautiful sight it was. I had seen the Zeto Crystal perform miracles, but this was the biggest one yet.

Suddenly I could hear a muffled gunshot and a loud thump. The door opened, and Pierre Beaumont entered the Royal Tomb, accompanied by a group of four armed agents. "*Impressive! I love what you did to this room!*" Pierre said with his villainous Swiss-French accent.

"*Why did you shoot our guide, Javier?*" I asked angrily.

"*Javier? Oh, you mean your bugger of a guide. Well, we cannot leave any witnesses. It matters little if we eliminate tiny specks of dust. By tomorrow this country will descend into chaos and civil war,*" Pierre responded with his thick Swiss accent.

"*So, are you starting a civil war in Mexico just because I am here?*" I asked.

Pierre shook his head and spoke to me with a mocking voice. "*Don't be ridiculous, little girl. The war in Mexico happens because the Mexican government refused to pay what they owe us. We cannot have that, nations must fear us.*"

"*But they won't be able to pay you back, if the country is ruined by war,*" I replied.

"*What an idiot, how could we have lost so much money to this clueless woman,*" Pierre muttered to himself and then spoke to me: "*The money doesn't matter. Money is just an artificial symbol to signify power. When war occurs, it causes creative destruction and pushes humanity to do better. Human progress is not caused by peaceful altruistic people, economic developments are caused by greedy and power-hungry people, such as I.*"

"*But why would you choose to make money from funding wars and destruction, yet you said there was no money to be made from cleaning up the oceans to save the world,*" I remarked.

"*When there is a major war, like the coming civil war in Mexico, every major nation will get involved one way or the other. They'll buy and develop weapons, which we do. To make weapons, you must mine ore and be ready to do some damage to the planet, which we are. Once the war is over, there will be a rebuilding effort, which we will finance with money for the world to keep developing. Every step of warfare is benefitting the World Bank and its benefactors, and thus, we will continue to support them.*" Pierre Beaumont explained.

"So why are you coming after me? Cleaning up the oceans doesn't interest you, but it doesn't harm you either. Why are you pursuing us on our private mission?" I asked.

"We didn't come after you. You came after us. Did you really think we would let you beat us in our own game, and take our money doing shady online trades?" Pierre replied.

"And what about the monocles you wear? What is up with that?" I asked.

"Oh, you mean this one?" Pierre said, tapped his monocle lightly on its side of the rim and took it off effortlessly. *"We found a few of these monocles many years ago. They are amazing out-of-the-world technology, which we believe is of alien origin. Unfortunately, we haven't been able to reverse-engineer them, so we couldn't make them ourselves."* Pierre disclosed.

I looked at Pierre's face. His right eye, that had been covered by the monocle, was glowing in a purple voracious luminous glow. It reminded me of the eye colour of Rangda, my ultimate enemy that destroyed the entire Milky Way Galaxy, which forced me to be born during this epoch to change the destiny of humanity. I decided to tackle the issue head-on. *"How is Rangda these days? I take it, you must be one of her worshippers?"* I asked mockingly.

Pierre shrugged his shoulders and replied. *"I am afraid I cannot answer that question. There were nine of us, and you caused the deaths of Ben Yehuda, Szymon Yehuda and Sandra Santiago. Ask Martin Al-Sham when you see him in the afterlife!"*

Pierre was interrupted when one of his accomplices addressed him: *"Pierre, we need to wrap this up, Mexico will descend into chaos within hours."* Pierre nodded, turned towards me and said, *"While I enjoyed talking to you, I am afraid our time is running out. Give us your magical artefact, the Zeto Crystal, or I'll kill your husband!"* Pierre said with a menacing grin and aimed his pistol at Alex.

Chapter 52: Pierre Kills Alex and is Incinerated by Holy Fire.

"*I am not giving you the Zeto Crystal! You are going to try to kill us, regardless of what I do.*" I exclaimed angrily. Pierre burst into diabolical laughter and replied, "*You are right, but I won't just try to kill you. I'll succeed, like I always do. Neither of you will leave the Royal Tomb alive!!*"

"*No, you won't. Your evil reign will soon end, Pierre. This is your last chance to repent and save yourself!*" I stated affirmingly. Pierre turned towards Alex, pulled the trigger, and shot him in the kneecap. Alex fell to the ground screaming in pain. "*Ha-ha! Oh, poor little Alex. That looks like a nasty wound. Here, I got some medicine for it.*" Pierre said, and poured some toxic chemical acid into Alex's wound. Alex writhed in extreme pain as the acid dissolved into the wound, causing his blood to bubble, and his physical body went into shock.

Pierre turned to me and spoke: "*Now, I don't have all day, but I can spare some time to make your husband's death excruciatingly painful if I have to!*" Pierre burst into diabolical laughter. Suddenly, the sight of The True Maker showed up as a hazy mirage, in the form of Keila Eisenstein, and spoke to me: "*The Zeto Crystal can set evil men who touch it ablaze, just give him the crystal and utter the phrase: 'Simba, Zetani, Humanis.' And he will burn!*"

The vision of The True Maker disappeared. I took the Zeto Crystal out of my pocket, and I spoke to Pierre. "*You are right, there is no way I can stop you. Here you go, take the crystal!*"

After saying this, I tossed the Zeto Crystal to Pierre, and he caught it with his left hand. The moment Pierre caught the crystal, I quickly uttered '*Simba, Zetani, Humanis*' and Pierre was set ablaze with a bright white flame. Screaming and screeching in pain, he dropped both the Zeto Crystal and his pistol, and he dropped dead to the ground. I leapt for the Zeto Crystal and picked it up with my left hand while I grabbed Pierre's pistol with my right hand, and in true Matrix-style, I rapidly shot Pierre's four bodyguards who were in shock from witnessing the luminous white flame burning Pierre's body.

I crawled over to Alex, to see if he was okay. He was dead. A stray bullet shot during the chaos, had hit him straight through the heart. I collapsed to the ground; my knees instantly went numb.

I was heartbroken. In the last week, I had turned from an optimistic environmentalist and a confident career woman, in a happy and beautiful sweet marriage, to a mass-murdering, sad, angry widow. In a bout of grief and madness, I turned the gun towards my own head, ready to commit suicide. It didn't work as the gun jammed. Damn the True Maker! Of course, the gun jammed! I would have to live with causing the death to the love of my life. All that was left for me, was to continue with the mission that I was born for. I lost all my energy and I passed out.

Chapter 53: Love is the Death of Duty.

When I woke up from the blackout, the True Maker, embodied as my beautiful mother of the 29th century, Keila Eisenstein, was glowing very luminously, in the darkness of the Royal Tomb. She looked peaceful, and she smiled gently at me. *"You did it, Sabina. You brought a charged Zeto Crystal to a Portal to Divine Dimension. Now, you can travel to the Divine Dimension and fulfil your destiny; To stop Rangda and save the future for all of us."* The True Maker said with a tranquil and a beautifully haunting voice.

I looked at the mirage of my future mother and sobbed, *"But... what about my happiness? What about Alex, the love of my life? What about our future happiness together? What about the murderous monster that I have become?"*

There was a long pause, and the True Maker changed form to an enchanting aura of pure energy. The True Maker's lingering whisper echoed in the air, *"You shall fulfil your purpose, which is the reason for your reincarnation. Alex is now dead, and while I understand your grief, it's insignificant. Your irrational emotions are just a part of your human nature."*

"So now, I must go through the portal to the Divine Dimension, leaving this world, and sacrifice my happiness and my life to stop Rangda from destroying the future?" I sobbed.

"You have already made your sacrifice, Sabina. Rangda is kept in a prison cell, it is the best time to end her life. And you'll outlive Rangda, she is still weak and in captivity. You are young and still learning your true potential, you must follow your destiny." the True Maker responded.

"Tell me, are you really omniscient?" I asked with a sad voice.

"As far as I know, I am. But people have the power to make their own decisions. Among each one, there will be a different ending. How could I possibly know for certain; it is your choice." The True Maker responded calmly.

"So then, you already know, that I am not going to sacrifice Alex to fulfil my destiny!" I asked defiantly.

"I am aware of your mindset, but you must reconsider. There isn't enough energy left in the crystal to both resurrect Alex and open the portal. You must choose either one or the other. Sabina, you must follow the path you were born to do..." The True Maker urged me.

"I will find a way to resurrect Alex and keep the galaxy alive," I responded.

After that, I squeezed the Zeto Crystal, and used its energy to resurrect Alex. He woke up with shock and terror on his face, *"Zuuhhh...... what happened?"* Alex exclaimed while rubbing his eyes.

"You died, but I resurrected you with the power of the Zeto Crystal. You'll be fine." I responded with a reassuring voice and smiled to him ever so sweetly.

"Urrm.... I remember I was somewhere... It was so cold and dark, was it the afterlife?" Alex asked in bewilderment, with cold sweat clamming his body.

"You are with me now, that is all that matters," I said and kissed him gently.

I used my empath powers to calm Alex down. He got up on his feet, studied the dead bodyguards, and the pile of ash that remained of Pierre Beaumont. *"What happened here, Sabina?"* Alex asked.

"There was a secret command that I uttered. It was a verbal encryption code that allowed the Zeto Crystal to incinerate an evil person that touched it. I voiced the command and set Pierre ablaze. I quickly grabbed his pistol and shot his bodyguards. You were killed by a stray bullet during the firefight, but I managed to revive you."

"So, you are a murderer just like them?" Alex said in resignation.

"I did what I had to do to survive, I never wanted anyone to die," I replied defensively.

"I know. And yet I wish there was another way..." Alex said and sighed.

I walked up to him and gave him a hug. *"It's okay Alex, everything is going to be fine."*, I muttered to him.

"Be careful of hunting monsters, lest you become one yourself. For when you stare into the Abyss, the Abyss also stares back into you." Alex said with an afterthought.

"Huh? What are you talking about?" I replied with a confused voice

"It's a quote by Nietzsche. We have become the very evil that we tried to prevent...", Alex responded with sorrow in his voice.

"No, we haven't. We simply had to realise that we cannot save everyone!" I replied defiantly, while I secretly wondered if Alex was right.

We stood silent for a while. There was a lot of tension and unresolved issues, but this was not the time nor the place to resolve them. "So, *did you travel to the Divine Dimension to stop Rangda and save the future?*" Alex asked.

I shook my head and replied: "*No, there wasn't enough energy left in the Zeto crystal for both travelling to the Divine Dimension and saving your life. I chose love over duty.*"

"*So you sacrificed the future, to save me? You shouldn't have...*", Alex said solemnly.

"*No, the crystal will recharge, and I will get more chances to fulfil my destiny later. But I only had one chance to save you.*" I said and kissed Alex passionately.

Our passionate kiss was interrupted when a nearby explosion rattled the Sun Pyramid. "*The war has come. We better get out of here!*" I shouted, and we ran towards the exit. As we crawled out of the tunnel and reached the exit, we saw one of the World Bank's helicopters, ready to take off. The pilot looked apprehensive; he was eager to take off but was unwilling to leave his boss behind. I pulled up a pistol and was ready to engage the pilot when I felt Alex's hand on my shoulder. "*No more killing, Sabina.*" He whispered gently in my ears.

"*Not if I can avoid it,*" I replied, comforted that Alex was still the good-hearted person who I had always loved. Alex always wanted to avoid bloodshed.

I snuck up on the helicopter and I entered the backdoor stealthily. The pilot, who was waiting for Pierre and his guards, hadn't noticed me. I placed the pistol against the back of his head and yelled, "*Don't move!*"

"*Who are you??*" The pilot asked with a terrified voice.

"*I am the person that your boss, Pierre, set out to kill. Don't repeat his mistake.*" I said with a chilling voice that scared myself.

"*Please don't kill me. I got a family.*" The pilot replied.

"*Good, follow my instructions, and you'll live. Try anything dumb, and I will pull the trigger. Understood?*" I warned the pilot. The pilot nodded, and I spoke again, "*Take us to Cuernavaca Airport.*"

The pilot agreed, and he flew us to Cuernavaca airport. On the way to the airport, I witnessed the bloodshed that the civil war had caused, and I regretted that I hadn't gone after Pierre Beaumont at an earlier stage.

Chapter 54: He Chose His Own Destiny.

Half an hour later, we reached the Cuernavaca airport as the sun was rising. I hadn't realised it before, but I must have been unconscious for several hours dozing on and off, after my clash with Pierre and his guards. Damn, I was really fatigued.

Now, I was struggling with a moral dilemma. The pilot could tell the others what had happened if I spared his life, and that would make more people come after me. But I couldn't murder him in cold blood, since I had promised Alex to not kill anymore. I decided to let him choose his own fate. I touched his left shoulder and felt my empathic power surging over me.

"Benjamin William Cook. You'll have to make a difficult decision about life and death." I said firmly.

"Wait... How do you know my name??" Benjamin stuttered in shock.

"Don't you worry about that. Just answer my question." I replied.

"Okay...So what do you want me to decide?" Benjamin asked.

"Whether you prefer to get permanent amnesia or to die," I replied coldly.

"Can't you just let me go? I promise to not tell anyone what happened," Benjamin pleaded.

"I can't hold you to a promise conjured at gunpoint..." I replied.

Benjamin nodded and replied, *"Then, I choose death."*

"Death?" I said in surprise, not expecting him to reject the other option.

"I love my family very much, I cannot live with myself if I forget about them," Benjamin said with a broken but firm voice.

"Very well, then I will kill you", I replied and aimed my pistol at Benjamin's head.

As I was about to shoot, Alex pushed my hand and stopped me. *"Sabina, this is not who you are, I know you are a good-hearted person, you promised to not kill again!"* Alex exclaimed with an upset voice.

"But, if I don't kill him, he will alert the others," I responded coldly.

"No, he will not. I vouch for him." Alex said and continued. *"Benjamin, would you like to start a new life, a life where you can do good for the world?"* Alex looked at him with innocent eyes.

"Yes... Yes, I do.", Benjamin said weakly.

"Excellent. As the CEO of Building a Better World Pty Ltd, I will hire you as my personal pilot. Your first job is to fly our private jet to Hawaii."

"Thank you, sir. I accept this offer." Benjamin replied.

We got on the plane and took off before the Mexican government found out about the death of Pierre Beaumont. As the aircraft reached the Pacific Ocean, I felt a deep sense of relief, but could also sense a terrifying premonition. Alex's act of mercy towards the pilot would cause us more pain and suffering in the future. I turned to Alex and whispered into his ear, *"You shouldn't have done that, he will turn against us."*

"No, he won't, and besides I couldn't let you murder him in cold blood." Alex responded defiantly.

"He chose his own destiny," I responded coldly.

"No, he chose the least bad option for him. Choosing death over forgetting the ones he loved, proved to me that he is a good man." Alex replied.

"I am not convinced," I replied solemnly.

"Neither am I," Alex responded, paused, and continued, *"But I would rather die again, than losing my morality."*

Chapter 55: Alex's Disappearance and Martin Al-Sham's Return.

After landing in Hawaii, we decided to stay there for a few days to recover from our terrible ordeal in Mexico. While we enjoyed our time on the resort, Alex and Benjamin became friends. While I was happy for them, I was less pleased about the rift between Alex and I. Being brought back from the dead, and witnessing my transformation, had changed Alex's attitude, causing him to withdraw from me. Perhaps he was right, maintaining one's morality was the only way to fight evil, but I had chosen another path. I sipped my Pina colada, and I was submerged in deep thoughts.

I thought back on my time in Mexico, I secretly wondered if I had made the right choice, to choose love over my duty. I had failed with the goal that I set out to do. The crystal was now de-energised, the beautiful luminous glow that it once had, was now gone, and it had turned dull. It had looked just like the boring blue stone that was sitting in my safe for years. Rangda was still a threat to the future. Had I chosen the right path when I forsake my duty to save my loved one? Or was, choice an illusion? Was I just following the path that the True Maker had chosen for me, and was I meant to save Alex?

I read a news article about the civil war in Mexico. The fighting had ended after less than 72 hours, when Jesus Ortega was found dead, mauled by his own dogs. I had caused that to happen, and my choice to influence his dogs to kill him had saved countless lives. Yet, it made me feel horrible. I knew the decision to release the dogs and influence them to attack Jesus made me a murderer. I could have found another way to get out of Jesus' compound without causing his dogs to kill people, but I have chosen that road. So, was I good, or bad, or, something in between? Perhaps, I was just a tiny force with a crazy delusion of grandeur, believing in my ability to alter the future

I heard a noise, and I turned around. *"Alex, is that you?"* I heard myself asking until I realised who the person in front of me was. It was Martin Al-Sham. I could see that Martin wore the same type of monocle as the other conspirators had worn.

"*Humph! I reckoned that you would show up, eventually.*" I said, puzzled by Martin's motive.

"*Did Benjamin Cook, that son-of-a-bitch, tell you to come here?*" I continued.

Martin looked flummoxed and replied, "*Benjamin Cook? Who is that?*"

"*Pierre Beaumont's helicopter pilot, whose life Alex spared. I suspect he must have told you about our whereabouts*", I replied.

"*I have no idea who that is. I have other ways of finding you, and we got a job to do.*" Martin replied.

"*What do you want me to do? And why are you wearing the same monocle Pierre wore?*" I asked.

"*Never mind about the monocle. I need you to fulfil your destiny. I need you to activate the portal with your Zeto Crystal and travel to the Divine Dimension. This is crucial for our destiny.*" Martin replied.

"*So, you want to help me stopping Rangda?*" I asked, hoping that Martin was not an enemy.

"*Yes... I want to... stop Rangda*" Martin replied with a deceptive tone.

Martin's tone of voice gave me a sinister feeling, so I decided to grab his hand and use my empath powers to find out if he was hiding something. Just like with Pierre Beaumont, I couldn't access his mind. Martin shook his head and spoke, "*I wouldn't try those empath powers if I were you. This artefact blocks your powers.*"

Martin pushed away my hand and retreated a few steps. He tapped the monocle gently, and removed it, revealing his purple right eye.

"*So, you really are one of them!?*" I burst out.

Martin shook his head and replied: "*I'm not one of them. Nine individuals came across advanced alien artefacts that heightened our awareness. I am one of the nine. We do not share the same goals, although we are aware of each other.*"

"*So, what about your right eye? Your eyes were blue, and I had never seen you wearing that device in the past?*" I asked sceptically.

"*I was wearing tinted lenses, don't ask stupid questions, Sabina.*" Martin scoffed at me

Martin re-attached the monocle to his eye and spoke again. *"But enough talking for now. I have a task for you. The others hold Alex in captivity, so we better get going."*

"What? Is Alex kidnapped? But my crystal is de-energised!" I replied.

"I found a solution to that while you dealt with Pierre and Sandra in Mexico," Martin replied.

"How are you going to charge the crystal?" I asked.

"You'll see, I'll show you once we are in Kiribati. But for now, I need you to follow my instructions." Martin requested.

"What if I refuse to help you?" I asked.

"Then I'll let you go, but Alex will die. I am not foolish enough to attack a woman protected by the True Maker. How unlucky that Alex doesn't have divine protection." Martin said and smirked at me.

"Okay, I'll come willingly. We share the same goal. You did ask me to stop Rangda and save the future for all of us." I replied.

"Excellent! I have a plane waiting for us at the airport. We leave at once!" Martin said.

Five hours later, I was on a plane heading towards Kiribati, on a mission to the Micronesian island's ancient underwater sunken pyramid. As I studied the beautiful beaches and lagoons from above, I thought about the destiny that lay ahead of me. Would I manage to stop Rangda and save the future? Would I ever meet my beloved husband again? The questions were many and the crystal was still out of its supernatural energy. I sighed and prayed to The True Maker. Without Alex by my side, I felt empty, but I knew what I had to do. What I was born to do! My future lay ahead of me, on the island of Kiribati, deep under the surface of the Pacific Ocean.

Chapter 56: Approaching Kiribati.

I was sitting in the Gulfstream private jet, watching the beautiful islands of Kiribati. I loved the Pacific Islands, and it had been a different feeling the last time I visited, during my honeymoon with my dear Alex. This time, everything was different. Alex was not with me, he was the prisoner of the man sitting opposite me in this luxury private jet, a Swedish man in his mid-50s, dressing as a Middle Eastern Knights Templar. His name was Martin Al-Sham.

Born as an empath, I can usually read people like an open book, but Martin Al-Sham was an exception. I had no clue what was going on in his mind or what his real intentions were. The man who had saved my life on several occasions, turned out to be a part of the conspiracy against me! And now, Alex was his prisoner.

I studied Martin quietly. He looked tired and old. A lot older than when I first came across him in Jerusalem, four years earlier. I had noticed on the way to the airport that he was walking with a limp, presumably a side effect from the bullets he took when he helped me escape Israel. But I knew that he was a dangerous man. He had killed seven people that I knew about, and probably others that I didn't know about as well.

Eventually, I could not handle the awkward silence anymore, and I felt compelled to speak to my malefactor to find out his real motives.

"So, I take it that you were a part of the Mossad conspiracy, after all?" I asked.

Martin shook his head and responded with a tired and irritated voice. *"I told you already. There is no real conspiracy. Just nine individuals that came across alien technologies many years ago. The steam-punk monocles enable us to know each other's whereabouts and elevate our minds to a higher level of intelligence. But we don't work together. Ben Yehuda and Pierre Beaumont were part of the Mossad conspiracy, I just came to help Keila Eisenstein."*

"So how do you afford all of this on your own? Kidnapping Alex, hiring a private jet?" I asked suspiciously.

"Believe it or not, I am actually wealthy," Martin replied.

"Oh, really? You never told me," I replied.

"You never asked," Martin said, smirked, and looked outside the window of the private jet.

I nodded at Martin in silence. His tired gaze, stern yet strangely kind-looking, gave me a kind of feeling that I have known him for decades. He sighed deeply and looked a little hesitant. Eventually, he took out an old worn-out photograph from his leather wallet and handed it to me. I took the photo from his hand and studied it carefully. It was a photograph of Martin in his thirties, and an Asian woman, standing side by side. They were both looking profoundly serious, almost like Martin was crying over someone's death, while holding a cheque from one of the major lotteries, having won a tremendous amount of money.

I returned the photograph to Martin and spoke to him, *"Who is that woman, and why did you look so sad when you have won over 120 million dollars?"*

"Her name is Elaine. I was unhappy because I knew that my fortune would come at a cost," Martin replied solemnly.

"And, where is Elaine now?" I asked.

"That is none of your business!" Martin lashed out at me.

I nodded and didn't reply. Martin Al-Sham's love life wasn't particularly important to me, and besides, my mission was to save Alex. I had learnt one of thing about Martin though, his real family name was Orchard, and not Al-Sham.

I sat silently for the remainder of the trip. A short while later, the plane landed on Kiribati's international airport, located on the main island Bonriki, close to Kiribati's tiny capital, Tarawa.

Chapter 57: On the Way to the Kiribati Volcano

An hour later, the private jet had landed, and we had made our way to the harbour. As we were about to hop on to the rented ship, Martin was talking loudly with the captain of the private yacht, but I didn't want to get involved. From the discussion, I concluded that the captain was worried about an imminent volcanic eruption. Eventually, Martin handed the captain a large wad of cash, and they seemed to come to an agreement.

Martin approached me and spoke: *"Get on the boat, Sabina. We are heading to Banaba Island."*

"The captain was talking about an imminent volcanic eruption. What's up with that?" I asked, feeling concerned.

"Well, the volcanic eruption is the reason we are going there. But once we are there, the captain will leave," Martin replied.

"So, the $10,000 couldn't convince him to stay and pick us up?" I asked.

Martin shrugged his shoulders and replied: *"He won't have much use for money when he is dead, will he?"*

"And what about us?" I asked tentatively.

"We'll be alright. Only an adrenaline junkie or a delusional visionary would go to a volcanic island just before it's about to blow up." Martin replied and smirked at me mysteriously.

"And you consider yourself a visionary?" I asked sarcastically.

"I know that I am. The raw thermal energy from the erupting volcano is just what we need to recharge the Zeto Crystal. Besides, I have the Chosen One with me. The True Maker wouldn't let you die, would he?" Martin asked rhetorically.

I didn't respond to Martin's statement. His cynicism sickened me, but I had to comply with his commands. Alex was his prisoner, and he was correct about one thing. The True Maker didn't care whether Alex lived or died, so it was up to me to save him. Besides, Martin and I shared the same goal. We both wanted to energise the Zeto Crystal, so I could activate the Portal and confront Rangda. I silently questioned his real motives for activating the Portal, as Martin was an assassin and had killed numerous people in the past.

We boarded the yacht in silence, and I felt anxious as we approached the massive volcano bursting in ashy hot clouds, just ahead of us. As we got closer to Banaba Island, the captain became agitated and stopped the yacht, refusing to approach the dangerous volcanic eruption. I smelled the thick volcanic smoke, and I felt sick from inhaling the thick ashy stench, a mixture of sulphur and phosphate everywhere. Martin approached me and spoke. *"Sabina, do your thing if you want to save the captain's life."* Martin opened his jacket, showing the pistols he had holstered under his coat.

I struggled against the impulse to steal Martin's pistol and shoot him with it. I was younger, fitter and had divine protection from the True Maker. I would undoubtedly get out of such confrontation alive. But then I stopped myself. If I were to shoot Martin, what would I do with the captain? I couldn't just murder an innocent man to cover up my crimes!

I nodded at Martin to acknowledge his request. I got up and approached the captain. I grabbed the captain's arm, used my empath powers to calm him down, and convinced him to go to the island. It was easier than I remembered it to be, perhaps my abilities had increased over time with the help of the Zeto Crystal?

As we approached the burning hellscape that was Banaba Island, I felt slightly guilty. If the volcano were to erupt, Captain Ahohako wouldn't have a chance, and he was an innocent man who was just desperate for money for his daughter's kidney surgery. Such was the plight of being an empath, feeling too much of other people's pain and suffering was painful to bear. As we stepped off the yacht, I exclaimed to the captain: *"Go back to your family with the money Martin gave you, Ahohako. Ailana needs her kidney transplant urgently!"*

As Captain Ahohako took off, Martin looked at me in disbelief. *"You never cease to amaze me, Sabina. You complained over the captain leaving us on the island. And now that you managed to subdue him, you sent him away!"* Martin said.

"Captain Ahohako is a good man. I couldn't risk his life to save my own skin. I wouldn't think twice about throwing you under the bus, Martin Orchard." I replied.

Hearing this, Martin laughed loudly, as if chuckling to a silly daughter, and replied, *"Very well, good to know that we are on the same page. Put on this gasmask, if you please. It won't be a pleasant walk ahead of us."*

Without a word, I put on the gasmask, and I followed Martin for the hellish trek ahead.

Chapter 58: A Hellish Hike.

We walked towards Banaba Island's ash spewing volcano cautiously. There wasn't much to say, and besides, the gasmasks covering our faces made it impossible to have a proper conversation. I thought about Dante's Inferno, and its various depictions of hell. I realised that being in the vicinity of this erupting volcano, was the closest to hellfire one could be on Earth. The thick and hot sulphuric gasses burned my skin, and a yellowish powder of sulphuric dust covered my entire body.

My only comfort was that the volcanic eruption didn't destroy Banaba Island. Instead, human greed and phosphate mining had damaged the surrounding islands decades earlier, and in a way, it was a fitting end that nature reclaimed what humanity had destroyed.

As we reached the erupting volcano's peak, Martin pulled off his gasmask and exclaimed, *"Give me the Zeto Crystal!"*. I handed Martin the crystal, and he wrapped it into a mysterious veil that shimmered like a thousand stars. Martin started to chant in Zetan language, which I recognised due to my connection to the True Maker, although I didn't understand it. When his chant was done, Martin threw the crystal, still wrapped in the luminous veil, down into the volcano's dome-shaped crater. After this, he collapsed to the ground and started coughing blood from inhaling the noxious fumes.

Immediately after that, the ground shook violently for a couple of seconds, and then it suddenly stopped, and no more smoke came out of the quickly-cooling volcano. Using an abseiling rope, I made my way half-way down to the volcano's bottom crater and was amazed by what I saw. The magma in the volcano had solidified, revealing a bright orange and sparkly golden hue of gleaming solid ground, and just above the solid volcanic rock, was the Zeto Crystal elevating mid-air, sparkling, and emitting the strongest blue rays of light. It was the most beautiful thing that I had ever seen.

"Did it work?" Martin yelled from the top of the crater towards me.

"Yep! It did. I have never seen the Zeto Crystal so energised before, it is glowing extremely brightly!" I exclaimed in amazement.

"Go down, get the energised crystal and give it to me. I don't have much time left," Martin gasped before he passed out.

I looked down the volcano, the crystal was still ten metres down, and I wasn't a particularly good climber. But then again, there was not much reason for me to be afraid. If I were to fall and break my bones, I just needed to get some energy from the crystal, and it would heal me.

Overcoming my fear of heights, I made my way down to the glowing Zeto Crystal. As I picked it up, I felt immensely powerful, and I realised that the energy level was almost to its full potential. Holding the Zeto Crystal, I instantly leapt 10 meters up from the bottom of the crater and landed close to Martin Al-Sham. Martin was unconscious and breathing weakly.

I was stuck in a dilemma. I didn't want to save Martin's life, but if I didn't, how could I save Alex? I realised that with my internet hacking abilities, and my knowledge of Martin's real name, I could access the Dark Net and potentially find some clues. But I didn't know how long it would take to find and save Alex before Martin's accomplices found out that something was amiss.

I searched through Martin's pants, and I found his phone. As I unlocked it with his fingerprint, it automatically called a number. An Asian woman answered the phone. *"Hello. Martin is that you?"* Hearing the voice, I froze. What had I gotten myself into? The voice spoke again: *"Sabina. If anything has happened to Martin, Alex will die!"*

Hearing this, I panicked. I revived Martin with the Zeto Crystal, and I handed him the phone. *"Tell Elaine that you are fine,"* I hissed at him.

Martin nodded and did as instructed: *"I am fine, Elaine. We just had a misunderstanding. Proceed as planned."* After that, he hung up the phone and looked at me. *"So, did you plan to leave me to die?"* he asked coldly.

"I never promised to protect you when you're hurt. You are a cold-blooded murderer, and you kidnapped my husband," I replied coldly.

"If you had known the truth, you'd be more eager to keep me alive. Regardless, how lucky for Alex that I am still among the living," Martin said.

"What truth? I doubt many truths comes from your duplicitous lips!" I replied irritably.

Martin shook his head and replied *"Tsk, tsk, tsk.... such a temper from a pretty young thing! Your feisty attitude reminds me of someone I..."* Martin bit his lip and didn't say anything more.

"What are you talking about, you weirdo?" I asked angrily.

"You have reminded me of my youth, perhaps," Martin replied knowingly. *"But enough of this. I need to organise a helicopter to take us to the next destination. The Sunken Pyramid of Kiribati!"*

I didn't reply. Martin called the helicopter hiring company on his satellite phone, and an hour later, a helicopter came to take us to our next destination.

Chapter 59: A Deep Dive to the Sunken Pyramid of Kiribati.

Half an hour later, the helicopter was hovering over an area of the Pacific Ocean. Martin Al-Sham was studying a sonar report on his tablet, and he turned towards me. *"This is it, Sabina. The Sunken Pyramid of Kiribati is right below us, located at a depth of 100 metres,"* Martin said.

"Are you sure? How come there is no information about this pyramid on the Internet?" I asked sceptically.

"Yes, I am certain. I sent an unmanned submarine down there a decade ago." Martin replied.

"So, you knew of this pyramid, yet you decided to not share the revelation to the rest of the world?" I asked in disbelief.

"Exactly. That wouldn't benefit my interests," Martin replied coldly. I nodded and said nothing in return.

After a period of silence, I decided to address the elephant in the room. *"So, if the Portal is down there, how do I get to this sunken pyramid?"* I asked.

"Well, I must disappoint you, but I didn't bring any scuba equipment," Martin said.

"So, you want me to dive down there, without an oxygen tank, find the pyramid's entrance, and activate the portal on my own?" I asked hesitantly.

"Smart girl, you read my mind!" Martin said mockingly and continued. *"You have the power of the re-energised Zeto crystal in your hand. Unfortunately, I cannot come with you. I don't have divine protection and would never survive such a deep dive."*

I hesitated. The Zeto Crystal had saved my life many times, but diving to a depth of 100 metres and finding a portal located within a sunken pyramid in total darkness? The thought scared me, and I wasn't even sure that Martin would keep his promise and release Alex. I decided to address the issue. *"Okay, I will dive down there on one condition,"* I said.

"I am listening," Martin replied.

"I request that you release Alex first. Once he is safe, I'll uphold my part of the bargain," I stated with conviction.

Hearing this, Martin looked anxious and afraid. After a few seconds of silence, he objected to my request, *"Well, if I release Alex, I have no bargaining chip against you. Nothing is stopping you from killing me once Alex is free."*

"Perhaps, but we still share the same end goal, which is to open the portal, and I wouldn't kill someone if I promised not to," I replied.

"Okay. Do you swear by the power of the True Maker, to not harm me, and to activate the portal if I release Alex?" Martin asked.

"Yes, I swear by the True Maker, to leave you unharmed, activate the Kiribati Portal, and confront Rangda," I replied in confidence.

"Very well, I'll make the arrangements," Martin replied.

Martin picked up his satellite phone and made a few calls to Elaine and her mafia underlings. Five minutes later, he handed me the phone. It was Alex. His voice was meek, but he seemed to be relatively okay. He said, *"Sabina, are you safe? An Asian gang kidnapped me, but I am safe now."*

"I am okay. Don't worry about me, Alex. I am with Martin Al-Sham in Kiribati. I must dive to a sunken pyramid, activate the portal, and fulfil my destiny. If we don't meet again, always remember that you were my one true love," I said solemnly.

"Sabina, please don't go! The world needs you. I need you!" Alex pleaded.

"I know. But I must fulfil my destiny and save the future. I love you, Alex. Goodbye!" I said and turned off the phone.

As I put the phone away, I looked at Martin Al-Sham. He was aiming a pistol at me and spoke with a panicky voice, *"I don't want to do this, but I can't have you back out now! You must swim down there and activate the portal straight away!"*

"Oh, no! what about being too cold-hearted to the Chosen One? Weren't you dictating me this whole time" I asked sarcastically.

"If you are the Chosen One, you will swim down there and activate the portal. If you are not, the True Maker will no longer protect you," Martin said with a mysterious gleam of sadness in his eyes.

I thought about asking Martin what had prompted him to be hostile, but I refrained from doing so. There was something compelling about having a pistol aimed at my face, and besides, I had never intended to back out from fulfilling my destiny. I took up my Zeto Crystal and held it to my chest. *"After this, I hope to never see you again,"* I said. After these words, I backflipped out of the helicopter, down to the surface of the water below.

I swam down deeper and deeper towards the pyramid, pushing with my feet and letting the light of the Zeto Crystal guide my way. It was an incredible feeling. While the semi de-energised Zeto Crystal had allowed me to swim underwater without breathing, when I escaped Szymon Yehuda and the Mossad assassins at King Street Wharf, it was different this time. Last time, I had felt like a scuba diver diving without a tank, feeling the coolness of the seawater flinching on my skin. This time, I felt magical, as if I was one with the water, swimming like an energetic young dolphin. I swam down quicker than a beautiful sea-mammal, and I reached the sunken pyramid in no time.

Chapter 60: Activating the Portal Inside the Sunken Pyramid.

Guided by the luminous blue light of the Zeto crystal, I navigated towards the tunnels of the pyramid, 100 metres below the surface of the Pacific Ocean. Although it should have been terrifying, swimming around in the pitch darkness through the passageways, I felt very relieved, and I intuitively knew the way to the portal. Eventually, I saw a sepulchre, where there were millions of rare and exotic fish, and a bed of ancient seaweed-covered stones stacking on top of each other. Harrowing through the foundation of algae rocks and curly sea plants, I found a tiny empty hole hidden between the ancient seaweed-covered stones. The hole was fitted precisely to insert the Zeto Crystal.

A realisation came to me just before I was about to insert the Zeto Crystal, and I was filled with doubts. What would happen to me if I inserted the Zeto Crystal in the tiny hole? I wouldn't be able to breathe, and I was a hundred meters below the surface! I would drown! I calmed myself down and reasoned about my predicament ahead. I had come here for a purpose, and surely, I wouldn't die before confronting Rangda? Perhaps, this was all a ploy, Martin Al-Sham had lured me into a trap? How easy it would be for him to swim down with high-tech scuba gear and enter the portal once I was out of his way.

I brushed my paranoia aside. Martin could have killed me in Jerusalem, and instead, he shot his accomplices when we were in the Solomon Temple. Whatever his end goal was, it clearly wasn't to kill me. I inserted the Zeto Crystal into the slot. I could hear a loud click, and the crystal disappeared. As I no longer was protected by the power of the Zeto crystal, I felt suffocated and could feel the immense pressure of the surrounding water pushing towards my body. My eardrum was about to implode from the extreme pressure, and I couldn't see anything anymore, as the whole area turned pitch-black. With all my willpower, I held on to the breath that I had kept inside my lungs, the air that I had while I was still holding the Zeto Crystal, before I had inserted it to the slot.

"Calm down, Sabina!" I repeated to myself multiple times. I could survive several minutes with the air in my lungs if I only kept calm and didn't hyperventilate. If I panicked, I'd instinctively breathe out this last breath of air, fill my lungs with water and die in seconds. I stayed motionless while knowing I only had a few minutes until I ran out of air. I entered a meditative yoga pose to bring myself to the yogic state of mind. Suddenly, I felt a jerky movement, and the ground started to shake from the pyramid vibrating and dismantling itself from ocean floor. The whole structure was moving upwards, alongside the grounds around it, ascending towards the surface, as fast as a lighting jet.

Suddenly, the pyramid stopped moving, and I was slung towards the stone wall, hitting the back of my head, knocking me out temporarily. When I woke up, the water was gone, and I could breathe again, but I was bleeding from a wound on the back of my head. The wound stung severely from all the salt in the ocean, but I was alive, and that was all that mattered! The Zeto Crystal had ejected itself from the tiny slot, and one of the walls had turned into a blue wall of shimmering light.

I struggled to get back up, and when I saw the big pool of blood next to me, I realised why. I was severely injured. I felt lightheaded and wanted to lay back and rest, but I knew that there was no help around, and passing out under these circumstances would lead to my death. I mustered all my energy, and I crawled to where the crystal was. As I grabbed it, my wounds healed, and I felt a lot better.

I looked up and saw how the blue light in the portal was flickering. Evidently, the entrance was closing when it no longer had an energy source. It was now or never. I sprinted towards the portal and jumped towards the gap, getting through just before it closed behind me.

As I entered the portal, I had a fantastic flight. I was flying inside a dimensional rift tunnel, my sheath was protected by a space bubble, floating in the timelessness between the two dimensions. I saw the entire Milky Way Galaxy from inside the space bubble craft, and I could zoom in and out as I wanted, watching everything as I wanted. I felt extreme peace and feelings of joy. Was this how it felt to be a deity? I didn't have much time to think about it, before I crashed down on the other side of the portal and landed in a strange world. The world was an endless white plane, with buildings sporadically scattered throughout the otherwise featureless landscape. I recognised the place from my dreams and visions, I was in the Divine Dimension.

I touched the back of my head, where I had suffered a fracture and a big gaping wound before. The wound had healed perfectly like it was never there, but my clothes, which were covered in blood, proved the opposite. I was lost and felt exhausted. The tension had drained all my energy, and I couldn't fight it anymore. I lay down on the ground and passed out from overexertion.

Chapter 61: Meeting up with Brahma.

When I woke up, I was on a stretcher in a beautiful garden. An angelic creature was studying the Zeto Crystal, which was placed on a shining pedestal. I realised that the humanoid must be one of the Zetans, the advanced alien species that altered humanity's DNA to make us what we are. The Zetan had bright white aura vibrating with psionic energy, and he looked like a creature full of wisdom. I couldn't communicate with the being telepathically as I, unlike my first mother Keila Eisenstein, have only a tiny fraction amount of Zetan DNA sequences in my blood. The Zetan was staring at the Zeto Crystal, which he had put on the pedestal in the middle of the courtyard. He was absorbed by the crystal and did not even notice me.

Suddenly, I felt angry. The Zetans had manipulated humans for eons, making people believe that they were deities to be worshipped, and I hadn't come here to facilitate their return to Earth. I had come to stop Rangda from destroying the future of humankind. *"Hey, don't touch that!"* I shouted as the old and pale-skinned Zetan mage put his hand on the Zeto Crystal. He turned around and looked at me in surprise. *"Art thou alive?"* The Zetan said with a strange Shakespearian accent.

"You didn't bother checking?" I replied with an irritated voice.

The Zetan nodded towards me and responded: *"Forgiveth me, my lady. The tranquil beauty of the Zeto Crystal hath me mesmerised. I go by the name Brahma. What shall I calleth thy?"* said Brahma.

"I am Sabina. Why do you speak with that ancient English accent?" I replied.

Brahma didn't say anything. Instead, he took my arm and established a telepathic connection with me. His eyes were flickering for a few seconds, and then he spoke again, *"Okay, Sabina. My bionic microchips have absorbed your local accent now. You are from a place called Australia?"*

I nodded and replied *"Impressive. We humans haven't advanced that far even in the 29th century!"*

"29ᵗʰ Century? Have I slept that long?" Brahma said in amazement.

I smiled at him and replied. *"No, it's the 21ˢᵗ century now. The year 2041 to be precise."*

"Oh, thank the True Maker for that. I slept for a few days, not 800 years!" Brahma said with a relieved voice.

"Sleeping for 800 years? How would that happen?" I asked curiously.

"The Divine Dimension is timeless, so the outside time flows erratically from our perspective. Thus, I could sleep for two minutes or two years without knowing the difference," Brahma explained.

I nodded and didn't comment on Brahma's explanation. I didn't understand what he meant, but I was here on a mission, not to discuss philosophy and physics. But how would I explain why I was here?

I was interrupted from my thoughts when Brahma spoke, *"So tell me, Sabina. How did you get here, and how did you survive losing so much blood?"*

I wondered the same thing, and I told Brahma what had happened: *"I found the Terran Zeto Crystal and I used it to activate the portal in the Sunken Pyramid of Kiribati. I hit my head badly when the pyramid started moving. When I woke up, I used the Zeto Crystal to heal my wounds."*

Brahma stared at me in awe and took a few steps back. After that, he exclaimed, *"That's impossible. Humans don't have that much proficiency with the Zeto Crystals. Not even we Zetans do!"*

"Not normal humans, but I am not normal. I am the reincarnation of the Chosen One from the 29ᵗʰ Century, the daughter of Keila Eisenstein. My name is Sabina Eisenstein."

Brahma stared at me in disbelief. After a moment of silence, he spoke: *"How can you be the reincarnation of someone from the future? Have humans invented time travel? That's impossible, all our experiments concluded that time travel was impossible."*

"So did humanity's experiments in the 25ᵗʰ century. But I wasn't sent back in time with technology, but by the True Maker herself. I come from the times ahead of you, as Rangda Kaliankan, the Zetan/Xeno hybrid that the Zetans have imprisoned will escape, absorbing and corrupting all the Zeto Crystals into dark crystals and cause the destruction of the Milky Way Galaxy." I stated gravely.

I looked at Brahma, he didn't say anything, but his face was full of guilt, and he was bursting in tears. Instinctively, I grabbed his arm and tried to use my empath powers on him, but to no avail, as he wasn't a Terran lifeform. Brahma wiped his tears, looked at me, and spoke: *"I understand. You have interesting and unique powers, Sabina. But our Zetan abilities only work if you have complete Zetan DNA sequences. You don't. I take it your powers stem directly from the True Maker?"*

"Perhaps. But please tell me. Why are you crying?" I asked.

"Because all of this is my fault. I was seduced by Rangda, enabling her to infiltrate our culture and destroy our civilisation. I was the one that convinced the other Zetans to imprison her instead of killing her, as I believed that she could repent," Brahma said.

"Why did you want to imprison her instead of killing her?" I asked.

"I had to save her life. I loved her. I hoped it would all be a nightmare that I would wake up from. I sincerely wished that my beautiful mistress wouldn't be our worst enemy in disguise." Brahma said and sighed painfully.

"Love is the death of duty," I said thoughtfully.

"Yes, and now I must do my duty and kill Rangda. I have been putting this off for too long." Brahma said with determination.

"I am coming with you. I was too young and innocent during my first lifetime, but now I have seen the world as it really is and realised that sometimes mercy isn't the answer. Rangda needs to die!" I said and surprised myself over the toxic, hateful tone I spoke with.

Brahma nodded and replied: *"Very well, Rangda's prison is 2000 kilometres walk that way"*. Brahma pointed to a faint cell-like object in the background. I was amazed over being able to see something so far away.

I said nothing, and Brahma handed me a beautiful blue dress laden with sapphires and gemstones. *"Wear this. It's not your size, but I cannot stand seeing a beautiful woman wearing those blood-stained clothes."* Brahma said.

"Thank you, Brahma. It's a beautiful dress." I replied. *"Who does it belong to?"* I continued.

I regretted my question when Brahma looked at me with sad eyes and responded, *"It was meant for Rangda. She was meant to wear it at our wedding."*

I bit my tongue and felt very reluctant to put on the dress. But what choice did I have since my other clothes were covered in blood? I put on the dress;

the bottom of the dress was almost dragging along the ground. It was clear that Rangda was a tall being, roughly two metres tall. I picked up the Zeto Crystal, and I walked in silence behind Brahma. Sometimes, ignorance is bliss!

Chapter 62: Finding Out About Alex's Infertility.

A few days later, I collapsed to the ground. My mouth was so dry, and I felt like I was dying from thirst. *"Water... I need water."* I said weakly.

Brahma looked at me with a bemused voice and replied: *"Sabina, it has only been a few days. You'll be alright. We still have 50 days to go."*

"Only a few days? I'm a human, and humans die from dehydration in a just a few days, you buffoon!" I snapped at Brahma.

Brahma laughed loudly at my outburst. *"What's so damn funny?"* I asked.

"You are funny when you are angry." Brahma said, smirked and continued speaking *"Don't worry, my child. You are in the Divine Dimension. Hunger or thirst won't kill you in this dimension, so you better get used to the pain."*

"Get used to it? I am too weak to move anymore!" I replied and burst out into tears. The hunger, thirst and exhaustion had turned me into an emotional wreck.

Brahma stopped laughing and gave me an encouraging smile. He got down to the ground and sat next to me. *"Give me your hand,"* Brahma said with a kinder voice.

I did as Brahma instructed. I could feel the gentle psionic energy flowing from his body to mine. *"What you must realise, Sabina, is that in this dimension you are not dependent on your body, but only on your mind,"* Brahma said gently.

"But how can I focus my mind, when my body is suffering?" I asked.

"Your body isn't suffering. Your mind makes you think that your body is suffering. You think you have been here for days, but only a few minutes have passed in your dimension." Brahma explained.

"And what about you?" I asked.

"I have been here for thousands of years. If I were to leave now, thousands of years of thirst, hunger and aging would affect my physical body in your realm. I would mummify and die on the spot. My physical body has long been gone; I can

only stay in this Divine realm for eternity." Brahma revealed, full of wisdom and kindness.

I wasn't satisfied with Brahma's answer. I had seen how he looked at the Zeto Crystal, and although he hadn't said anything when I picked it up, I knew that he yearned for it.

I decided to not let my paranoia affect my mind. I needed to recuperate my mental energies, and since I was too weak to move, I had no choice but to trust in Brahma. Martin Al-Sham motives also puzzled me, as I remembered that he revealed to me that he spoke to Zetan gods and was shown the secret Zetan code to open the portal. Brahma held my hand, and together we entered the most profound meditation I have ever experienced.

When I came back to my senses, my mind was refreshed, and Brahma smiled at me. *"Are you feeling better now?"* Brahma asked.

"Yes. I feel more energised than I have ever felt before," I replied.

"And yet something is bothering you?" Brahma asked.

I hesitated for a second. Something had bothered me for a while, but I wasn't sure whether this was the time or place to bring it up. As I saw it, my problem had nothing to with the mission ahead of me. *"It is nothing of your concern,"* I said.

"And still, I think I know what is bothering you," Brahma said.

I sighed audibly. A part of me was angry with Brahma for using his powers for spying on my mind, but it was the same that I had done to Alex, my friends, and my family. I realised that I might as well be open about my feelings. *"I have been married to Alex for over a year, and yet I haven't fallen pregnant,"* I revealed.

"And not for lack of trying?" Brahma asked.

Brahma's question reminded me of the multitude of attempts I had made in the last year. *"Definitely not for lack of trying,"* I replied truthfully.

"And when was your last attempt?" Brahma asked.

I froze for a second. I wasn't keen on sharing my sex life with a Zetan. Avoiding his intimate question, I responded with *"By the way, how long has time passed in the outside world?"* I asked and reminded myself what Brahma had told me just before, that a few days over here was only a matter of minutes over there.

"It's been exactly one day since you got here," Brahma stated.

"Wait a second! You said that only a few minutes had passed when I asked you before?" I remarked.

*"We've meditated for months in this dimension. That's the equivalent of a day on Earth. "*Brahma replied.

I didn't know what to make of Brahma's statement, but I didn't want to ponder on it further, so I decided to answer Brahma's previous question, *"Okay. If we have been here for a day, the last time I had sex with Alex would be two days ago. "*

"Excellent. Take this probe and insert it. I am sure you'll figure out how to use it." Brahma said, smirked and handed me a tiny alien device, which glowed and vibrated softly.

"Hmmm... Alright, look away and give me some privacy, please!" I replied sheepishly.

I inserted the device into my body, and I felt a tingling sensation of discomfort when the device sprang into action. A few minutes later, Brahma turned around and spoke. *"I have good news and unwelcome news."*

"How can you have any news at all? How did you collect the data from the probe?" I asked.

"I have bionic microchips in my brain that communicate with the probe. Both are run on bioelectricity. We used to have battery-operated devices like you humans use, but they ran out of batteries a millennium ago." Brahma replied.

"Okay, so what news do you have?" I asked him seriously.

"Well, on the bright side, you are very fertile. On the negative side, Alex is infertile." Brahma replied.

The news confirmed what I had suspected all along. Before I started dating Alex, I had tried to use my premonitory powers to determine who was meant to be Keila's father. I had never met that person, and eventually, I had questioned whether it was something I should even look for. When I first hooked up with Alex, it was to lose my virginity and be a normal young female. After a while, I had learnt that he was my soulmate, but my premonitions had never shown him to be the father of my future daughter, something that I had denied to myself and hidden throughout the years. At least now, I knew why my visions showed me what they did.

But what would I do now? I pushed those thoughts aside. I decided to focus on something much more important. I needed to stop Rangda before it was too late. *"Thanks for telling me this Brahma, we need to continue with our mission,"* I said as I got up and started walking to Rangda's eternal prison.

Chapter 63: Seducing Brahma to Fulfil my Destiny.

The next few days, we continued walking with a brisk pace. Our minds were rejuvenated from the lengthy meditation session, and I didn't want to waste more time, knowing that I needed to stop Rangda and get back to Earth before my body took too much damage from thirst and starvation.

Although my mind was energised and our pace was brisk, things were not okay with me mentally. After finding out what I subconsciously knew all along, that Alex wasn't meant to be Keila's father, I experienced recurring sexual visions of Eric Orchard and me. The problem with this was that Eric Orchard was my secret half-brother, in fact, it was so secret that not even Eric knew. My present mother Ellen Hines had an affair with Marvin Orchard, Eric's dad, which resulted in me being born.

I recalled the disgust I had felt when Eric tried to hit on me when I was 17 years old, not knowing that I was his half-sister. It had put me in a problematic predicament back then, as I loved him like a brother, and I didn't want to hurt him. Eventually, I had influenced Lindsey McGowan to be Eric's girlfriend so that I could maintain a platonic relationship with Eric.

Brahma turned around and looked at me. *"What's wrong? You don't look well at all!"* Brahma said. Before I told him, he grabbed my hand and established a telepathic connection. I pushed his hand away and looked at him sternly and said, *"Great, spying on me again, are you?"*

Brahma backed away a few steps, made an apologetic gesture and spoke, *"I am sorry, Sabina. I just want to help. I can see that you are suffering."*

I sank down to my knees and pleaded with a weak voice, *"Help me, please. Am I going insane?"*

Brahma didn't respond. Instead, he turned around and walked away. In my desperation, I ran up to him and stood in front of him. *"You must help me!"* I pleaded in desperation. Brahma sighed and responded: *"I don't know, Sabina.*

With visions, it's hard to say what is true and what is the fabrications of an over-stimulated mind."

"Please give me clarity. I am losing my mind!" I exclaimed.

"Okay, so there are two likely scenarios. Either stress and lack of nourishment have made you lose your mind, and you better disregard your visions for now." Brahma said

"What is the other option?" I asked.

"Well, have you ever considered that Eric Orchard might not be your brother?" Brahma asked.

Brahma's statement struck a nerve in my mind. I had never verified my belief that Eric was my brother. I had just assumed that Eric Orchard and I shared the same dad, although only my mother Ellen knew of this affair. Perhaps Brahma was right. In any case, no matter if Eric and I were biologically related or not, I would always perceive Eric to be my brother.

Another thought struck me. Eric's sudden appearance in my visions might be an indication of something else. Now that I knew about Alex's infertility, my purpose would haunt me until I dealt with the issue. But I could never see myself having sex with another man except for Alex! Suddenly, I had a wild idea. What if Brahma were meant to father my child? Keila was meant to have Zetan DNA and abilities, and Brahma was a Zetan. My destiny wanted this to happen.

I turned towards Brahma but didn't dare to look him in the eyes. I spoke silently. *"I was thinking... Would you like to father Keila, Master Brahma?"*

Brahma looked at me with a mix of surprise and excitement. *"I don't know. I haven't fathered children for 4000 years, and never with a human. I might be too old."* Brahma said.

"Well, you might still be up to the task. No harm in trying?" I said and smiled, hiding my disgust, but full of hope.

Brahma nodded and replied, *"I guess we both love people who cannot give us what we desire. You remind me of the Rangda that I fell in love with, when you are wearing that dress."*

"Well except that I am not over two metres tall?" I asked jokingly.

"Well, that's a clear distinction. But you possess a charm and wit, an innocent beauty," Brahma said.

I took off the dress and Brahma touched me. It was the strangest feeling I have experienced. On the one hand, I felt a complete oneness with Brahma's soul and bliss over fulfilling my destiny. On the other hand, my body froze and stiffened from the physical repulsion I felt from being touched by the pale-skinned alien.

"Would you prefer I looked like this?" Brahma asked and snapped his fingers. In the blink of an eye, my handsome Alex was standing in front of me.

"How did you do that??" I asked in amazement.

"Outer layer DNA modifier. With that technology, I can replicate the looks of anyone I like," Brahma explained.

"That is much better!" I exclaimed and kissed Brahma. After that, we proceeded to have the best sex of my life, combining Alex's incredibly handsome and masculine body with the spiritual and meditative abilities of Brahma, the old Zetan mage. After what felt like a blissful eternity, we finished, and I got dressed, ready to fulfil my destiny.

Chapter 64: Rangda Tricks and Kills Brahma.

A month, or less than an Earth day later, we stood outside Rangda's prison cell. Standing outside this spooky and terrifying place, covered in a dark aura, terrified me, and I wondered why we hadn't brought others to help us.

Brahma seemed confident and walked towards the main gate of the prison complex when I interrupted him. *"Wait! Don't go in yet!"*

"What is the matter, Sabina?" Brahma asked in surprise.

"I just had a foreboding feeling. What if Rangda wants us to come after her, so she can kill us and get out?" I said anxiously.

"Hmm, I don't think so. I am one of the mightiest Zetan warriors, and besides, we have a Zeto Crystal to amplify our strength." Brahma said reassuringly.

I thought about Brahma's claim. I felt that there was something that clouded Brahma's judgement. Was it his single-minded obsession with Rangda, which made him too proud to ask his Zetan peers to help him? As for myself, why hadn't I insisted that we brought others before this crucial battle? I realised that my unwillingness to seek help had the same root cause as Brahma. Did I think too highly of myself? Anyways, I didn't want to argue with Brahma about it. We were here, and it was time to get the job done.

"Yeah, you're right, no need to worry, but let's prepare ourselves," I said with determination.

"Good. Take this plasma pistol," Brahma said and handed me a futuristic handgun.

"Thanks," I replied.

"Do you know how to use a gun?" Brahma asked.

"Yes, but only the version you would find on Earth," I replied.

"Very well. Grip it like you would a ballistic pistol. The difference is that with our plasma pistols you'll need to hold down the side button with your thumb before pulling the trigger. Try shooting at that wall to get a feel for it." Brahma said.

I did as Brahma instructed and fired the pistol at the wall. The gun made a loud laser noise and fired a green bolt of energy that fizzed when it hit the wall, it looked like a Tesla weapon. *"Good enough! Stay behind me when I deal with Rangda."* Brahma commanded.

Brahma unsheathed his plasma sword and activated the biometric panel at the main gate with his handprint. The door opened, and it led to a tunnel-like black void. I felt a deep sense of discomfort when I entered the area. This was a place with a dark aura that was ridden with hatred and *wrath*. I didn't have time to feel uncomfortable though, as I had to keep up with Brahma who was moving with haste. As we crawled in the tunnel and reached Rangda's cell, Brahma took me aside. *"Sabina, this is it. Rangda is behind that door. Be prepared for anything!"* Brahma said, and he opened the biometric lock on the door.

We got into the cell, and unexpectedly, we saw Rangda shivering in a corner, crying. She was incredibly beautiful, not at all like the beastly and vicious creature, which I had seen in my visions. Brahma was right, she did look like me. *"Brahma, is that you? You were right. I was deceived by my misguided hatred. I want to set things right."* Rangda said with a soft, pleading voice.

"Don't listen to her! Remember why we are here!" I urged Brahma and aimed my pistol at Rangda.

"Shut up, Sabina. Let her talk." Brahma commanded.

I realised that I had to act. Brahma was still in love with Rangda, and the world was at risk. I fired my pistol at Rangda, but Brahma pushed my hand in the last second, so the plasma bolt only grazed Rangda's arm instead of killing her. Brahma struck me in the face, which knocked me to the ground. Then he kicked my pistol away. I was concussed and unable to prevent what would happen next. Brahma rushed over to Rangda and held her tight.

"You saved me against that evil woman," Rangda said to Brahma.

"Sabina is not evil, just misguided. She thinks you are incapable of change, but I know you are. I know that you regret the evil deeds that you did to our people. "Brahma said.

"No, she tried to kill me. You must kill her. She holds the Zeto Crystal, which is crucial for us to escape from this place and the other Zetans." Rangda said.

"But where would we go? There is nowhere for us to stay together." Brahma said in desperation.

"We can go to Xenora. From there we can find my hidden Xeno army, and build a new galactic empire ruled by the two of us." Rangda urged.

"No, we must do this the right way. I'll bring you to the other Zetans, and we'll convince them of your regrets. It's the only way to build an empire for the future. I'll promise to stand by you to the end." Brahma replied.

"Do you promise to love me until the bitter end?" Rangda asked.

"I do!" Brahma replied

"Thank you!" Rangda said.

Suddenly, Rangda pulled up a small corrupted Zeto Crystal, it was so black, and eerie, that it absorbed all the light in the room, like a black hole. Rangda pressed the corrupted crystal against Brahma's head, uttered a command and caused Brahma's head to explode, spreading his silvery-blue Zetan blood all over the prison cell.

Rangda uttered another command and fired a blast of dark energy against me with her corrupted Zeto Crystal. I got to my senses and deflected her blast through holding my pure and shining Zeto Crystal in front of me. While the Zeto Crystal saved me from the explosion, it wasn't enough to protect my mind from the terror I felt.

I got up and ran in panic as fast as my legs could carry me. I crawled out of the tunnel and realised that I couldn't close the main gate. Fear or no fear, I had to stay and fight. I couldn't be the one who caused Rangda's escape!

Chapter 65: The Showdown Against Rangda.

I squeezed the Zeto Crystal with my right hand and braced myself. I regretted that I had lost my gun, but I had no choice than to stand my ground and stop Rangda with no weapon. I saw Rangda storming against me. She had reverted to her true hideous form, and she was burning with dark flames of hatred. She held her corrupted Zeto crystal in her left hand and the gun that I had dropped in her right hand, ready to shoot at me.

Without a word, Rangda fired a barrage of plasma shots towards me. I held up the Zeto Crystal that shielded me against the projectiles, and Rangda threw away the empty gun in frustration.

"Impressive. You are a lot more proficient with the Zeto Crystals than I thought!" Rangda exclaimed.

"Yes. And I have come to stop you. Any last words?" I replied defiantly.

"Stop me? And how is that going? Brahma is dead, and you just set me free. I planned all along for you to come here and "stop" me. That's why I took control over Martin Al-Sham to serve me on Earth. I instructed Martin to protect you, and to make sure that you would get here. Your real purpose was to bring me out of prison!" Rangda said.

"So Martin Al-Sham was serving you all along? What's in it for him?" I asked.

"With humans, it's usually about money. I promised him great riches if he agreed to insert a bionic mind-control chip into his brain. He agreed, and now I own him!" Rangda revealed.

"And you deceived him?" I asked.

"No, I gave him exactly what he asked for. Unfortunately, being rich and serving me didn't make him happier." Rangda scoffed.

"And what about the connection I feel to him. Is that also your doing?" I asked.

"That Sabina... Is something you'll die wondering!" Rangda exclaimed and fired off a bolt of dark energy from her corrupted Zeto Crystal.

I deflected the bolt with my Zeto Crystal, but I felt the terror from the darkness touching my soul. Rangda attacked me furiously, firing multiple bolts of dark energy at me. While I managed to deflect the bolts, I was terrified by the darkness, and all I wanted to do was to run away in terror!

Suddenly, time slowed down, and I got a déjà vu from my first battle with Rangda in the 29th century. I couldn't beat Rangda because I was too noble and kind. I couldn't beat such a wicked creature by being kind. To beat her, I needed to lower myself to her level. To win, I needed to deceive Rangda, the Deceiver!

"Stop!" I shouted.

Rangda stopped and taunted me. *"Are you about to say your last words, Sabina?"*

"I have seen the truth. You were right all along. If you spare me, I promise to serve you. Together we can build a better world where only the strongest survives!" I exclaimed.

"But why should I spare you since you are weak?" Rangda mocked.

"Because, I am the Chosen One. Making me yield, will be your greatest triumph. Greater than the destruction of the Zetan Empire!" I shouted.

I studied Rangda's face. She was swallowing the bait. How could she not? Her entire being was about power and dominance. She wouldn't be able to turn down the opportunity to subvert the girl sent by the True Maker.

"Very well. Give me the Zeto Crystal, and I'll let you live and serve me!" Rangda said with a menacing voice.

"Sure. Catch!" I said and threw the Zeto Crystal towards Rangda.

As Rangda caught the crystal, I quickly exclaimed: *"Simba, Zetani, Xenoris"* to activate the Zeto Crystals defences against evil possession. The command set Rangda ablaze with a holy white flame. I took a few steps back. I felt relieved as I watched Rangda burn, while listening to her vile screams of pure agony.

The fire ended, and I realised that my plan had failed. Rangda was still alive, with fourth-degree burns all over her body. She hissed a terrifying hiss, threw away her corrupted crystal and charged at me with her sharp claws. She leapt on top of me and pierced my right shoulder with her razor-sharp claws. She stared into my eyes and screeched. *"You'll die a terrifying death for deceiving me. I will eat you alive. You'll wish you were never born!!"*

I saw the plasma sword hanging by Rangda's side. It was now or never. *"No, you won't,"* I said defiantly. I grabbed Rangda's sword, angled it towards her back and used all my strength to roll on top of her. Once on top of Rangda, I activated the plasma sword, causing the superheated sword to cut through Rangda's body like a hot knife through butter, cutting Rangda in half, parallel to her body, just under her chest.

I pushed myself away from Rangda, grabbed the sword, and moved a few steps back. I was so close to fulfilling my destiny.

Chapter 66: Dealing with the Monocle Conspiracy, Once and For All!

I walked over to the Zeto Crystal, which was glowing faintly, and I used its powers to heal my injured shoulder. I watched Rangda as she was hissing nonsense, moving in and out of consciousness with her fatal wounds. The True Maker appeared as a mirage, as always taking the appearance of my future mother, Keila Eisenstein.

"*You did it, Sabina. Now kill Rangda and fulfil your destiny!*" Said the True Maker.

I shook my head and replied, "*No. I cannot kill Rangda yet. There is something I must do first.*"

"*What is that?*" The True Maker asked.

"*I need to access Rangda's mind and find out the identities of her accomplices on Earth. I must kill them pre-emptively.*" I stated calmly.

"*You want to murder people in cold blood, without giving them a chance to redeem themselves? This is not you, Sabina. Don't do it!*" The True Maker said to me.

"*Yes, I cannot live with the stress knowing that powerful people are out to murder me. I need closure!*" I replied.

"*This is not your mandate as the Chosen One!*" The True Maker roared.

"*Then smite me! I will fulfil my mission, but I will also make sure that I can raise my future daughter in peace together with Alex.*" I replied defiantly.

The True Maker disappeared from my vision without saying a word.

I knew what I had to do. Regardless, if the True Maker condoned it or not, I had to deal with the villains in the Monocle Conspiracy to save myself and my family.

I walked over to Rangda, kneeled next to her body, and grabbed her dying head with both hands and squeezed her cranium. I then focused my psionic capabilities to access Rangda's bionic microchips. It worked; I had entered Rangda's evil mastermind. After searching for a while, I found the identities of Rangda's remaining accomplices on Earth. They were:

- Martin Al-Sham: My mysterious guardian, whose real motives Rangda had revealed before our final confrontation.
- Elaine Orchard: Martin's wife. A successful business tycoon in Asia. The owner of the Harapan Conglomerate. Responsible for kidnapping Alex, ruthless business practices using underground Asian mafia, and environmental destruction.
- James Winter: A security adviser to the American president, responsible for causing several wars and increased paranoia and distrust within humanity.
- Vladimir Kravchenko: A Russian serial killer who had murdered hundreds of people, and avoided getting caught, due to the heightened awareness of the futuristic monocle.
- Josefina Fiero: Brazilian business tycoon whose company had caused the collapse of the Amazon rainforest, severely impacting earth's biodiversity.

I thought about the True Maker's words. Was I meant to seek out these people and convince them to change their evil ways? I didn't believe it would be a successful venture. I couldn't leave them alone as they either would come after me, or if not, keep destroying the planet. I knew what I had to do. I searched through Rangda's bionic microchips and reprogrammed all the monocles to kill the users. Even if they survived the self-destruct sequence like I did in Mexico, they would at least lose an eye, and no longer have the heightened awareness from the alien technology.

I released Rangda's head and picked up the plasma sword. I chopped Rangda's body to pieces, to make sure she couldn't regenerate. After that, I picked up the Zeto Crystal and left the gruesome scene behind me. It was time to return home. In solitude and silence, I started the long walk back to the Terran portal.

Chapter 67: Getting Stripped of My Powers.

A few months later in Divine Dimension time, I returned to the Terran Portal. I had spotted several groups of Zetans in deep meditation, but I had left them alone. I knew that they desired the Zeto Crystal, and wanted to return to Earth as gods, but I didn't want to facilitate their return. The Zetans were not actual deities, they were advanced aliens that stole the True Maker's glory and played around with humanity for their own bemusement. If I facilitated their return to Earth, it would cause more division among us instead of unity.

As I held up the Zeto Crystal to open the portal, the True Maker appeared like a mirage. Her return made me feel irritated, and I lashed out sarcastically at her: *"Look who is back. Have you come to thank me, for killing Rangda and saving the Milky Way Galaxy?"*

The True Maker sighed and replied, *"It seems that you are a lost cause, Sabina. You are too full of yourself. I never tasked you with stopping Rangda. In your former life, you begged me to turn back time so you could set things right. Sending you back, was a mercy to you, and all living things in the Milky Way. Your fates are irrelevant in the grand scheme of things."*

I pondered what the True Maker had told me, and I realised that she was right. *"I am sorry for my tone. This has been an arduous expedition, and I just want to go back to Earth and be with my family,"* I pleaded.

The True Maker nodded and replied, *"I'll grant you that request. But it won't be the same life that you led before."*

"Why is that? What will change?" I asked anxiously.

"I will strip you of the Zeto Crystal, and all your powers. You'll return to Earth and live like a normal woman." The True Maker stated.

"But, look at the work I have done. I can do so much good for the planet if you just let me." I pleaded.

The True Maker left my statement unanswered and looked at me with judgemental eyes. Her gaze was too much for me to handle, and I broke out into tears. *"Please spare me,"* I squirmed.

The True Maker smiled at me and responded, *"I was never about to kill you. In fact, I don't ever kill anyone. I am incapable of doing so. That's why I needed your help to kill Rangda."* The True Maker replied gently.

"But people die all the time?" I objected.

"Yes, I created a world where life is created and ends every second. It is just part of the system. I am the creator of the Universe; thus, I can heal and create lifeforms, but I cannot destroy and kill."

I pondered the True Maker's statement for a while and then I replied. *"But why do you want to strip me of my powers? I can carry out your will on Earth, doing the things you cannot do."*

"You mean murdering people in my name?" The True Maker asked sarcastically.

I bit my tongue realising the implication of what I just had said and tried to defend my statement. *"But sometimes killing people can make the world a better place."* I defended myself.

"Yes, but the problem is the ripple effect that divine intervention creates. You stopped Ben Yehuda and Pierre Beaumont during your adventures. But what effect will that have on the future timeline? Perhaps, your attempts at creating a better world will actually destroy it." The True Maker stated.

"That doesn't seem likely," I replied.

"Perhaps. But I learnt in previous versions of the universe that my interventions caused more problems than they solved. Thus, I have chosen a policy of non-interference." The True Maker stated.

"So, that is why you don't answer prayers?" I asked.

"Yes, that is why I don't even listen to them," the True Maker replied.

I stood silent for a while and took in everything that the True Maker had told me. Eventually, I decided that I needed to know about my future. *"So, what will happen to me?"* I asked.

"I'd rather not tell you, as revealing your future will alter it," The True Maker replied.

"But I need to know. Please tell me more?" I pleaded.

The True Maker replied, *"You will give birth to Keila, and the two of you will die together. The two of you will die on your 112th birthday, on the 20th of October 2131".*

I pondered what the True Maker had told me. I felt determined to get on with my new life as a normal woman. *"Okay, I accept what you have told me. Please open the portal, so I can go back to Earth,"* I said.

"I will. On one condition." The True Maker replied.

"I am listening," I replied.

"I will relocate the Terran primordial Zeto Crystal to a new location on Earth. You are not allowed to look for it." The True Maker urged.

"Okay, I promise to not look for The Zeto Crystal," I replied.

After that, the portal opened. As I entered the gateway, I passed out, and everything became black.

Chapter 68: Waking Up from a Coma.

After what felt like an eternity, I eventually woke up in a hospital bed in a private hospital in Sydney. Alex held my hand and smiled at me. *"Welcome back, Sabina."* He said.

"Ugh, what happened? How did I get here?" I asked with a weak voice.

"There was a tsunami in Kiribati, damaging a local village. When I got there, I found out that you were missing, and a sunken pyramid had risen from the bottom of the sea. I added two and two together and went to the pyramid to look for you. I found a bed of rocks with a sepulchre in the Kiribati Pyramid, and I realised that it looked exactly like the Royal Tomb in the Sun Pyramid. I couldn't find you, but I didn't want to give up hope, so I hired a medical team to be on standby outside the Kiribati pyramid. People called me crazy, but I didn't care, I needed to cling on to hope. A few days later, you came through the portal and dropped unconscious on the ground. You have been in an induced coma ever since." Alex told me.

"So, you saved my life? How long have I been gone?" I asked.

*"Yeah, I felt that I owed you one, "*Alex said and winked. *"Five months,"* he continued.

Five months! I put my hand on my belly and felt relieved, noticing how it had grown. I burst out into tears of joy when I felt a tiny kick.

"Alex, I am pregnant!" I exclaimed.

"Yes. I know. It's a miracle!" Alex replied excitedly.

I grabbed Alex's hand to feel his joy, but there was nothing except the warmth and the touch of his soft skin. The True Maker had told me the truth. I had lost my empath powers. But how would I live in a world where I couldn't feel and influence people's thought. It was a sixth sense, that I had since I was born, not something that was easy to lose.

"What's wrong?" Alex asked with a concerned voice.

"I have lost it. I have lost my empath powers!" I cried.

"What do you mean?" Alex asked in confusion.

"The True Maker stripped me of my powers. I can no longer read or influence minds." I replied.

"So, for better or worse, you are just like everyone else now?" Alex asked with relief in his voice.

"Yes, but I don't know how to be like everyone else. It's the first time I experience it." I sobbed.

Alex wiped my tears and looked into my eyes. He smiled sympathetically and spoke, *"I am not going to lie to you. The coming months will be the toughest in your life. Your muscles have gone weaker from being comatose, and you are pregnant. Not an ideal combination."*

"Well, I figured as much. Any good news?" I sighed.

"I'll be by your side every step along the way. We'll get through this together." Alex said and held my hand.

"Thanks, Alex. Have you called my mother, Ellen, and her husband, John?" I asked.

"Not yet. We didn't know that you'd wake up today. I'll call your parents as soon as you need to rest." Alex responded.

"Thank you. I can't wait to see them," I replied.

"Why do you always refer to your dad with his first name?" Alex asked.

"Because, he is not my real dad," I said, and sighed.

"Wow, I never knew!" Alex exclaimed.

"Neither does he, but I just needed to get it off my shoulder. Please don't tell anyone. I need to rest now," I said weakly.

"Of course, I'll stick around and will be here for you when you wake up," Alex said and left the room.

As Alex left, I felt a sense of guilt. I had shared one secret with him, but I hadn't addressed the elephant in the room. I had not disclosed that he was infertile, and not the father of the child in my womb. I decided that Alex would have to wait to find out the truth, as I had to recover first. Once I had recovered, I could be honest, but for now, I really needed all the support I could get.

Chapter 69: Beginning My Rehabilitation.

"*One more step, Sabina. You can do it.*" My physiotherapist Sandra Stephens told me cheerfully. I focused my energy, and led by her gentle hand, I took the last step to the chair and sat down. Today's milestone achieved: 20 steps!

It frustrated me that I was struggling so much. I had always been a high achiever in everything I put my mind into, from yoga, music, and chess, to online trading and supporting charities. Not to mention that I had saved the world from several evil conspiracies, as well as an alien demon queen.

"*Why can't I recover quicker, I feel so worthless in this state!*" I complained to Sandra, who gave me a sympathetic look and replied. "*You are recovering very well, considering the circumstances. The doctors had never seen someone with so many scars on their brain tissue before. That you woke up, and we are talking now is a miracle.*"

I nodded and didn't reply. I suppose to the medical staff, my return to life was a miracle, but for me, it was boring and mundane. I had experienced real miracles.

I wanted to ask Sandra about her life, but I didn't know if I should. Did people usually ask their medical staff and physiotherapists about their lives? I had lived my whole life seeing everything, just a small touch away, but now I was blind and clueless. My lost empath abilities were what hurt me the most, but my intelligence had decreased, and my premonitions were gone as well. I could no longer beat the chess game on the Kasparov level, and I could no longer make almost unlimited money doing online trading. I guess what I experienced was what old people experience when dementia first strikes them, although, by human standards, I was still considered bright and with a high-level intellect.

I understood why the True Maker had chosen to punish me, and I accepted her decision. My premonitions and heightened intelligence had made me arrogant. Like the Zetans before me, I had tried to change to the world to fit my personal ideals. But the world wasn't just for me to form, it belonged to everyone, something that I had to humbly accept, now that I was just like everyone else.

I looked at Sandra and spoke: *"I want to take 40 more steps before I rest today."*

She shook her head and replied. *"I don't want to strain you too much considering your condition."*

I pushed myself up from the wheelchair and stood unsupported on my feet. *"Thank you, Sandra. But although I might not have the ability, I still want to put in the effort."* I said, and suddenly I felt a lot better. It was as if the True Maker had noticed that I accepted my rightful punishment and allowed my body to heal from the damage that pride and arrogance had caused it.

A few days later, I was released from the hospital, having experienced a miraculous recovery that surprised everyone.

Chapter 70: Seeking Advice from My Mum.

The day after I left the hospital, I was having tea with my mother, Ellen. It was a scorching day, but fortunately, the ocean breeze and the shade on the Iceberg Club's terrace, overlooking Bondi Beach, made the day bearable.

My mother was happy, excited to see her daughter well and back to life. Her joy made me happy, I had lost the chance to change the world, but at least I could make the people around me happy.

As the tea and our fruit salad arrived, my mum decided to break the blissful silence we had experienced together. *"So, how are you holding up these days? You must be excited over your pregnancy and your miraculous recovery?"*

"Yes, I am very excited for the future, and I am happy to be alive," I said, and smiled to make my mother happy.

"And yet your eyes are full of sorrow?" Ellen remarked.

My dear mother. I loved her, and I couldn't lie to her, not even when I intended to make her happy.

"I don't know. Since I lost my abilities, I don't feel complete anymore. I want everything to be like it was." I admitted.

"People always feel that way when they experience unwanted change. But it doesn't help. Change happens all the time, and like it or not, it is something we all have to deal with," Ellen replied.

"I guess, but that's easier said than done, isn't it?" I sighed.

"Well, at least I am always here for you when you need me," Ellen said.

"There is one more thing," I admitted.

"There always is," Ellen said and smiled sympathetically.

"Alex is infertile and not the father of my child," I admitted and stared down the floor.

"What are you saying?? Does Alex know about this, and if not, how do you know he is infertile?" Ellen said in shock.

"*No, Alex doesn't know. I suspected something to be wrong when I couldn't fall pregnant. In the Divine Dimension, I met Brahma, a Zetan. He ran tests that confirmed my suspicion,*" I revealed.

"*And Brahma is the father of your child?*" Ellen asked.

"*Yes.*" I replied.

"*Did you ever consider the possibility that Brahma was lying, to father your child?*" Ellen suggested.

"*Yes, I considered that for a long time. But I realised that Keila was meant to be half-Zetan. And Brahma was a Zetan, so it all fell into place.*"

"*I understand. I hope you are right.*" Ellen replied.

I nodded. I had omitted the real reason that drove me to have intercourse with Brahma. The recurring visions I had where Eric Orchard was Keila's father. Honesty or not, some thoughts were better left unspoken.

Suddenly I felt a pool of water rushing through my pants. Had I peed myself? "*Sabina! Your water has broken, we better hurry to the maternity ward!!*" Ellen exclaimed in excitement.

"*Oh my god, you are right. Let's hurry up!*" I said, and we left the restaurant and headed for Sydney Women's Hospital in Randwick.

Chapter 71: Double Confessions.

A few weeks later, I was lying on my couch at home, relaxing after the light morning run that I had made along Sydney's rocky coastline. I was happy that my body had made a full recovery. According to the medical experts, it was a miracle, as the amount of brain scarring, I had when I came to the hospital had rendered me brain dead.

As happy as I was that I had physically recovered, I was stressed by realising what this meant. I had to be honest. I had to tell Alex the truth.

I approached Alex in the kitchen. He was drinking coffee and looking joyfully at baby Keila O'Neill. I hesitated. I knew that Alex had a momentous day at work. After my recovery, he had resumed working for the charity that we started, although we were now solely focused on the ocean clean-up project, since I had lost the ability to make more money.

I pushed away my reluctance. I knew that I could always come up with a 'good' reason for not telling Alex the truth, but those reasons were just cowardice. If we were to live a happy life together, we had to be honest with each other.

Alex noticed me, smiled and spoke: *"She is beautiful, isn't she? Our baby daughter, Keila."*

I looked at the infant who slept peacefully in her cradle. Every baby was beautiful to their parents, but Keila was extraordinary even with that in mind. No doubt due to her half-Zetan DNA.

I hesitated, cleared my throat, and spoke *"Alex, there is something I must confess."*

Alex's smile disappeared, and he looked at me with a serious expression. *"I figured as much. I have a confession of my own to make. But I felt it was better to wait until you had recovered,"* Alex revealed.

I nodded and said with an afterthought *"I guess we are both thinking alike. What is your confession?"*

"When you arrived at the hospital, the doctor's said that you were brain dead. After a month of no progress, I thought of turning off your life support. That's when we found out that you were pregnant. I decided to keep you alive so that you could give birth to our daughter." Alex looked remorseful, and his voice broke.

"So, you almost gave up on me, and kept me alive only as a womb for our daughter?" I cried.

"Yes. I almost gave up on you. If you weren't pregnant while in a coma, you would be dead now. Now that you are back, I feel so guilty about ever thinking of giving you up!" Alex said and stared down the floor.

I thought about Alex's confession. I wasn't angry at him. Alex was just an ordinary human, and it made sense that he would give up on me, when the medical doctors had proclaimed me brain dead. I tapped his shoulder, looked him into the eyes and spoke, *"It's okay. Most people would have thought about giving up on someone under the circumstances. What matters is that I survived in the end."*

"Thanks. I feel better now that this burden is off my chest." Alex replied, and wiped away his tears.

A moment of silence ensued. The elephant in the room was still there. My confession to Alex. Although I had forgiven his transgression, I couldn't be sure that he would act in the same way.

"Uhm, I also got something to confess," I said quietly.

Alex nodded and replied, *"Alright, let me hear it."*

"Keila is not your daughter," I confessed.

As expected, Alex didn't take the news kindly, and in a mix of anger and disappointment, he yelled out, *"So who is the father then? Did that filthy Martin Al-Sham have his way with you?"*

"No, god no! Nothing like that!" I replied.

"So, tell me what happened then," Alex commanded.

"I will. If you calm down and let me. I forgave you just a minute ago, the least you can do is listen to me like a civilised person." I commanded angrily.

"Alright. Tell me what happened?" Alex replied in resignation

"When I travelled with Brahma to face Rangda, I had a lot of time for reflection. I thought about an issue that has gnawed in the back of my head for ages. Why I hadn't fallen pregnant with you. I asked Brahma for advice, and he ran an advanced Zetan test that proved that you were infertile. Some days passed, and I

realised that Brahma was bound to be the intended father for Keila. My mother in the 29th century had Zetan abilities, and Brahma was a Zetan. So, I put the two and two together." I explained.

"And what if Brahma was lying to you? You told me that Brahma was in love with Rangda, and that Rangda's beautiful form looked like you. What if you were just the substitute for the love he could never have again?" Alex speculated.

"Well if he was, it all happened for a reason. If I didn't come back pregnant, I wouldn't be alive today." I replied solemnly.

Alex pondered my statement, nodded, sighed and spoke, *"Yes, I guess you are correct. But I need to go now."*

Hearing this, I panicked at the prospect of losing him, and I went down on my knees and pleaded, *"Please don't go! Stay with me."*

Alex stroked my hair and smiled. *"Don't worry, Sabina. I am just going to the Great Barrier Reef Conference in Brisbane to find sponsors for our ocean restoration project. I'll be back in a couple of days. I am sure we'll resolve our issues when I come back."*

Hearing this, I smiled. Alex chose duty over love at the moment, but he would come back for me. It was the best solution for everyone. *"Okay, my love, good luck at the conference. I'll speak to you soon!"* I said.

"That's fine, Sabina. You had engaged in a sexual encounter with an outer realm being, it's not something I would feel threatened by." Alex said, grabbed his suitcase, and rushed for the Auto Driving Car that was waiting outside our South Coogee mansion, ready to drive him to the airport.

Chapter 72: A Celebration, Some Sad News, And a Reconciliation.

A few weeks later, Alex and I were celebrating that we had secured a big sponsor for our ocean restoration project. The new management of the Indonesian Harapan Conglomerate had pledged a hefty sum of money to undo the damage caused by their former CEO, Elaine Orchard, who had died mysteriously. Hearing this had relieved me. I had felt guilty over killing the remaining members of the Monocle Conspiracy, without giving them the chance to repent for their crimes. Knowing that something good came out of this debacle made me feel better about myself, although it was something that I would always have to live with.

"Cheers to us!" I said as we drank the exquisite French champagne at the beautiful fine dining restaurant where we were celebrating.

"You made all of this possible" Alex replied.

'In several ways' I thought, but I decided to not reveal my role in the death of Elaine Orchard, so instead I said *"I got the movement started, but this victory is all yours. You've done a brilliant job these last few weeks."*

"Thanks, Sabina," Alex said and started munching on a blue cheese and pear tart. I sensed that something was bothering him, but I didn't want to ask, and there was no way for me to know any more.

We had a delicious meal, but Alex was mostly silent throughout the evening. Eventually, I decided to ask. *"Is everything okay? I thought tonight was a night of celebration."*

"It is, but I received these letters before, and I have been too nervous about opening them," Alex replied.

He handed me the letters. One was from Alex's paternity test for Sabina. The other envelope was from his fertility test. *"Do you want me to open the letters for you?"* I asked.

"Yes, I am too nervous about doing it," Alex replied.

I opened the letters, and they confirmed what I already knew. Alex was infertile, and he wasn't Keila's father. *"I am sorry, Alex"* I said as I handed him the letters.

He looked at the letters sighed and replied. *"It's okay. I thought it was strange that you fell pregnant while you were in Kiribati, and I was worried that Martin Al-Sham would be the father. At least this way, I know I couldn't have a child any other way."*

I nodded, but I didn't say anything.

After some silence, Alex spoke again, *"But it's a shame we cannot give Keila a sibling."*

I smiled sympathetically at Alex and replied, *"Don't say that. We were both the only child, and we turned out fine. Besides, if you can love Keila like your own child, nothing is stopping us from having another child in the future."*

Alex pondered my statement for a while and replied, *"I guess you are right. The emotional attachment is more important than the biological connection."*

"But let's leave that for the future. I for one can't wait for Keila to get older so I can have a good night's sleep!" I said and winked at Alex.

"Oh yeah, sleeping is great. I can't wait to attend the next conference!" Alex teased.

"I'll definitely come with you. And I'll bring baby Keila as well!" I replied.

"Damn! I just lost my incentive to save the environment!" Alex exclaimed.

"You'll find the motivation. Speaking of Keila, we better go back home and relieve Ellen from her babysitting duties." I replied.

"Can't we wait another hour? I booked a hotel room upstairs for dessert." Alex suggested.

I looked at Alex and smiled. *"Yes, you are right. I'll message mum and tell her we'll be late."* I said and winked at Alex. After that we paid the bill and went upstairs for some excellent dessert!

Chapter 73: Attending Dr Tony Phillips United Nations Environment Prize Ceremony.

A few months later, Alex and I attended the United Nation Environment Ceremony in New York, to see Dr Tony Phillips receive a prize for developing the automated solar-powered marine vessel, which we intended to use for cleaning up the oceans. When I first found out about the award, I had experienced a short surge of jealousy.

I was the one who had provided the prototype to Dr Phillips, through my past life experience back when I was a highly intelligent being, and I felt that I deserved to be rewarded and get recognised for my efforts. After a short hissy fit, Alex had calmed me down. What mattered was that the automated ocean cleaning project received worldwide recognition and funding to achieve our goal. My ego was of less concern. Besides, I didn't blame Tony for not mentioning my contribution to the committee. I was in a coma, and unlikely to wake up, when Tony was nominated. It made sense for him to not share the glory with a "brain-dead" woman.

We watched Tony's thank you speech, and I was happy when he repeatedly mentioned our names and our project to clean up the Pacific Ocean. Despite losing my powers, there was still hope for us to build a better, cleaner world.

After the presentation, there was a press conference where Alex and I also took part. Usually, I didn't do much public speaking. I preferred to leave that part to Alex, and I was surprised when I received a question addressed directly to me, *"Miss Hines. Do you have any comments regarding your involvement in the rising of the Sunken Pyramid and the tsunami aftermath that killed 32 people in the village of Ambo, Kiribati?"*

I looked at the journalist. Her name tag said that her name was Elenoa Mariwati and that she was reporting for Micronesian news. I panicked slightly feeling that everyone was looking at me. After a slight pause, I responded. *"Miss*

Mariwati, I was one of the people injured in that tragedy. Apart from that I don't understand your question."

"Okay, I rephrase it. Did you make the pyramid rise from the ocean floor, causing the tsunami that destroyed my village?" Elenoa said sternly.

I panicked and felt guilty, knowing that it was me that caused it, but I realised that to everyone else, Elenoa's accusations must seem far-fetched and absurd. Before I had the time to answer, Dr Tony Phillips interjected. *"Don't be ridiculous. There is no technology available to lift a pyramid from the bottom of the ocean. What happened at the Sunken Pyramid of Kiribati was a natural disaster caused by earth's tectonic activity. An act of God if you will."*

I studied Elenoa. She took notes but didn't seem keen to give up yet. *"I have one more question, if I may ask?"* she said.

"Granted!" I replied.

"When do you intend to visit the village of Ambo and see the damage first-hand?" Elenoa asked.

"If it's important for you, I am happy to go to Kiribati straight after this summit," I replied.

"Very well. I'll see you in Kiribati then, Miss Hines." Elenoa said.

After my short exchange with Elenoa, the press conference continued with other questions where Alex and Tony answered to the best of their abilities, while my mind wandered around. Once we were back in our hotel room, Alex asked me about my exchange. *"So, are we heading to Kiribati? Why did you agree to that?"*

"That Elenoa woman. She is very peculiar. She knew that I caused the tsunami and the pyramid to rise from the seafloor." I said in confusion.

"Don't worry about it. No-one believed her. You'll be alright." Alex replied.

"Well, except that I did cause that pyramid to rise, inadvertently killing those people," I said while sighing.

"It's Martin Al-Sham's fault. You had no choice but to go. Don't blame yourself." Alex said kindly.

"I don't blame myself, but I know that I need to go to Kiribati to investigate further," I concluded.

"Of course, love. Let's sleep and fly there in a few days." Alex said, and we went to bed together.

Chapter 74: Elenoa's Revelation.

A few days later, I was sitting at the airport waiting to leave Kiribati. It hadn't been a fruitful destination, and I hadn't learned anything of value. The pyramid was still sealed off by several international agencies after it's strange and sudden appearance just a year earlier. While it would have been interesting to revisit the pyramid, we didn't have the permits to enter, and I no longer had the empath powers to convince someone to give us access.

We also visited the village of Ambo, and for the first time since I had lost my abilities, I was happy that I no longer had them. My former self would have been horrified and felt terrible to experience all the suffering, knowing that my actions had caused it. But my new jaded personality did not feel much remorse, it felt like it wasn't such a big deal. After inspecting the damages, I wrote a cheque and tried to leave it all behind me.

We decided that we didn't want to spend more time than necessary at Kiribati, and after the compulsory press conferences and public media posts, we were happy to head back to the airport for our private jet back to Australia.

Just before I boarded my flight, I was approached by Elenoa at the airport. *"Mauri e Kiribati!"* Elenoa greeted me cordially.

"Actually, we were just leaving" I replied irritably.

"But you just got here?" Elenoa complained.

"Well, I would have stayed longer if you had extended me an invitation, instead of guilting me into coming, through harassing me with baseless accusations on a press conference." I snapped at Elenoa.

"I am sorry if you feel that way. That wasn't my intention, and I am a huge fan of the work you are doing in the Pacific." Elenoa said apologetically.

I sighed. I was tired and didn't want to discuss the issue any further, but my curiosity got the better of me. *"So, why did you make those claims at the press conference?"*

"I was paid to do it. I got my visa, my press accreditation and my travel expenses all paid for by a mysterious wealthy white man. His only condition was that I asked you these questions," Elenoa disclosed.

"Oh really. What did he look like?" I asked anxiously.

"He was very tall, at least 190 centimetres. Blonde, in his 50s and he had a mask that covered half of his face." Elenoa revealed.

"A mask? How strange!" I said.

"Yes, but he was a nice old gentleman, and he helped us rebuild our village after the tsunami. He seemed to be mourning someone, or at least, he seemed very lonely," Elenoa recalled.

"Well, thanks for your help, Elenoa. I will make sure to stay longer on my next visit." I said, and I hurried to my private jet.

Elenoa's revelation filled me with fear. Martin Al-Sham was alive, and he had lured me to Kiribati so I would see the damage that the tsunami had caused. He was clearly after revenge, but I couldn't tell what my future would hold, and who else I was up against. I was no longer a woman with supernatural abilities, I was just a normal human being, full of worries and concerns. I called Alex on his phone and urged him to hurry up, I didn't want to stay here for a minute longer!

Chapter 75: A Troubling Talk with Keila.

Four years later, it was September 2047. Keila had grown up to be a beautiful five-year-old, and she had started her pre-school. Things were going well for Alex and me, we were both 27 years old, and we were exceptionally successful. I had come to terms with the loss of my abilities and appreciated my life as an average human. It was very relaxing to not know everything about the people around me, and once I had gotten used to it, I realised that ignorance really was bliss. I had come to terms with not being supernaturally smart or superbly influential. I was happy raising Keila, being a housewife and a part-time philanthropist, alongside my handsome and loving husband Alex.

The first year after realising that Martin Al-Sham was still alive, I was continuously nervous of his whereabouts, but as there was no sign of him in my life, I eventually relaxed. I concluded that he had either been killed by someone, or he was still alive, but had aged and changed his ways to live a retired life. In either case, he didn't seem interested in bothering me anymore. I was wrong about this, which I learnt the hard way on one wet and rainy September day.

It was 9 PM and a stormy night. Alex was away on a conference, and I was doing some cooking at home, when I suddenly saw Keila, walking past me with a kitchen knife in her hand, playing with it like a toy. What was going on? I shrieked and called her name, but she ignored me and walked towards her bedroom, so I ran up after her. When I found her, she was patting the family cat, Luna, with one hand, and holding the knife with the other. *"Keila, honey, what are you doing?"* I asked with a concerned voice.

Keila put the knife down and turned around. *"I was just thinking about something I want to do, mummy,"* Keila said while looking at me with innocent eyes.

"With a kitchen knife in your hand? Never touch the knives! They belong in the kitchen!" I said with a reprimanding tone.

"Okay. Sorry, mum" Keila replied and handed me the knife.

"Now that I've taken it off your hands, honey. What were you thinking about?" I said in amazement.

Keila paused and was looking for words, then she said something that shocked me. *"Mummy, you said that we shall love Luna. But I saw Luna kill a mouse the other day. Isn't that the natural order of things, the strong killing the weak? The cat killed the mouse because she is stronger. Likewise, I should kill the cat to prove that I am stronger than the cat!"* As Keila uttered these words, she was laughing, and her eyes were flashing purple in excitement.

"Who told you these crazy things? We are humans! We can, and shall, choose to be nice to other animals!" I exclaimed.

"Grandpa did," Keila replied.

"Don't lie to me, Keila. Neither John nor Andrew would ever say such a mean thing!" I said indignantly.

"I am not lying, mummy. It was the tall man with the mask that told me! He told me he was my real grandpa!" Keila protested.

I was petrified, and my legs went numb when I heard this. Had Martin Al-Sham re-emerged and started targeting Keila? What makes him think he could claim to be Keila's grandfather? I needed to find him and stop him immediately.

"Keila, don't believe a word that man says. He is a bad man. Where did you see him?" I said.

"Oh, he was in my room playing with me, while you were in the kitchen cooking. Okay, mummy. I will love and pet Luna now." Keila said, picked up the cat and brought it to the couch where she stroked it gently.

I picked up the knife, put it away in the kitchen and approached Keila. *"Keila, honey. Aside from seeing him today in this room, while I was in the kitchen, where else did you meet the bad man with the mask?"* I asked worriedly.

"I met him once before in the park when I was playing with my besties Jasmine and Jordan. They thought he was scary, but I thought he was cool! He looked like the Phantom at the Opera, but he didn't sing. Mummy, I thought you loved that show?" Keila said sweetly and innocently.

"Listen to Jasmine and Jordan and don't talk to strange men," I said with a grave voice.

"Okay. The old man with the mask also gave me this note. He told me to give it to you." Keila said and handed me a note.

I opened the note which had the following text: Sabina, we need to talk. My associates have your house under surveillance, try anything and Keila will die. Bring Keila to meet me in Trenerry Reserve, NOW. It is time for you to learn the truth.

/Martin Al-Sham.

I grabbed the pistol, which I had bought when I found out that Martin was alive and told Keila to get dressed. I needed to confront Martin for the last time.

Chapter 76: Martin Al-Sham's Revelation.

15 minutes later, we arrived at the pitch black, windy, and rainy Trenerry Reserve. The park, which was usually a beautiful spot in the day, with its majestic ocean views, was now a desolate, cold, and unwelcoming location. Martin Al-Sham stood tall over one of the high cliffs, watched the ocean below the sharp rocks, seemingly unaware of our presence. I approached him with my hands close to my pistol, ready to draw.

Martin turned around and shouted at me to overpower the wind. *"Sabina, we meet again. How unfortunate for both of us."*

I walked closer to him and replied. *"What do you want? "*

"Justice!" Martin replied.

"Justice? You tell my daughter to kill my cat, and you call that justice? What is wrong with you?!" I yelled.

"You got to her in time, and the cat survived. But the cat is irrelevant to me. What's important is, did you notice Keila's eyes?" Martin said and smiled wickedly.

"Yes, they... they were purple. How did you do that?" I asked in amazement.

"I didn't do anything special. I don't have any superpowers. But I did invoke the demonic Rangda that dwells within Keila." Martin said, and chuckled.

I stared at Martin in disbelief. I had no idea what he was talking about. Martin sneered at me and spoke again: *"Let's rewind the tape. Who do you think your father is?"*

"John is my father," I replied, knowing that it wasn't John, but it was a guy called Marvin.

"Don't lie to me. It won't benefit you." Martin Al-Sham taunted.

"Okay, if you want to know the truth, it was Marvin Orchard, a man my mother Ellen randomly had sex with." I sighed.

"Yes. And who is Marvin Orchard's son?" Martin asked rhetorically.

"Eric Orchard. But this is none of your concern, so why do you ask??" I snapped at Martin.

"Patience is a virtue, Sabina. I am getting there." Martin said and continued, *"Who did you always care about? Who did you see fathering your children in your visions, when you knew Alex wasn't the one?"*

"Eric Orchard. But why and how do you know this?" I asked, feeling puzzled.

"I know because I was connected to Rangda's mind, when you entered her mind to kill my accomplices and me. While you were studying her mind, I studied yours, and I know everything about you, things you desperately try to hide." Martin cleared his throat as if holding back a memory and looked towards the ocean.

I lost my patience with Martin. I wanted to shoot him to get it over with. But even if I somehow managed to shoot Martin, and avoided getting killed by his accomplices, I didn't want my daughter to see this. Instead I screamed at Martin *"So what if I had sexual fantasies about Eric? You are a murderer who served an evil alien demon!"*

Martin smirked at me and replied: *"I am not scolding you for fantasising about Eric. I am telling you that you should have acted on the fantasies. You see, Marvin Orchard wasn't your father. I am!"*

"Stop lying. That's impossible!" I yelled angry at Martin, while secretly fearing that he was telling the truth.

"Well, it was I, who fathered you. I had intercourse with your mother during her Egyptian holiday in January 2019. You were born in October 2019. Coincidence? I don't think so. Besides, I did a paternity test on some of your hair. There was a match." Martin revealed and handed me the document.

I read the letter that confirmed Martin's claim. *"But what about Marvin Orchard?"* I stuttered.

"I don't keep track of your mother's trysts! She is one deceitful swanky lady," Martin scoffed and continued, *"Either she copulated with a guy called Marvin Orchard during her holiday, or she just mixed up my name and told you a lie, and there was no Marvin Orchard!"* Martin suggested.

I considered Martin's claims. I realised that it didn't matter to me. John was the man who had raised me, and the question, whether my biological father was the villainous Martin Al-Sham, or the long-gone Marvin Orchard, was irrelevant. *"So, what if you are my biological father? It changes nothing. It's not like we are going to hang out and celebrate Christmas together."* I replied coldly, hiding my feelings of despair.

"I doubt that our Christmas celebrations would be cordial, considering that you killed my wife Elaine and tried to murder me." Martin sniffed. *"But you're wrong about the remaining statement. It changes everything!"* Martin continued.

"Why is that?" I replied.

"Because you turned down Eric, the man you were meant to be with, as you thought he was your brother. Instead, you pursued a relationship with Alex who was sterile. Upon finding out about Alex's infertility, you then mothered a child with Brahma." Martin stated.

"And why is this important?" I asked dismissively

"Because this was how Rangda's evil power comes back to life. Rangda Kaliankan was the daughter of Kalianka, Brahma's sister. By choosing Brahma as the seed bearer instead of Eric, Keila was reborn with a tendency towards evil and wickedness. Through Keila, Rangda's spirit will survive and cause a new dark era. So, in the end, you defeated your enemy, but you also gave birth to her malevolent reincarnation." Martin replied.

"You are lying. You must be!" I screamed in desperation.

"And yet you saw the purple glow in Keila's eyes when she spoke about killing the cat. She is just young, she'll get worse. In the end you must choose between murdering your own daughter or allowing Rangda's victory." Martin said.

I realised the implications. I collapsed to the ground, lying in a puddle, and crying uncontrollably. I must have been wailing for minutes, before I finally got back to my senses. When I got up, I saw Martin speaking to Keila with menacing words. *"Don't worry about your mother, she is weak. You are not like her. You are strong. You are destined to rule."* As Keila listened to Martin, her eyes were glowing purple, her pupils were dilating in delight.

"Why. Why are you doing this?" I moaned.

"Because of this!" Martin yelled and removed his mask. He revealed a big gaping hollow where his right eye had been and a massive scar along the side of his face. *"You swore by the True Maker to not hurt me if we released Alex. Yet, the first thing you did after defeating Rangda was to murder Elaine and attempting to murder me."*

"I am sorry!" I moaned.

"Bah. You are not sorry. You have known that I am alive for several years. Not once have you tried to seek forgiveness for what you did to me! You are only sorry because your actions turned out to have negative consequences for you!" Martin snapped at me.

"So, what do you want?" I begged.

"Justice! And I just got it. You'll have to live with this for the rest of your life." Martin replied. After that Martin said, *"Shoot now!"* and the last thing I remember was being hit by a tranquilizer dart before falling unconscious.

Chapter 77: I Choose Love and Hope.

I woke up the following day in a hospital bed. Alex and Keila stood next to my bed. Keila was back to her usual beautiful self with bright blue eyes, and clean complexion, unlike the demon I had seen the night before.

Alex looked at me with worried eyes and spoke: *"What happened last night? You and Keila were found unconscious in Trenerry Reserve. Keila said you were attacked by a man in a mask?"*

"Yes, Martin Al-Sham re-emerged," I said thoughtfully.

"What? Why? What did he want?" Alex asked in shock.

"He blames me for the death of his wife and his disfigurement. He revealed something to make my life miserable, as his revenge." I replied.

"That's absurd. Martin's wife kidnapped me, and he forced you to go on a dangerous expedition. Whatever happened to him and his wife while you were in a coma can't possibly be your fault." Alex said.

I thought about revealing how I intentionally murdered the remaining members of the Monocle conspiracy, after defeating Rangda, but I stopped myself. I didn't want to admit this side of myself to Alex, and besides it had nothing to do with him. At least that was what I had thought. Instead I replied, *"I know. Martin is a deluded madman. He even claimed to be my biological father!"*

"This is just getting worse and worse. We need to hire bodyguards to protect us." Alex said.

"There is no point in doing that. Martin is not coming back. He has made his statement." I replied thoughtfully.

Alex shook his head and replied, *"This is not negotiable. I need to know that my wife and daughter are protected when there is a madman out to hurt you!"* Alex insisted.

I smiled a tired smile at Alex. I was happy that my husband wanted to protect us. *"Okay, you win. We'll hire bodyguards until it is confirmed that Martin Al-Sham is arrested or has left the country."* I said.

Being a man of action, Alex picked up the phone and acted straight away. While I listened to his call, I realised that I had to tell him the truth about Keila. It was the only way, to protect my gifted and beautiful daughter from turning into the embodiment of Rangda.

Once Alex had hung up the phone, I signalled him to come closer. *"Martin Al-Sham revealed one more thing,"* I said.

"What did he say?" Alex asked.

"He revealed that Keila's father Brahma, was Rangda's uncle. Thus, Keila is Rangda's cousin, and they share an eighth of the same DNA." I said with a sorrowful voice.

"Don't worry. It's just more lies by a demented madman." Alex replied dismissively.

"Unfortunately, not. Martin tricked Keila into almost killing our cat, Luna. When she held the knife, I saw the mark of Rangda, the glowing purple eyes." I stated with a grave voice.

Hearing this gripped Alex with fear and he walked back and forth in the room. Keila broke the silence. *"What is going on, dad? And who are Brahma and Rangda?"* Keila asked innocently.

I felt stupid, Keila was a highly intelligent five-year-old, and I shouldn't speak about her in her presence.

"Rangda is your cousin and a friend of Martin. They are both bad people, that's why they tried to hurt us." I replied.

"Okay, mummy. I am hungry. May I have some fruit?" Keila asked.

"Yes, mummy is still hurt. Go with daddy to the canteen, and he'll give you fruit." I replied.

As Alex and Keila left my hospital room, I felt determined. I wouldn't let fear and hate take my loved ones from me. I would choose love and hope to form Keila into the amazing woman that she could be, and together we would work for a better world.

Chapter 78: Good Ending.

Time flew like it always does in retrospect. Many years later, on the 20th of October 2131 to be precise, I woke up and realised that it was my 112th birthday, and the day I would die. It felt bittersweet knowing that I would die, but it also felt glorious knowing that I have lived a fulfilled life. My visions had told me the date of my death many times, and now it was time. Nonetheless, I wasn't worried. I had led an incredibly meaningful life, and although I, like any living being with a healthy mind, wanted to keep living, I accepted that my time was up.

I looked at the photograph of my late husband, Alex. He had died peacefully in his sleep when he was 92, roughly 20 years earlier. I had mourned his passing for a while, but more than mourning for my dear Alex, I had celebrated his life. Alex had lived a wonderful life, and his peaceful and pain-free death was the ultimate blessing that the True Maker could have granted him. We humans were mortals, and a peaceful death at an old age was all we could hope for.

I never had any other children except for Keila. Before I found out that she was Rangda's cousin, I had discussed it at times with Alex, but after I found out, it was out of the question. Someone with Keila's capabilities, she was almost as gifted as I were, before I was stripped of my abilities, could make, or break the world. After finding out about her inner demon, I saw it as my mission to be her guide in life, to make sure that she used her powers for good, and not for evil. I think I did a good job, and we were closer than ever in our advanced years after we both became widows.

Keila had been married to a woman. According to herself, she was bisexual and had chosen to live a non-heterosexual life, as she was terrified of the prospect that she would give birth and spread Rangda's tainted genes among humanity. Keila's partner, Sara, had been a decade older than Keila when they met, and Sara already had children. Thus, Keila could have her family without spreading Rangda's legacy. It was the best she could do with the life she had been given. When Sara died, Keila had moved in together with me, and we were both happy old mother and daughter. Full of energy and best of mates, we enjoyed playing lawn bowling while overlooking the beautiful ocean.

Martin Al-Sham died ten years after our last encounter. I know, because he had included me in his will, and in his manifesto. I attended his funeral to make sure that he was dead, and I left his manifesto unread, and I used the pages for starting fires in our fireplace for those chilly winter nights.

There was a knock on my bedroom door, and Keila entered together with our housekeeper, Rose, who was carrying a cake.

"Happy Birthday, mum" Keila cheered with 'youthful' enthusiasm, or at least as youthful as an 88-year-old woman could muster. Oh, your children, they'll always be young in your eyes!

Rose put down the cake on the table in my room and was about to leave when I spoke to her. *"Hey, dear Rose, how would you feel if I give you this house to take care of when I die? "*

"That would be too generous, Sabina. And besides, you already gave me a house to care for. You and Keila need someplace to live, hopefully for many years to come." Rose replied.

"Thank you, Rose. Spend the day with your family. I am sure the laundry can wait." I replied, knowing that my laundry wouldn't be an issue anymore.

After Rose had left, we had some cake when Keila surprised me with a suggestion. *"Hey mum, how about we go to the Brazilian barbecue today?"*

Keila's suggestion surprised me. She had been a vegan, ever since we found out about her connections with Rangda over 80 years earlier, as she vouched to never eat meat again. *"Keila, honey. Do you know something that I don't?"* I asked.

Keila smiled and replied: *"I know that today is our last day on this planet, and I know that you love churrasco. So, let's celebrate!"*

"Celebrate? So, you are not sad and afraid?" I asked.

"It's a relief to finally fulfil my purpose. No more struggling with my inner darkness. Finally, just peace and tranquillity." Keila said and her face radiated of blissfulness.

"So, you know what is going to happen today?" I asked

"Yes, in ten minutes we will take an AutoCar to the Brazilian BBQ in Darling Harbour. There we'll fill up on the dishes that you love. After that, we'll head to Observatory Hill and meditate in stillness." Keila replied.

"Sounds like a busy day. Very well, beloved daughter. Let's go."

A while later, we entered an AutoCar, that took us to Darling Harbour for our lunch. We enjoyed a sumptuous lunch, and a few hours later we stood outside the venue. Keila spoke to me cheerfully. *"Hey mum, how about we walk to Observatory Hill?"*

"I don't know, Honey. A three-kilometre walk is not that easy once you reach my age!" I replied

"Well, it's the last chance for you to see the city you love," Keila teased me cheerfully.

"Okay, love. Let's go for a pleasant walk." I replied.

As we slowly walked through the city that we knew and loved, I felt a bit melancholic, but I was helped by Keila's cheerful retelling of our life stories. I couldn't remember all the events she mentioned, and I realised that lousy memory had started to affect me at last. I walked slowly, and the three-kilometre-walk took over two hours to complete!

Eventually, we reached Observatory Hill, and I started feeling anxious and running out of breath. Keila reassured me. *"Don't worry, mum. Let's just sit in the shade under that tree, hold hands and meditate."* I thought of protesting, but I was tired, so I agreed to Keila's suggestions.

Suddenly, I felt a massive spike of energy, and as I opened my eyes, our bodies were gone, and the universe had absorbed my soul. I was dead and I experienced the pure bliss of the afterlife. Keila was right. Our deaths had served a purpose, as the True Maker, allowed our bodies to absorb the massive energy spike of a gamma-ray blast, which would otherwise have destroyed Sydney.

"A mysterious death of two elderly women occurred today at Observatory Hill in Sydney. Witnesses and security cameras confirm, that there was a swift flash of light, and the women disappeared into thin air. It is speculated, that the deaths were caused by a malfunctioning orbital laser, but the army has refused to comment on the incident."

Nigel Orchard (Eric Orchard's grandson) The Sydney Morning Herald, on 20th of October 2131.

Chapter 79: Evil Ending.

(This alternative ending takes place straight after Chapter 76)

"*Justice! And I just got it. You'll have to live with this for the rest of your life.*" Martin replied. After that, Martin said, "*Shoot now!*".

I got down to the ground, grabbed my pistol, and shot Martin's accomplice, who was holding the tranquilizer rifle. I shot him just before the tranquilizer dart hit me. I quickly turned around and aimed my pistol at Martin. "*Time to die, Mother Fucker!*" I shouted as I riddled him with bullets.

The terrified Keila tried to run away, but I caught up with her and dragged her to the cliff's edge. I didn't want to do what I was about to do, but I had no choice. I couldn't allow Rangda to be reborn into this world. I lifted her up, shouted, "*I am sorry, my dear child*" with tears running down my cheeks. I pushed Keila down the cliff for a 20-metre fall. "*No, mummy....!!*" I could hear her little voice echoing as the sound slowly faded away.

I collapsed to the ground and was found unconscious, when the police came to arrest me. When I told the court what had happened, I was handed a life sentence in a mental health facility, for the murder of Martin Orchard and the attempted murder on Keila O'Neill and Jaime Sanchez, Martin's associate.

Keila survived the fall but ended up paralysed from the waist down. Surviving an attempted murder by her own mother, traumatised Keila and caused her to become angrier, filling her life with thoughts of hatred and rage.

Alex was unaware of Keila's connection to Rangda, and he refused to ever see me again. I tried contacting him about the danger that Keila posed to him and the world, but he never listened. Alex assumed that I had turned insane, and he never wished to speak to me again. I don't blame him, but his unwillingness to listen to me, and his love for Keila, ultimately caused his death. When Keila was sixteen years old, Alex died under mysterious circumstances, orchestrated by Keila, and she inherited our fortune. Equipped with her evil genius, she used her inheritance to make more money, and fund various nefarious projects.

Keila also funded several expeditions that were looking for the Zeto Crystal. One of them found it, and Keila used its powers to heal her body to peak performance, so she was able to walk again. Keila then corrupted the Zeto Crystal, to make it more useful for domination and terror, so that she could achieve her goals.

Once in peak condition, Keila set out to achieve a new goal. She wanted to spread her evil genes. Keila extracted her eggs and used many surrogate mothers to maximise her progeny. She funded this with the ill-gotten gains that she made from funding wars and destroying the environment. On 20th of October 2131, Keila was the most feared and powerful woman on the planet, and she had thousands of progenies spread across several generations. Both Keila and I, died on this day, as we were both in Sydney, but without the True Maker's blessing to stop the Gamma-Ray Blast, the entire city was destroyed in a massive explosion. However, Rangda's evil legacy lived on through her effect on the human genome.

A few hundred years later, every human on the planet had their genome tainted with parts of Rangda's genes. This changed humanity forever. Gone was the love and respect for living things and the environment. Instead, humanity was driven by brutality and endless greed. Acting this way and aided by technological advancement, humans became the new Xenos of the Milky Way Galaxy. Ever-expanding, and always destroying everything they came across. Without any Zetans to resist them, humanity eventually spread all over the galaxy. Death and destruction always followed in humanity's footsteps, wherever they went.

The True Maker, could only watch, cry, and hope that one day, another Chosen One, would be born to save the galaxy from humanity's greed and wrath.

This is the end of Sabina's Story. Stay tuned for the final part of the tetralogy following Martin Al-Sham's life.

Don't miss out!

Visit the website below and you can sign up to receive emails whenever Martin Lundqvist publishes a new book. There's no charge and no obligation.

https://books2read.com/r/B-A-QIOG-CTKBB

Also by Martin Lundqvist

Divine Space Gods
Divine Space Gods: Abraham's Follies
Divine Space Gods II: Revolution for Dummies
Divine Space Gods III: Rangda's Shenanigans

Sabina Saves the Future
Sabina's Pursuit of The Holy Grail
Sabina's Quest to Open the Portal in the Sun Pyramid
Sabina's Expedition to Stop the Apocalypse

The Divine Zetan Trilogy
The Divine Dissimulation
The Divine Sedition
The Divine Finalisation

Standalone
Matt's Amazing Week
James Locker The Duality of Fate
The Portal in the Pyramid
Money Laundering in the Laundromat
Pyramidportalen

Matts Fantastiska Vecka
Divine Space Gods Trilogy
Sabina Saves the Future: Complete Trilogy
Diez Historias Aleatorias y Muy Cortas
Ten Random and Very Short Stories
Dieci Storie Casuali e Molto Brevi
Dix Histoires Aléatoires et Très Courtes
Zehn Zufällige und Sehr Kurze Geschichten
Cinco Historias Aleatorias y Muy Cortas
Five Random and Very Short Stories
The Fall of Martin Orchard
Masa Depan Putri Sabina

Watch for more at martinlundqvist.com.